WHITE HOUSE AUTUMN

WHITE
HOUSE
AUTUMN

ELLEN EMERSON WHITE

Feiwel and Friends　New York

This one, is for my father.

A FEIWEL AND FRIENDS BOOK
An Imprint of Macmillan

Library of Congress Cataloging-in-Publication Data

White, Ellen Emerson.
    White House autumn / by Ellen Emerson White.
        p. cm.
    Summary: Seventeen-year-old Meg's surging emotions after her mother, the United
States President, is shot, threaten her relationship with boyfriend Josh and best friend
Beth, but she strives to maintain control to help her father and younger brothers.
        ISBN-13: 978-0-312-37489-1 / ISBN-10: 0-312-37489-5
    [1. Presidents—Family—Fiction. 2. Assassination—Fiction. 3. Family life—
Washington (D.C.)—Fiction. 4. Celebrities—Fiction. 5. Schools—Fiction.
6. Washington (D.C.)—Fiction.] I. Title.
PZ7.W58274Whi 2008
[Fic]—dc22

                                                                    2008006883

Originally published in the United States by Scholastic Press.

Feiwel and Friends logo designed by Filomena Tuosto

First Feiwel and Friends Edition: August 2008

10 9 8 7 6 5 4 3 2 1

www.feiwelandfriends.com

WHITE HOUSE AUTUMN

1

MEGHAN POWERS SLOUCHED in the back of her Political and Philosophical Thought class, incredibly bored. Her friend Alison yawned at her from across the aisle and Meg nodded, feigning death from ennui. Top *that*, Camille.

"Miss Powers?" her teacher asked. "Do you have a problem?"

Meg sat up hastily, death scene arrested. "Sir?"

"I realize," he spoke with some sarcasm, "that a discussion of the Presidency can hardly be expected to hold your interest—"

Most of the class laughed.

"But," he said, "I would appreciate it if you would try to pay attention."

Meg blushed. "Yes, sir." She was going to add, "Forgive me, sir," but he might not find that as amusing as she would. One of the many problems with being the President's daughter was that she had to watch every single thing she said—and did—in public. Rise above her natural inclination to be—well—a jerk. Her mother had only been in office about nine months, and Meg was still trying to get used to it. Hell, her whole *family* was.

She slumped down into her turtleneck. Turtlenecks were good to hide in. But, this was a nice skiing shirt, and she shouldn't stretch it out. She sat up, turning around to check the clock. Ten minutes to go. Major drag. It was only October, and she wasn't supposed to have senioritis yet.

However.

Maybe she would look at Josh for a while. She liked to look at Josh. Except that he was looking at her, and it was too embarrassing to stare back. Besides, gazing lovingly was sort of a public display of affection, and one wanted to maintain decorum whenever possible. That made up for the times when it *wasn't* possible. Like during the last song at dances. Amorous embraces seemed rather appropriate at such moments. Except for White House dances. Although officials who had had a little too much to drink had been known to break that rule—like Raul, the prince who had taken their association as dinner partners as an engagement or something, and spent the whole night trying to kiss her, until Preston, her father's press secretary, had tactfully tangoed her away. Meg was exceedingly fond of Preston.

The bell was ringing, and she closed her notebook. That was the good thing about thinking—it was an excellent way to kill time. Not that she ever accomplished much. *Reflections*, by Meghan Winslow Powers. Swell. She and Rod McKuen could walk off into the sunset together. *Admiring* the sunset.

"You coming?" Josh asked.

"Yeah." She zipped her books into her knapsack and smiled back at him. He had a very nice smile. And nice hair and nice eyes and a nice nose—the kind of guy people asked for directions, although knowing Josh, he would get rattled, blink a lot, and send them blocks out of their way. Not miles, just blocks.

"What are you thinking about?" he asked.

She grinned sheepishly. "I don't know. Things."

"Interesting things?" he asked.

"Not really." She walked closer to him in the hall, smelling his aftershave. It was pretty funny to imagine him putting it on in the morning when she knew he didn't shave. Or, as he put it, he shaved every three weeks, whether he needed it or not.

"I'm sorry I can't come to the match," he said.

"It's no big deal." She automatically swung her arm, as if she were holding one of her tennis racquets. "I don't think we're going to win, anyway."

He grinned. "You mean, you think *you're* going to win, but the rest of the team isn't."

Well—yeah. Pretty much.

"Nice attitude, captain," he said.

"Well," she glanced around, "don't quote me."

He made his hand into a microphone. "Yes, fans, you heard it here. Miss Powers concedes that—"

"Funny," she said, pushing him off-balance. Actually, it was too true to be funny. Reporters were always showing up at her matches, and even members of opposing teams sometimes took pictures of her. The one which seemed to be making the rounds recently was a terrible photo which had shown up in some tabloid, of her hitting a drop-shot. On the run, mouth open, eyebrows furrowed. Really most attractive. And embarrassing. It was like, she spent thirty five hours a day trying to get people to forget who she was—and one stupid picture would blow it in about ten seconds.

"Melissa Kramer's *really* going to want to win today," he said.

Her opponent, who was ranked fourth in the 18-and-under, USTA, Mid-Atlantic Section—and seemed to think that meant she would be heading off to Wimbledon, sooner rather than later. Meg nodded. "Yeah, but she's all hat, no cattle." Or, more specifically, all serve, and no ground-strokes or cogent strategy.

And had made the grave error, earlier in the season, of popping off on the sidelines after winning the first set they played, 6–2— whereupon, Meg had won the final two, 7–6, and then, 6–1. After which, Melissa complained that it "wasn't fair" that she had to play someone famous. It had taken a great deal of effort for Meg to do nothing more than smile pleasantly and say, "Oh, I'm sure I just got lucky."

Yeah. Right. *Lucky.*

"You gonna smash them or what, Meg?" their friend Nathan shouted down the hall. Nathan was six-four, and one of the few football players she'd ever genuinely liked—and trusted. He had huge shoulders, a close-cut Afro, and always wore those baseball shirts with brightly colored sleeves.

"Six-love, six-love," she shouted back.

"Boy, some people sure are conceited," Josh said.

Meg laughed, and pushed him again. "You're really a jerkhead, you know that?"

He nodded. "Yeah, you tell me all the time."

"Mrs. Ferris says for us to get ready as fast as we can," Alison said, meeting them at Meg's locker.

Meg missed the last number of her combination and had to start over. "Big pep talk?"

"And how." She looked at Meg, then at Josh, and grinned. "I'll see you in the locker-room."

Meg flushed. "Uh, yeah, I'll be right there."

When she had her books and her tennis gear, and was waiting for Josh to get his stuff, she wandered down to the corner where Wayne, one of her Secret Service agents, was.

"I'm just going to change, and then head out to the bus," she said.

He nodded. On days when she had away matches, her security detail was increased, with two agents riding *on* the bus, plus follow cars, and other agents doing advance work. At the beginning of the season, the Secret Service had wanted her to ride in a separate car, away from the rest of the team, but Meg had protested so vehemently that, luckily, they had agreed to compromise. Having agents on the bus was bad enough, especially when everyone was talking about sex—which was most of the time. No wonder they lost so many matches.

Josh walked her to the locker-room, and they paused outside.

"I'll call you tonight," he said.

She nodded. "Have a good lesson." Two afternoons a week, he worked with his piano teacher, preparing for auditions for the conservatories he was applying to, even though he insisted that he would never get in and would end up majoring in history somewhere.

"Have a good match." He leaned over to kiss her, and Meg made sure that no one was around before relaxing against him. Well, her agents were around, but they never looked. She didn't *think*. "Do it for the Gipper," he said against her mouth.

"I'll try my best, Knute." She hugged him, then pulled away. "Talk to you later?"

He nodded, kissed her one last time, and she went into the locker-room.

HER TEAM LOST almost every single one of their matches, and someone from the *Washington Post* took pictures of her perspiring and lunging for cross-court shots. Melissa had apparently been practicing like a mad thing, because her placement was much better than Meg remembered, and the match went to three sets before she managed to pull it out with some of her hardest serves.

Leaving Melissa, of course, very disgruntled.

When she had originally been assigned to the top rank on the team, she had worried that it was only because she was the President's daughter. In fact, when she'd first tried out, even though she knew she could beat the reigning number one player, Renee, easily, she carefully lost her challenge match, so she would come in second and not have to feel as though she had been given special privileges. But, her coach had not been fooled and kept her after practice to accuse her of throwing the match. Meg had allowed as how maybe she could have done better, and Mrs. Ferris said that if she wasn't going to put out her full effort *every single match*, she couldn't play at all. Awkwardly, Meg explained the situation, and her coach had sympathized—sort of—but still said that she couldn't be a member of the team with that attitude. Meg decided to adjust her attitude, but she still threw points sometimes, because most of her opponents were uneasy about having to play her, and she didn't want any unfair advantages.

Nothing like winning a few easy points to make people stop feeling uneasy.

She and her agents parted in the North Entrance Hall, with its shiny checkerboard floor, marble pillars, and flashy main staircase.

Meg usually went up the main stairs, instead of the private staircase, because the main one ended up outside the Center Sitting Hall, near her bedroom. There was an elevator, but she never took it, since one of her many mottos was: when in doubt, burn up calories.

She dumped her tennis bag and books on the bed, messing up the quilt and pillows a little. She made her bed before she went to school in the morning—her parents insisted—but the maids always changed the sheets and remade it, much more neatly. Neat beds made Meg nervous.

"Hi," she said to her cat, Vanessa, who was asleep among the pillows. Vanessa purred, extending a soft grey and white paw, and Meg smiled. "Pretty cute," she said, and batted her hand against the paw a few times. Vanessa liked games.

She changed out of her white and maroon tennis shirt, and into a very old green chamois shirt that had once belonged to her father. Her shower could wait—first, she had to have a Coke.

"Here, come on." She picked Vanessa up, balancing her in the crook of one arm. "Let's go see what's going on."

"Miss Powers?" Pete, one of the butlers, came down the hall to meet her. "Maybe I can bring you something? A Coke? Some Doritos?"

Meg grinned. Nothing like having someone make the offer before she even had to ask. "Sounds great, thank you," she said, and followed him down to the kitchen, so she could at least take the glass out of the cupboard and feel as though she was helping. The White House staff preferred that the First Family *not* to help them, but Meg felt funny about being waited on all the time.

Armed with a delicate crystal glass of Coke and a silver bowl of Doritos, she went up to the third floor solarium where her brothers were slouched in front of the television, watching—*again*—one of their Brady Bunch DVDs, and eating chocolate cake.

"Hi," Steven said, and gave her a more arrogant grin than usual. He'd always been a cocky kid, but being in the eighth grade *really* seemed to have gone to his head. "You sure look ugly."

"Yeah, and everyone thinks we look *just* like each other." Meg sat down next to Neal, who was eight, and hadn't learned about arrogance yet.

"I think you look pretty," Neal said, smiling at her, and Steven pretended to throw up on a cushion.

"Oh. Yeah." Steven lifted his head. "Stupid Beth called before."

"Beth's not stupid," Meg said automatically. Beth was her best friend from home, and when they weren't emailing and texting each other, they talked on the phone a lot. "Did she leave a message?"

"Something about the essay questions for Wesleyan, I don't know." He picked up his cake. "Hey, d'ja win or lose?"

"Got her in three sets," Meg said.

"It took you *three*?" Steven shook his head. "You suck."

Yeah, yeah, yeah. She swung her legs onto the coffee table. If there was anything she enjoyed wearing, it was sweatpants. She infinitely preferred herself in sweatpants and old flannel or chamois shirts. "Which one is this?" she asked, indicating the television.

"When they go to the Grand Canyon," Steven said with his mouth full.

Meg nodded, looking at him, and then at Neal. It was funny the way the three of them did—and didn't—resemble their parents. She and Steven were like their mother, with dark, thick hair and narrow, high-cheekboned faces. Neal was more cherubic, with light brown hair and a gentle smile like their father's. Even so, people could always tell that they were related—probably because they all slouched the same way. It had to be more than that, but the slouching was obvious. Her parents were always bugging them to shape up on their postures.

"I like the one where they go to Hawaii better," Steven said, and went into the little kitchenette to wash frosting smudges off his hand. He had this habit of not using plates or forks when he ate cake. A rather disgusting habit, in Meg's opinion, but then again, she only ate the creamy part of Oreos, so she figured she wasn't one to criticize. "What's for dinner?" he asked, coming back out and using Neal's head for a towel.

"Roast chicken," Meg said. "And I think, plantains and stuff."

"Blech," Neal said.

Meg shrugged. "Mom likes them." She liked them, too, actually—especially when they were caramelized.

"Does that mean she's coming to dinner?" Neal asked.

Did she look as though she'd committed the President's daily schedule to memory? "I don't know," Meg said. "I guess so, if that's what they're making."

"What about Daddy?" Neal asked, taking another hunk of cake without—Meg noticed—bothering with a plate or fork, either.

Steven grinned. "He had to go shake hands with Miss Cherry Blossom."

Neal giggled, and Meg had to laugh, too, even though she felt sorry for her father, because of all the annoying things he had to do—cut ribbons at new buildings, plant trees with Cub Scouts, address the Senate spouses, and so forth. An endless stream of ceremonial, and often, silly, events. In real life—well, life before the White House—he had been a senior partner at his law firm, specializing in taxation.

They sat through another episode, and had just switched over to *The Simpsons*, when their father came in, dignified in a grey worsted suit, with a muted red tie, for contrast.

"How was Miss Cherry Blossom?" Meg asked.

"Very excited," he said wryly.

"Did you kiss her?" Steven asked.

"We shook hands." Their father took off his jacket, and Steven put it on, sitting up and trying to look like an adult. Then, their father loosened his tie and frowned at the television. "Filling your little minds with garbage again?"

Meg looked at the ceiling. "Forgive him. He knows not what he says."

Their father smiled. "You all could be in your rooms, reading Dickens." He tilted his head at Neal. "How was school?"

"Fun," Neal said. "We played kickball."

"All day long?" their father asked.

Neal giggled, then nodded.

"Great," their father said. "Even the school's not giving you Dickens." He looked at Meg. "Did you beat her?"

Meg nodded.

"Excellent," her father said. "Was she a good sport?"

Meg shook her head.

"Were *you*?" her father asked.

Well, except for the part where she'd smirked.

"How about school?" her father asked.

"I don't know." She slumped down in her best teenage punk imitation. "Got drunk again."

"Terrific." He tipped her Coke to the side to study what was left of the liquid, and Meg jerked the glass away, guzzling it and falling back in a drunken stupor. He laughed, then turned his attention to Steven. "How about you? What did you do today?"

"Read Dickens," Steven said solemnly. He got a snicker from Neal, a smile from their father, and a groan from Meg, whereupon he glanced away from the television just long enough to cross his eyes at her.

"Ah," their mother said, from the doorway. "There you all are." She came in, tall, and as ever, beautiful, in a blue silk dress, slimly belted in at the waist, and wearing graceful high heels.

No wonder her father hadn't kissed Miss Cherry Blossom.

"Guess what, Mom?" Neal said. "We played kickball! All day!"

"Well, that sounds productive," she said.

"Did you play kickball, too?" Meg asked.

Her mother nodded. "Yes, indeed. Hank and I were out in the Rose Garden for hours."

Hank, being the Vice President, Mr. Kruger.

Watching her cross the room, Meg meditated vaguely about the fact that she would probably never meet another woman with her mother's skill on high heels as long as she lived. Meg generally fell off espadrilles, forget high heels. She also fell off things like sneakers and Topsiders, and if it happened in public, would pretend that she suffered from a severe inner ear problem.

"Hey, Prez," Steven said.

"Hi." Their mother smiled at him, as she bent down to accept the hug Neal offered.

"Madam President," Pete said from the door, "may I bring you anything before dinner?"

Her mother decided on a scotch and soda—*and* a double espresso, which was not an unusual combination for her, and her father asked for a beer. Pete left, returning a few minutes later with the drinks, and a platter of crackers and artisanal cheeses—most of which *did not look American*. The voting public would, presumably, be appalled.

Their mother let out a sigh—which meant she was planning to relax for at least five full minutes. "I must say, I've been looking forward to this all afternoon."

"More than another round of kickball?" their father asked.

"Surprising as it may seem, yes." She closed her eyes for a brief, apparently rejuvenating, second, then opened them, looking at Meg and her brothers. "So. Tell me what you all did in school today."

"Dickens," Meg said.

2

MEG SAT IN bed that night, patting Vanessa and reading a very trashy, but entertaining, political conspiracy novel. She was supposed to be working on her college essays, but after an hour on the phone with Beth—who kept saying things like, "How about we blow off this whole college thing and just go to Colorado or someplace and be disreputable for a few years?"—she wasn't in the mood anymore. Besides, questions like, "What message, in twenty-five words or less, would you send to the inhabitants of another planet?" were kind of holding her back. What did they want her to write? "Hello from Earth. Having a wonderful time. Wish you were here." Of such answers, college acceptances were not made. Not that the President's daughter wasn't going to get into any school where she deigned to apply. Terrific. Nice to be accepted, or rejected, on her own merits—or lack thereof.

Someone knocked on the door and she considered hiding her book and running to her desk to hunch industriously over essays—but figured she wouldn't be able to pull it off.

"May I come in?" her mother asked.

It would be sort of fun to snap "Hell, no!" and see what happened. "Yeah," Meg said. "Sure."

Her mother opened the door, closing it behind her. The President, in her lounging gown. Yes, Virginia, Presidents *do* wear bathrobes.

"What are you reading?" she asked.

Meg held up her book and her mother nodded.

"The man has a very depressing view of it all," Meg said.

"The man is not completely off-base," her mother said.

Meg arched one eyebrow, putting on a "pray, continue" expression. "Oh," her mother waved that aside, "I'm just tired. Long day."

Meg flipped her right hand over to use as a make-believe notepad. "Would you like to talk about it?"

Her mother grinned. "No, thank you, Doctor."

Meg kept the notepad ready. "Do you feel alone? Friendless? Persecuted?"

"You read a few too many books, my dear," her mother said.

"Yeah, I finished a really swell one yesterday." Meg reached onto her night table for *Witness to Power*. "It was about this President named Nixon, see, and—"

Her mother sighed.

"It was really good," Meg said.

"I can imagine." Her mother sat at the bottom of the bed, with top-notch posture. "How's everything going?"

"Fine, thank you," Meg said politely. "And you?"

Her mother leaned over to cuff her. "Seriously." She recrossed her legs. "How are things going?"

Had she and her mother talked much lately? Not really. Less so than usual, since the President had been on the road a lot and had, among other things, only gotten back from Ottawa late the night before. Meg tried to think of her recent Life Highlights—other than beating Melissa Kramer, about which she had preened a bit during dinner. "Josh asked me to the Homecoming Dance."

"Big surprise," her mother said.

Meg nodded. "I said yes."

"Even bigger surprise," her mother said. "What are you going to wear?"

Because, naturally, it was semi-formal. "Can I borrow your Inaugural gown?" Meg asked.

"Well," her mother said, "don't you think it might be just a trifle sophisticated?"

Meg sat up straight, trying to look as mature as she could in her "What'll Ya Have" t-shirt from the Varsity in Atlanta. "Maybe a trifle."

Her mother nodded. "I'm sure we can come up with something more appropriate."

"I prefer black evening wear," Meg said.

Her mother looked dubious. "We'll see."

Which almost always meant no. Meg shrugged. "I'm not leaving the house in pastels."

"Oh, but I had my heart set on rose," her mother said.

Did she need to repeat the obvious? Meg frowned at her. "I'm not leaving the house in pastels."

Her mother laughed.

"Well, I'm not," Meg said.

"Fine," her mother said. "We'll just have the dance here."

It was a potentially humorous concept, but Meg sighed deeply, anyway.

"In all seriousness." Her mother leaned back against the bedpost, folding her arms, and Meg pictured the caption that would go with that pose: the President, caught in a rare moment of leisure. "I thought we might discuss your interview."

Meg shuddered. *People* was coming to interview her the next day, and she could think of about nine thousand ways she'd rather spend the afternoon. Like raking leaves, or cleaning the cat box, or having her appendix out, or—

"Preston will be sitting in with you, of course," her mother said, "but I thought you might want to talk about it."

Actually, Meg had been thinking along the lines of contracting a rare, and very contagious, disease—so that the interview would have to be canceled.

"You'll be fine," her mother said. "And once you do this one, we really *can* turn down all of the others." Since, apparently, the press office was regularly bombarded with requests to interview one—or any combination—of the President's children. "Just remember to count to three before answering questions."

Meg grinned. "What if I forget and count to four?"

Her mother also smiled. "You'll look rather daft. Three is just long enough to plan your answer."

"May I quote you?" Meg asked.

"What, and give away my trade secrets?" Her mother reached over to give her another cuff, to which Meg reacted as theatrically as possible, lying dazed and unconscious against her headboard. Her mother kept talking, giving no indication that she had even noticed. "You might want to watch your grammar. If the woman has a poor ear, you could come across as a bit of a ruffian."

Meg frowned. "You mean, I can't say 'ain't'?"

Her mother shook her head. "I meant 'going to' and 'have to,' as opposed to 'gonna' and 'gotta.'"

"I don't say 'gotta,'" Meg said, offended.

"If you were speaking quickly, you might. Just be careful," her mother said.

Meg nodded, the thought of this interview making her feel very sulky. Not like a good little trooper at all.

Her mother looked at her carefully. "It's not too late to call it off, Meg. We can just—"

And have a major national magazine think that she was a delicate little flower, incapable of handling a puff piece interview? Meg shook her head.

Her mother looked at her some more, and then nodded. "Okay, but if you change your mind, all you have to do is say so. Anyway, I'm sure you'll be fine, and Preston will be right there, if you need help."

She had always been pretty comfortable—sometimes *too* comfortable, she had been told—making off-the-cuff comments to reporters, but a formal, sit-down, solo interview was different. "I probably can't make jokes or anything, either, right?" she said, feeling fretful enough to give her mattress a small kick.

"You might want to watch it," her mother agreed. "It's altogether possible that she won't appreciate your sense of humor."

Meg grinned sheepishly. Sometimes, she had the feeling that there were a lot of people like that.

"Not that *I* don't appreciate your sense of humor," her mother said.

Meg made her grin shy.

"To a degree," her mother said.

Meg made her grin sad.

"A small degree." She glanced at Meg's empty desk. "How are your essays coming along?"

Meg patted Vanessa.

Her mother frowned. "Have you even started them?"

"Well, the one to the Barbizon School's almost finished," Meg said.

Her mother humored her by nodding.

"Would you like to read the one I'm doing for Julliard?" Meg asked.

Her mother sighed. "You don't play an instrument."

"Oh, but I sing," Meg said. "Haven't you heard me sing? Want me to do 'I Got Rhythm'?"

Her mother shook her head. "No, thank you."

Meg pulled in a deep breath, to center herself. "'I got rhythm, I got music, I got—'"

"It *is* October," her mother said. "Those applications are going to be due before you know it. And—well, I think it would be a good idea if you started taking the whole thing more seriously. Particularly the, um, Ivy League schools."

In other words, Harvard. Her mother's alma mater, and the only place she *really* wanted Meg to go. Especially since the Vaughns—her mother's maiden name—had been going there for several generations. Her father had graduated from the law school, so he was very enthusiastic about the idea, too.

Not that they were pushing her or anything.

"I don't know, Mom," she said. "I mean, I'll apply there, and

Yale, and Brown, and all, but—well, there are a lot of places I want to apply, not just the Ivy League."

Surprisingly, her mother didn't faint. "Well, then, you really *do* need to start working. That's a lot of essays."

Since almost all of the schools had supplemental forms, in addition to the Common Application. "You want to see the one I wrote for Bob Jones University?" she asked.

Her mother laughed. "No, thank you."

"Well," Meg said, "how about the one for Oral Roberts, or—"

"Have I ever told you that you are perhaps the most annoying person I know?" her mother asked, not unpleasantly.

Meg shook her head. "Not that I recall."

There was a knock on the door.

"Madam President?" a male voice said. Frank, her primary personal assistant. "Secretary Brandon, for you."

"Thank you." She kissed the top of Meg's head. "Excuse me."

"Tell him I think it's time we show China *exactly* who's in charge," Meg said, imitating her mother's presidential frown of concern.

Her mother smiled again. "I'll give him the message."

AS USUAL, THE conversation at lunch the next day centered around where people were applying to college, who was going to get in—and why, what schools were good, and what schools were a joke. Meg usually kept her mouth shut during that sort of conversation, although sometimes she felt as if she spent a good portion of her *life* keeping her mouth shut.

She looked around the table, sipping some skim milk. Except for Alison, most of her friends were male, which was strange, because at home in Massachusetts, the opposite had been true. She had always been kind of nervous around the opposite sex. Shrinking Violet. *Stuttering* Violet, even. But here, a lot of girls seemed to see her as a competitor, especially insofar as guys were concerned. Meg had assumed that that would die down after a few months, but even now, she would see girls take their boyfriends' arms when she walked by.

Not that she had *ever* moved in on someone else's boyfriend—or planned to do so, in the future.

She spent most of her time hanging around with Josh, Alison, Nathan, and another friend of theirs, Zachary, who was a basketball and baseball jock, as well as a serious trombone player.

"So, you getting the cover, or what?" Nathan asked.

Meg stopped sipping milk, seeing that he was looking at her. "Who, me?"

"*People*," he said.

"God, I hope not." She glanced at Alison. "You doing anything after practice?" From which she, unfortunately, had been excused today.

"Going to the dentist," Alison said.

"Want to pretend to be me, and *I'll* go to the dentist?" Meg asked.

"Meg Powers, Young Woman in a Hurry," Zachary said solemnly, and they all laughed, Meg imagining a picture of herself in a floppy hat and raincoat, fleeing madly.

"Here." Josh handed her a chocolate chip cookie. "Maybe if you eat this, you'll have cavities by two-thirty."

"No such luck," she said. Especially since she'd only had one cavity in her entire life, despite sometimes being lazy about flossing and such.

The bell rang, and after they threw away their trash, Josh put his hand on her arm.

"Are you really that nervous?" he asked.

She nodded. "Yeah, kind of."

"You've done a bunch of interviews before," he said.

"Yeah, but not anything this big," she said. Her parents had always said that they thought "focused publicity" was looking for trouble. Preston sent out occasional, vague news releases—"Today, Meghan took her SATs," or "Steven was three for four, and struck

17

out twelve batters, in his most recent baseball game," but her parents wanted the three of them to have as little exposure as possible, for both security and privacy. She wasn't supposed to know about the percentage of letters and emails, out of the hundreds—sometimes *thousands*—she got every week, and usually spent Sunday afternoons trying to answer, that were obscene, or threatening—or both. The correspondence staff, as well as the Secret Service, screened everything first, but she had overheard people talking about some of the sick letters she had gotten. No one ever mentioned it directly.

Except once. In July, some horrible fundamentalist revolutionary group had decided that they wanted to kidnap her, and had mailed all kinds of detailed threats and made phone calls and posted all over the Internet and everything. She had been confined to the White House for over a week, everyone treating her like a little bundle of dynamite. She wasn't supposed to go out on the Truman Balcony, she wasn't supposed to walk around on the lawn, she wasn't supposed to do *anything*. What she did, was pace nervously around the house. Her parents had been extremely upset and, to counteract that, Meg tried to be cheerful and make jokes and pretend that none of it was happening. Since they had yelled at her for taking it too lightly, she was pretty sure the bravado had worked. She had tried to handle the whole thing with a certain panache. Humphrey Bogart all the way. Luckily, no one knew that she had gotten sick to her stomach almost every time she ate. Even now, when she thought about it, her stomach hurt.

But, nothing had happened, and gradually, her security eased back to its normal level. She really only worried about it once in a while—usually when she was alone in a car with her agents, and they were at a red light. If a van pulled up, she would get scared to death, gripping the door handle, expecting terrorist commandos to come leaping out with machine guns and drag her inside. Drag her inside, and—God, she didn't even want to think about it.

Anyway, her parents had decided to sign off on the interview with *People*, because they thought it seemed pretty safe—and that it would be a one-time-only event. Little things would still be printed, of course—like photos of Neal playing soccer, or Steven and her father shooting baskets. The first time Steven's picture had shown up in a gossip magazine, describing him as "a new teen heartthrob," he had been impossible to live with for a couple of weeks.

Pictures of her doing things like walking out of movie theaters with Josh, who was always described as "regular escort Joshua Feldman," popped up in the tabloids all the time, but more often, it would be a trumped-up shot of her—with some movie star she had never met, but with whom she was purportedly madly in love. After her mother had thrown out the first ball at Fenway Park in April, quite a few players had come over to their seats to say hello and shake hands with all of them—Steven had been absolutely overjoyed—and for a couple of weeks, photos of her kept surfacing, assuring the general public that she was currently dating *several* members of the Boston Red Sox.

Which actually didn't sound so bad to her.

Naturally, Josh had been somewhat less amused.

One pretty funny picture had been when some photographers took pictures of the three of them swimming in the White House pool for part of a story about her mother, which was going to include "The President's children at play." Meg had been wearing a somewhat skimpy two-piece bathing suit at the time, and had to stay underwater so that they wouldn't be able to get her from the neck down. The photographers thought she was a bad sport.

"What are you thinking about?" Josh asked, holding the cafeteria door for her.

Meg sighed. "The stupid pictures I'm going to have to pose for."

"What are you wearing?" he asked.

Good question. "I'm supposed to 'dress conservatively,'" she said. "Anyway, that's what my parents said."

"They're right." He rested his hand on her waist. "The country would get too excited, otherwise."

She shook her head. "Yeah, right."

"Would I lie to you?" he asked.

Good question. "I don't know," she said.

He smiled at her, the sweater she had given him for his birthday—a sort of coppery russet—bringing out the color in his eyes. "What do you think?"

"I think you're cute," she said.

3

CONSERVATIVE CLOTHING. SHE decided on a blue plaid wool skirt, a white Oxford shirt, navy blue nylons, and black flats. She was going to wear a headband, but it would make her look about eleven. So, she would have to stick with wavy and wild.

The phone next to her bed rang and she picked it up.

"I have a message from Mr. Fielding, Miss Powers," the chief usher said. Mr. Fielding was Preston.

"Is the reporter here?" she asked.

"Correct," the chief usher, Mr. Bryant, said. He was the man who pretty much ran every aspect of the Residence. "Shall I tell them you're on your way?"

"Yeah," Meg said. "I mean, please. I'm just going to brush my teeth and everything."

For one last touch, she yanked a blue crewneck out of her bottom dresser drawer to drape around her shoulders to complete the "casually conservative" image—although it took her three tries to make it look casual. Sporty, even.

"You want to come?" she asked Vanessa, who was sound asleep on her computer keyboard. Except that was pretty contrived. If she was going to go for the cat cuddled to her cheek, she might as well wear the damn headband.

Preston and the reporter were waiting in the solarium, with a bearded photographer. The reporter was an earnest-looking woman with curly brown hair and tortoise-shell eyeglasses, who was wearing a khaki pantsuit which might as well have *shrieked* "sleek, but practical." Preston had on a pair of leather ankle boots, black slacks, a light grey shirt with a skinny black silk tie, and a darker grey jacket over it,

21

his handkerchief perfectly folded in the outside pocket. Very stylish man. He saw her, and stood up.

"Meg, this is Kelly Wright," he indicated the woman, "and this is Ed Crouthers," he motioned towards the photographer, who nodded at her.

"How do you do, Ms. Wright," Meg said. "Mr. Crouthers."

"Please," the reporter said, her smile friendly. "Just call me Kelly."

Her mother's press secretary, Linda, had often said, grimly, "when they smile at you, *run*."

Meg nodded. "Okay, thank you. I'm Meg."

Although they probably already knew that.

"I had them bring a Coke for you," Preston said, pointing towards the tea tray.

Drinking Coca-Cola was *very* all-American. And well-adjusted. And non-controversial. Except, perhaps, for Pepsi devotees. "Thank you." Meg picked up the glass, noticing that everyone else had coffee. She was going to have to learn to like coffee. Holding it made her feel older.

Preston sat in an easy chair perpendicular to the couch, and Meg hesitantly took the place he had vacated, very self-conscious, trying not to flinch as the camera flash went off. She would not do well at the Barbizon School.

"You have a beautiful view," Ms. Wright said.

"Yeah," Meg said, looking out the windows at the South Lawn, and the Washington Monument and Jefferson Memorial beyond it. "I mean, yes, we do."

"I gather you all spend a lot of time in this room?" Ms. Wright asked.

"Yeah—I mean, yes," Meg said. Maybe her mother was right about the ruffian. "Pretty much. I mean, what with the television, and the little kitchen, and all." She coughed nervously, glancing at Preston, who gestured with one hand for her to relax.

Ms. Wright drank some of her coffee. "What I thought we'd do, Meg, is sit here and talk for a while, and I'll just ask informal questions. Does that sound all right to you?"

Meg nodded, her hand tight in her lap. Publicity definitely wasn't all that it was cracked up to be. At least Preston was here, instead of being off running interference for her father—which took up most of his time, since, even all of these months later, people didn't seem to be quite sure what to think about the reality of having a First Gentleman. There had been a big media splash when her father had chosen him—the very young, cool and charismatic destined-for-the-West-Wing black guy to be his press secretary, and Meg was pretty sure that her mother would much rather have given Preston a high-ranking position on her *own* staff, but obviously, it hadn't worked out that way. Preston was always making fun of her father—whom he called "Russell-baby" in private—for being bourgeois, and for Christmas, had given him subscriptions to several men's fashion magazines. It always amused Meg to see her father on a Saturday morning, slouching in old corduroys and a sweatshirt, reading *GQ*. Steven took a picture of him once.

"How do you feel about living in the White House?" Ms. Wright asked.

"Uh, well." Meg tried to think of something profound, or at least interesting, to say. "I don't know. It's, uh, it's pretty big." Great. That put her in the finals of the Inane Remarks of the Year contest.

If only she had some anecdotes. They probably wanted anecdotes.

Kirby came nosing out from underneath the coffee table and without thinking, Meg handed him a butter cookie from the tea tray.

"You have five animals?" Ms. Wright asked.

Meg almost said, "Six, if you include Steven," but was able to stop herself. "Yes. I think the cats are all downstairs."

Kirby wagged his tail, and she gave him another cookie. When they had gotten Kirby seven years earlier—at the pound; her parents believed in that—they had been assured that he was a German shepherd, but he had grown up into a large brown shaggy dog with odd splotches of white. Her mother said he was a collie; her father thought he was mostly retriever; Steven insisted that he was part Airedale. Meg usually just said that he was brown and white.

"Let's see." Ms. Wright checked her notes. "You have two Siamese, a tiger cat, and the grey one is yours, right?"

Meg nodded. "I found her at the Chestnut Hill Mall when I was thirteen."

Ms. Wright smiled. "What was she doing at the Chestnut Hill Mall?"

"She was in Bloomingdale's," Meg said, forgetting to count to three. She blushed. "I mean, I guess someone abandoned her, and the ASPCA said it was okay for me to keep her."

Mr. Crouthers decided that he would like a photo of Meg with her cat, so Meg went downstairs to get her, returning and posing for a few pictures. Cute and contrived. Then, Ms. Wright began asking more directed questions—about her friends, hobbies, and White House routines.

Meg answered them, saying that she liked skiing, tennis, and reading. Reading what? Oh, anything—political novels, classics, whatever was around. No romances? No, Meg said. What would Josh Feldman say about that? He'd laugh, Meg said—which was true, and then went on to answer questions about Josh; about how he was in her class, and he was a really good pianist and baseball player, and yeah, it was kind of serious, but not really serious. She looked at Preston to see if she should maybe elaborate on that, but he shook his head.

The questions got harder. Like, how did it feel to be the only daughter of the first female President of the United States. Unique, Meg was going to say, but she counted to three, and said "challenging," instead.

"In what way?" Ms. Wright asked.

Maybe she'd outsmarted herself by not going with her original response. "Um, well." Meg thought. "I guess everyone has to work harder. To be a family, I mean. To make time for everyone else."

Ms. Wright nodded, and wrote that down. "Would you say that you have a good family?"

"Well, yeah." Meg shifted uncomfortably. "I mean, *I* think so."

"How do you and your parents get along?" Ms. Wright asked.

"Fine," Meg said. Classic, cautious answer.

Ms. Wright raised her eyebrows. "You never argue?"

What a no-win question. Either she had to air a bit of dirty laundry—or lie. "Well, sometimes," Meg said. "It's nothing major, though."

"What sort of things do you argue about?" Ms. Wright asked.

Foreign policy. "Well." Meg glanced over at Preston, who nodded. She sipped some Coke, planning an answer. "I don't know. About bedtime." She looked at Ms. Wright, who motioned for her to continue. "I mean, I usually stay up pretty late, and sometimes my parents grump and say I'll never be able to get up in the morning."

"Are they right?" Ms. Wright asked, seeming a little disappointed by the very tiny scope of the answer.

"Sometimes," Meg said. Lots of times. *Most* of the time. Her mother, who always woke up instantly, couldn't understand why other people might have trouble.

"What else do you argue about?" Ms. Wright wanted to know.

Damn. The smiling reporter had finally decided to dig her cleats in. "I don't know." Meg broke a butter cookie in half, and then, in quarters. "If my room's a mess. If I'm screwing around"—she flushed—"I mean, fooling around, instead of doing homework." She looked at Preston, who indicated for her to relax, that they knew what she meant.

"What about drinking and marijuana?" Ms. Wright asked.

Meg counted to six. "What about them?" Steven had once told a really obnoxious reporter that he was a methadone addict, and it had taken some quick work on Preston's part to keep it from getting printed.

Ms. Wright shrugged. "Well, a lot of young people today—"

"I don't," Meg said. That would be all she needed—to show up in the tabloids, or on the Internet, drunk at a party.

Ms. Wright nodded. "I see. Because of your position?"

Enough already. "Because I don't want to," Meg said, barely keeping the irritation out of her voice. "The people I hang around with aren't into that."

"What *are* they into?" Ms. Wright asked pleasantly.

Whips and chains. "I don't know," Meg said, and shrugged. "Movies, parties, sports. The same as anyone else."

Ms. Wright picked up her coffee cup so casually that Meg was immediately on guard. "What about your boyfriend?"

Hadn't she just answered that? "Well," Meg said. "We go to movies, mostly." A couple of times, they had gone to hear jazz— which kind of bored her, but Josh was really into it, so she always pretended to be having an *excellent* time, even during really monotonous solos.

"Do you and your parents discuss your relationship?" Ms. Wright asked.

Meg nodded. "Well, yeah. Sure."

Ms. Wright put her coffee cup down. "Are your parents as liberal in practice as they are on paper?"

And, the mild-mannered reporter moved in for the kill. Meg counted to three. And then, to five. Her mother was right; the trick to handling an interview was to control the pace. "Of course they are," Meg said. "They wouldn't be very honest, otherwise."

"What about premarital sex?" Ms. Wright asked.

Whoa. Now, she was getting mean. Meg looked at her as benignly as possible. "In what sense?"

Ms. Wright smiled back. "What do you think about it?"

Meg coughed so that she wouldn't say that she thought about it constantly. "I think it's a subjective issue."

"How do you feel about it personally?" Ms. Wright asked.

"It would depend on the situation," Meg said.

Ms. Wright actually leaned forward. "How so?"

Upon which, Preston stepped in. "Come on. Are your readers really interested in that sort of thing?"

"How many teenagers do you know?" Ms. Wright said, but then raised a hand to show that she knew she had overstepped her bounds. "What about college, Meg?"

Whew. She was back on solid ground, for the moment. "I'll probably be applying to seven or eight schools," Meg said, "and then, it'll depend on where I get in."

Ms. Wright looked at her over her glasses. "You're not really expecting to have any trouble getting in, are you?"

Well—no. Which sucked, regardless of whether anyone believed her about that. "College admissions are a pretty subjective thing," Meg said.

"Like sex?" Ms. Wright asked, and Meg laughed.

The interview got a little better after that, and Meg answered questions about her parents, her brothers, and about how they all considered Trudy, their former housekeeper, to be their grandmother, since they didn't have any grandparents of their own anymore. She also said that having Secret Service agents didn't bother her—which wasn't true, that the White House was actually very homey—which was *sort* of true, and that no, she had never resented her mother for having spent so little time at home over the years—which wasn't even *close* to being true.

Ms. Wright scanned her notes. "Just one more thing. Do you have any advice you'd like to give to other teenagers?"

Meg stared at her. "Advice? Like what?"

Ms. Wright shrugged. "You tell me."

For starters, she would advise them all to buy low, and sell high. Meg laughed. "What, you mean like, something inspirational? You're kidding, right?" She saw that Ms. Wright wasn't laughing. "You're not kidding?" What was she supposed to talk about—good citizenship? Family values? Her personal relationship with Christ? She could spout about economic recovery, but Preston would get mad.

"You can't think of anything?" Ms. Wright asked, sounding faintly disappointed.

"Well—no." Meg played with her Coke glass. "If I start talking about—I don't know—social responsibility, I'm going to sound like a real jerk."

Ms. Wright immediately seized upon *that* one. "Do you think there's a need for social responsibility?"

Meg hesitated. "Is this on the record?"

Ms. Wright laughed, shutting her notebook and capping her felt-tip pen. "No. It's not on the record."

Meg smiled uncertainly.

They ended up going downstairs, where they ran into Steven and two of his friends, who were eating ice cream and laughing raucously, while Neal tagged along after them. The photographer took some pictures, Ms. Wright asked some questions, and then, finally, they left. After accompanying them to the East Wing Lobby, Meg sank down on a small settee in the Garden Room, exhausted.

"Well." Preston sat down next to her. "That wasn't so bad, was it?"

Meg just groaned.

4

"PRESTON TELLS ME you were quite the political kid today," her father remarked at dinner.

He had also said that her outfit had not only looked conservative, but downright *Amish*. "Yeah," she said, briefly. "Neal, can you pass the salt, please?"

Her mother, who had been taking phone calls and going out to the West Sitting Hall every so often to confer with various aides and advisors, looked up. "How did it go?"

Meg shrugged. "Okay. Kind of embarrassing."

"Boy," Steven reached across the table to take the salt after Meg finished with it, "you should have seen Meggie when they started taking pictures. Throwing her hair and everything." He imitated her. "She loved it."

Meg blushed. "I did not. I hate having my picture taken."

"So, how come you were throwing your hair?" he asked.

"I wasn't," she said.

"Yeah, sure." Steven stuffed half a roll into his mouth. "When that photographer guy asked you to, you did."

"Well, he asked me to," Meg said defensively.

Her mother lowered the report she was reading. "What *else* did the photographer ask you to do?"

"What," Meg said, "you mean, other than dance topless and sing 'I'm Just a Girl Who Can't Say No'?"

Her parents laughed, but nervously.

"D'ja tell them about the centerfold yet?" Steven asked with his mouth full.

"Steven, cut it out." She tried to kick him under the table.

Neal laughed. "I saw her. She was throwing her hair."

"Neal, shut up." She tried to kick him, instead, but he moved his legs out of the way.

"It wouldn't hurt to have a sense of humor, Meg," her father said mildly.

Meg scowled at her brothers. "It wouldn't hurt to have them shut up, either."

"Steven, have you decided whether you're going to try out for basketball?" their mother asked.

Ever the diplomat.

Steven shrugged. "Dunno. Coach says I'm too short."

"Yeah, really," Meg said. "Talk about munchkins."

"Shut up!" Steven tried to kick *her*. "It's not my fault!"

"Meg, act your age," their father said.

"Oh, yeah," she said, picking up her fork. "He harasses me for ten hours, and I get in trouble for saying one thing. Yeah, that's fair."

Their mother sighed. "Come on, let's not fight at the table."

Logic which had never made any damn sense to her, no matter how many times she heard it. Meg put her fork down. "Can I ask you something? Why's it matter if we fight at the table? I mean, what's the difference if we fight *away* from the table, or at it?"

"The difference," their father said, very patient, "is that your mother and I like to relax at dinner, not listen to a lot of wrangling."

"But, we like to wrangle," Neal said.

Their mother closed her eyes for a second, passing her hand across her forehead.

"Want some of my Valium?" Meg asked.

"No," her mother said. "I do not want some of your Valium."

What a shame. "I've got Librium, too," Meg said. "You want some Librium? Or OxyContin?"

"What's Librium?" Neal asked.

"Remember those blue pills I was giving you the other day?" Meg asked. "Those were—"

"Wait," Steven interrupted. "You were giving him red pills. I don't remember any blue pills."

"Really? Hmmm." Meg frowned. "Maybe they were amphetamines, then. Are you sure, Steven? I really thought I was giving him Librium."

Steven shook his head. "No, you were giving *me* Librium."

"Kate, why don't we go have some coffee before you have to head back downstairs," their father said, looking across the table at their mother, who responded with a tired nod.

"You'll be missing out," Steven said. "We're going to take this act on the road."

Their father stood up. "The sooner, the better."

"Yeah, see if *you* get tickets," Steven grumbled.

When their parents were gone, he stopped slouching, sitting up with his elbows on the table. "What's with them?" he asked. "They're pretty cranky tonight."

"We were pretty bratty," Meg said.

Steven shook his head. "No way. I thought we were being funny. Funnier than usual, even."

Neal looked worried. "Are Mom and Dad mad?"

"No." Meg finished her squash. "Mom just had a bad day"—and, judging from the stream of phone calls and conferences, quite possibly a tough night ahead—"and Dad thinks we gave her a headache. You know how he is."

"But, is he *mad*?" Neal asked anxiously.

"I said no, already." Meg held out her plate. "You want my beets, Steven?"

Steven made a gagging sound.

Meg held the plate under the table. "Want my beets, Kirby?"

Kirby sniffed the cold purple vegetable, then went back to sleep.

"Would any of you like dessert?" Felix asked, coming in to clear the table.

"I'm all set, thanks," Meg said, carrying her plate to the kitchen, Steven and Neal following suit.

"Do we have any cookies or anything?" Steven asked.

Felix smiled a nice grandfatherly smile. "I'm sure we can find something."

After hanging out in the kitchen for a while to eat cookies, Meg left to see what her parents were doing. She found her father by the fireplace in the Yellow Oval Room, drinking coffee.

She sat down in a yellow and white antique chair. Louis XIV. Or maybe it was Louis XVI. She wasn't into furniture. "Where's Mom?"

"In the Treaty Room," he said. Which was her upstairs office. "She's trying to get some work done, so don't bother her."

Steven was right; they *were* unusually cranky tonight. "I wasn't going to," Meg said, feeling very defensive. "Why are you in such a bad mood?"

Her father looked annoyed. "I'm not."

Yeah, right. "Well." She stood up. "Sorry I came in here."

"I didn't say for you to leave," he said.

Maybe not directly. Meg shrugged, stiffly. "You don't look too thrilled about me staying, either."

Her father sighed, then smiled, patting the soft cushion next to him. Meg gave brief consideration to storming out of the room anyway—but then, sat down.

"I'm sorry," he said. "Your mother and I are just tired."

Which made her feel very guilty. "I'm sorry we were being jerks at dinner."

"You weren't being any jerkier than usual." He let out his breath. "Your mother has a very high-pressure job."

"So do you," Meg said.

"I wouldn't say there's a comparison." He leaned back into the cushions, staring up at the ceiling.

Out of all of them, he complained the least—but had probably been affected the *most* by her mother winning the election. "Do you hate it here?" she asked.

He turned his head just enough to look at her. " 'Hate' is a rather strong word."

Okay. "Do you intensely dislike it here?" she asked.

He laughed, reaching over to ruffle her hair. "I'm fine. How about you? Preston said they gave you a pretty rough time."

She nodded.

"He also thought that you handled it like a pro," he said.

Albeit, an *Amish* pro. Meg shrugged, looking at the small fire in the fireplace.

It was silent for a long minute, her father seemingly deep in his own thoughts.

"I worry about you," he said. "You're—very hard to shelter."

As far as she was concerned, that was one of the best things about being a senior, and with college looming in the very near future, she was starting to have moments here and there when she felt a genuine—if fleeting—sense of autonomy. Which she liked. *A lot.* She looked up at him. "Dad, I'm seventeen. I don't need sheltering."

"I just don't want to see you change," he said quietly.

She tilted her head, confused. "What, you mean, grow up?"

"I don't want to see you turn into a politician," he said.

All she did was *read* about politics—and, admittedly, watch C-Span and CNN and all. Still, that didn't make it a *vocation.* "You married one," she said uneasily.

He nodded, looking in the direction of the Treaty Room.

Oh, no. "Are you guys having a fight?" Meg asked. She hated it when her parents argued. They almost never did it in front of anyone, but there would be taut antagonism in the air, buried anger which made her feel as if she were in an invisible maze where she couldn't bump into any of the walls or open any of the doors.

"No, I just—I don't know." He picked up his coffee cup, drinking some. "They don't have any bright ideas about putting you on the cover, do they?"

Jesus, she *hoped* not. "I don't know," she said.

He nodded. "Good. Your mother and I wouldn't permit that."

Meg grinned. "Because I'm too ugly?"

"Well, that, too," he said, putting an affectionate arm around her shoulders.

That meant that he thought it would be dangerous to have her on the cover. She folded her arms across her stomach, concentrating on not remembering the week she had been confined to the White House.

The Treaty Room was just next door to the Yellow Oval Room, and she knew her mother would be in there sitting behind the walnut table, right hand clenched around a silver pen, telephone balanced on her shoulder, papers everywhere. Maybe switching from her contact lenses to her glasses, while she waited for the ibuprofen to work on her headache. The headache Meg and Steven and Neal had given her.

"Thinking great thoughts?" her father asked.

Not by a long shot. In fact, she was starting to get a little headache herself. She looked at the connecting door leading to the Treaty Room—which was tightly closed, and actually rarely used; her mother almost always went in there through the Stair Landing entrance. "Does she like being the President?"

Her father nodded. "Most of the time. In fact, I think she's a little surprised by how *much* she likes it."

On good days, in fact, she practically seemed to *glow*. "What about you, though?" Meg asked. "Do you wish she wasn't?"

"That would be like wishing she were a different person," he said.

Which she decided to take as a no.

Now, *he* looked at the closed door, which was painted pale yellow, to blend in with the wall. "Hard to share her with the rest of the country," he said.

Extremely hard.

"But, I think it's worth it," he said. "Don't you?"

Personally, her jury was still out on that one. "I guess," Meg said, without much enthusiasm. The country seemed to be getting a pretty good deal, but it would certainly be a lot less stressful for her family, if her mother were a teacher or a lawyer or something, and they lived quietly in Massachusetts, like regular people.

"Think of your friends, Meg," her father said. "Every family has situations to which they have to adjust."

Meg considered that. Josh's parents were divorced, and so were Beth's. Nathan's little brother was autistic, Alison's mother had recently been diagnosed with multiple sclerosis—yeah, every family definitely had challenges. Her family just had—an unusual one.

"Is Josh coming over tonight?" her father asked.

She nodded. "Yeah. We're going to study." Maybe.

He looked at her curiously. "He's certainly over here a lot these days. How are things going with him?"

"Good. I mean—" She searched for a better way to phrase it. "He's my best friend here." Which maybe wasn't very romantic, but was the truth.

Her father nodded. "That's the way it should be."

"Is it with you and Mom?" she asked.

"Absolutely," he said.

5

JOSH SHOWED UP a little before nine, and they went to the West Sitting Hall, because her parents were pretty strict about them *not* being alone in her bedroom together. A rule they had been known to break, but not egregiously so.

The West Sitting Hall had a huge, double-arched window that looked out over the West Wing, the Oval Office, and the Old Executive Office Building. Kind of a nice view. It was also one of the only rooms in the Residence with furniture from their house in Massachusetts—the coffee table from their sitting room, the couch and love seat from the living room, various lamps, and even a couple of the plants. It was Meg's favorite place in the White House, except for the solarium—and, of course, the tennis court outside.

"The interview was okay?" Josh asked.

"Lots of fun," she said, starting to move her hair back off her shoulders. Then she thought about Steven making fun of her for throwing it around, and lowered her hand.

"When's it going to run?" he asked.

Good question. "I don't know. A few weeks, maybe." Unconsciously, she lifted her right hand to move her hair, saw what she was doing, and frowned at it.

Josh looked at her curiously. "What's wrong?"

She put her hand down, blushing. "Nothing."

"What are you so embarrassed about?" He moved the hair back for her. "I think it's cute when you play with your hair."

"I don't play with my hair," she said.

He grinned.

How could she have a habit that stupid—and not even know about it? "Well, it gets in my eyes," she said, self-consciously.

"I think it's cute." His hand moved from her shoulder to her face. "It's also sexy," he said, moving much closer.

"It is, hunh? Hmmm." She brought her hair forward, then whipped it back with a sweeping gesture. "How sexy?"

"*Very* sexy," he said.

"Oh, really?" She tossed it back again.

"Stop it," he said. "You're making me crazy."

She threw her hair back a third time.

"Okay." He put his glasses on the side table. "You asked for it."

She grinned at him. "For what?"

He pushed her onto her back, kissing her, both of them laughing.

"I may ask for it more often," she said.

"Well, let me tell you," he kissed her, "I'll—"

"Christ," Steven said, coming in from the Center Hall. "Is making out all you guys ever do?"

They sat up quickly, Meg straightening her hair, while Josh put his glasses back on.

"You're lucky I'm not Dad," Steven said.

"Yeah, well, what do you want?" Meg asked, trying to recover her dignity.

"I just came downstairs. Can't a guy come downstairs?" He grinned, and sat on the couch between them. "So. How's it going, Josh?"

"Fine," Josh said.

Steven put his arm around Meg. "You've got yourself a good little woman here. You know that, don't you?"

She ducked away from his arm. "Steven, will you get out of here?"

"I just want to know his intentions," Steven said. "Can't I ask his intentions?"

Meg shook her head. "You can get out of here, that's what you can do."

"Well, okay. I'll leave you two kids alone." He grabbed Josh's hand, shaking it firmly. "Come down to the office sometime, boy. We'll talk."

"Thank you, sir," Josh said. "I'll do that."

"Good." Steven nodded several times, starting for his room. "We'll talk."

Josh watched him go, walking like an elderly Supreme Court justice. "The kid's a maniac."

"The kid's a *pain*," Meg said.

Josh nodded, and she knew he was refraining from saying that he thought the two of them had the exact same sense of humor. They headed up to the solarium to watch television for a while—she was a *big* one-hour drama person—and then, switched over to the news at eleven, where the top story was about the President, and her response to the most recent flare-up in the Middle East.

"Do you really want to watch this?" Josh asked.

Would it be embarrassing to admit that the answer was yes? "I don't know. We could just go down and *ask* her, I guess." She took off his glasses, putting them on herself. "What do you want to do?"

He removed the glasses, putting them carefully on the nearest table, and then leaned forward.

"We could listen to music," she said, just as he was about to kiss her.

He stopped, his arms resting on her shoulders. "Do you want to?"

"If you do," she said.

He kissed her, and slowly, they moved until they were lying on the couch.

"We got a whole new shipment the other day," she said. The music companies—along with publishing houses, and Hollywood—almost always sent their latest releases to the President and First Family as a matter of courtesy, and there were literally thousands of recent movies and CDs in the White House collection, most of which was stored up here on the third floor. "I could just walk out there and pick out a few—"

Josh kissed her harder.

"Or," she said, when she got her mouth free, "I could stay right here."

He nodded. "You could do that."

"Unless you want to hear some inspirational gospel songs," she said. "You want to hear some gospel music? Or folk music. I bet I could dig up some really rousing folk music."

He moved to kiss her neck, and she decided that it would be much more pleasant to remain where she was.

"I'm going to take off my shirt," he whispered, after a few minutes. "Okay?"

She nodded, not even wanting to let go of him for that long, and he sat up, yanking the t-shirt over his head, then stretching out back on top of her.

Wow. She slid her hands over his shoulders and down his back, feeling the muscles and the warmth of his skin. Wow. Why did she always get excited so quickly? Maybe there was something wrong with her.

His breathing was faster, and Meg could feel and hear herself breathing almost as quickly. Practically panting, in fact. She blushed, embarrassed by the sound, a blush that made her face feel even hotter. His hand was inside her shirt, and she wondered if it was supposed to feel that good, or if there really *was* something wrong with her. Well, Meg, she could hear the White House doctor, Dr. Brooks, saying, I'm sorry, but it looks like a case of terminal libido. How long do I have, doctor? she would ask, choking back tears. Three months, he would say. Make them good ones.

Josh's heart was pounding, and she hugged him closer, affection and passion mixing somewhere inside her.

"I wish—" He sighed, resting his head against hers.

"What?" she asked, although she was pretty sure she could guess the answer.

"I don't know." He rolled onto his back, bringing her with him. "I wish we could go somewhere where I didn't have to be scared that the President of the United States was going to walk in."

Meg laughed. "I'd be more afraid of the First Gentleman."

"You know what I mean," he said.

Now, she sighed. "Yeah, I guess."

"You *know* what I mean," he said.

"Yeah." She turned her head enough to look at him. "If we went anywhere else, my agents would have to be there." And it wasn't as though they could be alone over at his house, because if his mother wasn't home, he was invariably babysitting for his little sister.

Josh nodded, looking very frustrated.

"It's not my fault," she said defensively.

"I know it isn't." He rested his hand on her face, running his fingers along her cheekbone. "I'm sorry."

"Don't apologize," she said, starting to feel a little testy.

"I'm sorry, I won't." He stopped. "I mean—"

She shook her head, amused. "I know what you mean." She ran her hand across his chest, very much liking the fact that he had hair on it. Not too much; just enough. "If you want, I could tell you some jokes."

He relaxed, too. "You don't know any jokes."

"I know lots of jokes," she said.

He grinned. "You always say that, but you never tell me any."

"I'm afraid of offending you," she said. "Most of them are anti-male, anti-Jewish, anti-musician, and anti-people-with-glasses."

He nodded. "That kind of cuts me out."

"Well, yeah," she said. "So I don't tell them, because I don't want to hurt your feelings."

He kissed her. "Thanks. I appreciate it."

"If you want," she moved to a more comfortable position, so her arm wouldn't fall asleep, "instead of listening to music, I could sing for you."

"You're getting in a weird mood," he said.

Seemed that way, yeah.

He sighed, and then sat up.

"I have these spells," she said. "It's because I was born in Salem."

He reached for his glasses. "You were born in Boston."

She nodded. "At the State House. My mother was giving a speech."

"And you finished it, because she was tired," he said.

She turned to look at him. "I've told you this before?"

"Lucky guess," he said.

They both laughed, and he leaned over to kiss her.

"I should probably go," he said. "It's pretty late."

Yeah. Unfortunately.

After walking him downstairs, and saying a very chaste good-bye, because of the doorman, and the Secret Service agents nearby, Meg went back up to the second floor. She walked down to the kitchen, deciding to get herself a couple of cookies, and maybe some cheese for Vanessa. When she came out, her mother was standing outside the Presidential Bedroom door, holding a cup of coffee.

"Did Josh leave?" she asked.

Meg nodded. "Yeah, a few minutes ago."

"I would have come out to say good-night, but," her mother gestured towards her bathrobe. Then, she glanced at her watch. "Does his mother mind him getting home this late on a school night?"

"I don't think so," Meg said.

"Were you two up in the solarium this whole time?" her mother asked.

Meg nodded.

"Was there something interesting on television?" her mother asked.

The President, being indirect, and not very subtle about it. "The news," Meg said.

41

Her mother looked at her watch again.

"And, you know, um, SportsCenter," Meg said, embarrassed to feel herself blushing. "And—homework."

Her mother wasn't doing a very good job of pretending not to be concerned, so Meg decided to change the subject.

"You want to see if there are any good movies on?" she asked. "Maybe we could—"

Her mother shook her head. "It's a little late. Don't you think you're going to have some trouble getting up tomorrow?"

So far, this conversation wasn't going very well. "Yeah, probably." She edged towards the Center Hall. "Guess I'll go to bed."

"All right, sleep well," her mother said.

Meg nodded. "Yeah, you, too."

"Thank you," her mother said, and paused. "You *are* as mature as I think you are, aren't you?"

Meg was very tempted to ask exactly how mature she thought she was. "I'm not sure what you mean," she said, taking an Oreo apart to eat the middle.

"Meg, I'm not trying to invade your privacy. I just—" Her mother frowned. "Worry."

"Well," Meg said, for lack of anything better to say.

They both stood there.

"Is that it?" her mother asked.

Pretty much. "Well, kind of. I mean, we—well, it's—" Meg sighed. "Want an Oreo?"

6

EVEN IN THE White House, life could be fairly routine. Meg spent the rest of the week concentrating on tennis, and having long discussions with her parents—which, on her part, mostly involved listening and nodding—about where she should apply to college. Right now, she had it narrowed down to Harvard, Yale, Brown, Princeton, Columbia, Williams, Stanford, and Georgetown, although Beth had been lobbying pretty heavily for Wesleyan, Sarah Lawrence, and Hampshire. Or, alternatively, hiking around Europe and getting into as much minor-league trouble as possible. In the meantime, her parents were still pushing Harvard—and only Harvard.

Right after school started, she and her father had visited a bunch of different colleges, mostly in New England—a trip the media adored. Like at Yale, Senator Quigley's son had taken her on the campus tour, which the press seemed to think made for a nice human interest spin, and photos of the two of them together showed up in numerous places, identifying him as her new boyfriend, and describing them—since Senator Quigley was the ranking member of the Senate Judiciary Committee—as "young Washington royalty."

In any case, Meg was sort of leaning towards Williams—off in the mountains, away from publicity, near skiing. Harvard would be pretty much exactly the opposite.

Her mother had been tense and distracted all week, worrying about the escalating problems in the Middle East, and the summit meeting which was going to be held at Camp David right after Thanksgiving. It was, essentially, a G-8 conference of world leaders, and there was a lot at stake. Her mother had made a number of foreign trips, including Berlin, London, Paris, and Madrid, as well as recent short visits to Canada and Mexico, but this was the first time that all of the major foreign officials were coming to the United States during her administration, and the staff had been working on all of the pre-summit negotiations for weeks.

Her father was mostly concentrating his efforts on housing and environmental stuff, and ever since her mother took office, he had regularly appeared at global warming conferences, and made trips to places like the Gulf Coast, to help with the still-extensive rebuilding efforts. Her mother had a great Secretary of the Interior, with whom her father had hit it off, and they had been making a point of coordinating their policy efforts. Even though everyone else in the family usually made a point to stay as far away from nature as possible, Meg had a theory that her father's secret ambition was to be a forest ranger.

Steven had made the basketball team and seemed to spend every waking moment dribbling, although he probably wouldn't get to play much. There was a half-court in a secluded spot on the South Lawn, so he was always out there for hours. The only place he was allowed to dribble inside the house was the North Entrance Hall. The doormen and guards really seemed to get a charge out of it, and kept giving him tips.

Neal was mad, because the Secret Service didn't want him to go trick-or-treating. Apparently, if he kept his mask on, he might be permitted to stop at a few, carefully selected houses, but he wouldn't be allowed to eat any of the candy, afterwards. Steven thought this was uproariously funny, until it occurred to him that this year he wasn't going to be able to go out and throw eggs or whatever delinquent thing he and his friends in Massachusetts would have been doing.

Her mother's solution to all of this was to have a Halloween party—a costume party—to which Steven's and Neal's friends could come. Meg thought *this* was hysterically funny, until her father came up with the bright idea that Meg and some of *her* friends could dress up and be chaperones. The press thought it all sounded wonderful, and the event had apparently already become so prestigious, that half of the offices on Capitol Hill had called, trying to wrangle invitations for their various bosses' progeny. For her part, Meg was kind of hoping to contract the flu that day, and conveniently be unable to attend.

On the morning that the tennis team was playing the one school with a first singles player whom she wasn't sure she could beat, she had a little trouble getting up, a problem which she suspected was Freudian.

The switchboard had to call three times before she said, "Okay, okay, I'm awake," and meant it. She crawled out from underneath her quilt, opened the draperies, and was instantly depressed. The sky was grey, with rain threatening. When she had checked the weather on the Internet, before she went to bed, all of the forecasts had said that it was *definitely* going to rain from midnight on, which would mean that the tennis match was canceled. From the looks of the sky, the storm wouldn't start until right after she lost.

Very grumpy, she opened her closet to find something to wear. There weren't any rules, but the President's daughter was supposed to try to look nice, if she could—not that Meg ever tried very hard. Today, she felt like looking mean as hell, but that was probably out of the question.

She stared at the dresses, skirts, nice pants, respectable jeans and disreputable jeans—then took a pair of blue sweatpants out of her bottom dresser drawer. She put them on with a light blue Lacoste and a darker blue chamois shirt as a jacket. Not in the mood for socks, she stepped into her Topsiders. All of this made her feel somewhat less grumpy, and she went over to one bookcase—she had two built-in cases on either side of the fireplace, plus a huge freestanding one—to find something she could skim a few chapters of and be completely cheered up. She pulled out *Daisy Fay and the Miracle Man*, which was an hysterically funny book by Fannie Flagg, and fell onto her bed to read.

"Hey, Meg!" Steven bellowed down the hall. "Dad says you'd better hurry up!"

She looked at the clock, scowled, and slammed the book onto the floor.

"Meg, come on!" he yelled.

"I'm coming already!" Twice as grumpy as before, she slouched down the hall to the Presidential Dining Room, reaching for the orange juice without bothering to say good morning to anyone.

"Snap it up," her father said. "You're going to be late."

Meg poured her orange juice so quickly that she spilled some on the tablecloth and had to blot it up with her linen napkin.

"Boy, talk about stupid," Steven said.

Meg kept blotting so that she wouldn't throw the glassful at him.

"What are you wearing?" her mother asked, and Meg could tell that she was in a foul mood, too.

"Sweatpants." She took the Frosted Flakes box from Neal, who was reading the back of it.

"Well, go change," her mother said. "I don't want you going to school like that."

"Like what?" Meg filled her cereal bowl and started reading the box herself, which made Neal kick her under the table. "I always dress like this."

Her mother frowned at her. "Not in public, you don't."

Meg ignored her, reading the box.

"Dad, make her give it back," Neal said. "I had it first!"

"Give him the box, Meg," her father said, sounding very irritated. "And go put on something presentable."

Meg let out a hard breath, returning the box as ungraciously as possible.

"Ground her," Steven advised, his mouth full of English muffin.

"Shut up," Meg said, "or I'll tell them you're the one who broke the eagle vase."

Her parents scowled at Steven, who mouthed the word "bitch" across the table at her.

Their mother put down the morning edition of the *Post*. "It was that basketball, wasn't it? From now on, you're not to use it anywhere in the house, got it?"

"Not even in the North Entrance Hall?" Steven asked. "You promised I could—"

Their mother picked her newspaper back up, her mouth tight. "I changed my mind."

"That's not fair," Steven said. "You promised!"

Their father pointed at him. "One more word out of you, and you're going to be the one who gets grounded."

Steven sat glowering for a silent minute, then looked across the table at Meg. "Bitch," he said, then grabbed the basketball which was on the rug next to his chair and ran out of the room.

"Steven!" Their father jumped up. "Get back here!" He spun to face Meg. "See what you started? I hope you're happy."

Meg shrugged. "I didn't start anything. He's the one who—"

"You started it," Neal said.

"I did not!" she said. "You just—"

Her mother's paper slammed down. "Meg, I don't know what your problem is, but I'm in no mood for it."

Since she was going to get herself grounded for about thirty years if she stayed in the room, Meg pushed away from the table.

"You're not to leave the house until you change," her father said.

She kept going, and he grabbed her by the sleeve.

"Starting right now, you're grounded," he said. "For two weeks, and if you don't shape up by then—"

"Big deal." Meg shook her arm free. "What's it matter if I can't go anywhere without a bunch of damn agents, anyway?"

"You want me to make it a month?" he asked.

Jesus, she couldn't *wait* to go away to college. "Do what you want," Meg said, and left the room. She got her tennis bag and knapsack from her bedroom, meeting her mother on her way out.

"I said for you to change." Her mother's voice was calm, but angry.

"I don't have time," Meg said. "I'm late."

Her mother moved her jaw. "I'll write you a note."

Meg looked at her, tall and determined in a grey flannel Brooks Brothers dress with barely visible white pinstripes. Then she sighed, went back into her room, put on a different pair of blue sweatpants, and came out again.

"Satisfied?" she asked, and her mother looked so furious that she backed up a step.

"Meg, I'd advise you to get back in there," her mother said, her voice quiet enough to be a little scary.

Meg swallowed, afraid to push it any further, but not wanting to back down, either.

"*Now,*" her mother said.

Meg hesitated, still not sure how to play this.

"I'm late," she said, and ran down the hall, taking the stairs to the first floor so quickly that she almost fell. Her agents were waiting, and she jumped into her car.

Wayne grinned at her. "Running a little late?"

The odds that the President would chase after her were low—since it would lack dignity—but, she didn't want to take any chances. "Yeah," she said. "Let's go."

Gary started the engine. "Trouble getting up?"

"Let's just go, okay?" she asked. "Uh, I mean—please."

When she got to school, she headed straight to her locker without pausing to talk to anyone, or even say hello. She opened it, not bothering to admire the decorations inside. Big-shot seniors always decorated their lockers, and hers had a mainly photographic motif. Postcards of old-time movie stars like Cary Grant and Humphrey Bogart, digital photos of her favorite Red Sox players—none of whom she was dating, and a couple of snapshots of Josh. There were also a few pictures of Boston, but it was essentially a locker full of men, and usually, opening the metal door cheered her up no matter what kind of mood she was in.

Not today.

Alison drifted over. "Ready for the big match?" she asked cheerfully.

Meg jammed her tennis bag into the locker. "Who cares about the stupid match."

Alison frowned. "What's with you?"

Her bag didn't seem to want to go in there, and she kicked the bottom to *make* it fit. "Nothing."

"If you say so," Alison said.

"I say so." Meg let her walk away, focusing on Cary Grant. Then, she sighed. "Alison, wait."

Her friend turned. Alison qualified as a big-shot senior by the way she dressed. Which was generally a distinct combination of being retro—and timeless. Today, she had on baggy corduroy pants, an Argyle sweater vest, an Oxford shirt that probably belonged to her brother Andrew, and a very long, gauzy scarf. Annie Hall was alive and well, and living in the District of Columbia, NW.

Meg kept her eyes on Cary Grant. "I'm sorry. I'm in a pretty lousy mood."

"I didn't notice," Alison said. Stiffly.

Meg sighed. "I'm sorry, I had a fight with my mother." She was going to say, "my stupid mother," but it was tacky to be publicly derogative about parents.

"Um, a bad one?" Alison asked. People were usually cautious when they asked questions about the President.

"I'm probably grounded for the next *year*." Meg searched through her English folder for the essay she had spent half the night working on. It wasn't there, and she frowned, checking her notebook, and then the rest of her knapsack.

"What's wrong?" Alison asked, as she began to go through her knapsack again.

"I forgot my stupid English paper." Because of her stupid mother. Meg gritted her teeth. It was okay to *think* derogatory things about parents. "Mrs. Hayes is going to kill me."

"Just tell her you forgot it," Alison said.

"Oh, yeah, great." Meg kicked her locker shut. "She'll probably flunk me."

Alison grinned, but sympathetically. "Not if you explain."

"With my luck? No way." Meg leaned forward against her locker for a second, resting her head on her arms. "You might want to stay away from me. I have a feeling I'm going to be mean to people."

She grouched her way through the morning, not participating in class, scrawling inane pictures in her notebook: jagged lines, people skiing, Vanessa sleeping. Everyone seemed to sense her mood, and no one bugged her much—which made it easier not to offend them by snapping and snarling.

"Cheer up," Josh said, as they walked into physics. "It can't be *that* bad."

"You weren't there," she said, taking her usual seat in the back. They always sat in the back.

"It's nothing to get worked up about," he said. "Everyone fights with their parents."

"Yeah." Meg twisted a pencil in her hands and—predictably—it broke. "But, I think I kind of went overboard."

He shrugged. "They'll get over it. Just be really nice when you get home."

Maybe. Although she knew that Steven was going to go out of his way to *remind* her at dinner how much breakfast had sucked.

"Hey, did you guys study for this?" Zachary asked.

Meg felt a nervous thump in her stomach. "Study for what?"

He grinned. "You're kidding, right?"

"No." She started to get scared. "Study for what?"

"We have that test today," Zachary said.

They had a test? Oh, God, they *did* have a test. She had completely forgotten. Meg closed her eyes.

"You have time." Josh opened her book for her. "It's just these formulas."

Meg looked at a page of unfamiliar material, then re-closed her eyes. What a day.

Her teacher came in right on time, and handed out Xeroxed exams which looked so difficult that even the people who had studied groaned.

She stared at incomprehensible motion and distance problems. Damn it, she should have figured that God would get her for being so rotten to everyone. Or maybe this was proof that there *was* no God.

She uncapped her pen, scribbling her name at the top of the sheet. The one good thing about physics was that her teacher always gave partial credit. She looked at Josh, who indicated that he would leave his paper in sight, but she shook her head and he looked very relieved. But, as she struggled with the first problem, she couldn't help wishing for an act of God or a fire drill or something. That way, the test would be invalid, and she could have another crack at it tomorrow.

Not getting anywhere, she glanced around and saw everyone else's pens and pencils moving. Terrific. She knew Josh would lift his elbow for her, but she would never stoop to that. Pretty tempting, though.

Of course, if she flunked the test, her parents would completely flip out, and maybe it would be better just to—no. She was above that. Or, anyway, above actually *doing* it.

She picked up her pen. It had been stupid to be so rotten to everyone. So her parents wanted her to change out of her sweatpants, big deal. She should have just put on some jeans and left it at that. But, no. Now the whole family was mad at her, and she couldn't blame them.

Circumlocuting her way through the third problem, she felt a sudden, unexpected jolt of guilt, picturing her mother's expression. Hell, maybe she *deserved* to flunk this test—even though it meant she might not graduate, or get into college, or ever be gainfully employed, or—she shook her head, trying to concentrate on physics.

There was a knock on the door as she struggled through the fifth problem, panicking because she was running out of time. She didn't even check to see who was there, and was surprised to hear her name.

"Meg," her teacher said again, and she looked up. There was something strange about the way he gestured towards the door, something *anxious* about it, and she gulped without knowing why, a tight coldness starting in her neck and throat.

She stood up, clenching her pen hard enough to hurt her hand, and crossed to the door, praying that nothing was wrong.

Her agents were standing in the hall, and feeling their controlled urgency, the coldness turned into a hard contraction of fear.

"Who is it?" she asked unsteadily.

"Your mother," one of them said.

7

FOUR SHOTS HAD been fired. Maybe five. Her agents hustled her past the police barricades, and crowds of reporters and cameras, into the hospital, which was grey and blue with Secret Service agents, and white and turquoise—from the surgical scrubs—with doctors and nurses. Everyone was yelling at once.

She was steered into a small, noisy waiting room and scanned the faces through incredible dizziness, searching for her family. Neal jerked away from the aides who were holding him and she bent to hug him.

"Shhh, it's okay," she whispered. "Don't worry, everything's okay."

He clutched her around the neck, crying so hard that his whole body shook.

"I know," she said, hugging him more tightly. "Don't worry, I'm here." She closed her eyes, afraid that she was going to cry, too. But, she had to be an adult. He needed an adult.

They were taken to another room, beige and windowless. Meg sat on a scuffed green leather couch, pulling her brother onto her lap. The hall was a babble of tense, excited voices and she tried very hard not to listen, afraid of what she might hear.

"I'm scared," Neal whimpered, his arms tight enough to half-choke her.

"I know." She rubbed his back, struggling to be comforting. "Don't worry, it's going to be okay. I promise." She didn't look at anyone in the room, not wanting to see a contradiction in their expressions.

They sat there, Meg holding and rocking him, whispering for

him not to worry. Hearing something at the door, she glanced up and saw Steven, looking as terrified as she felt, his hands tight fists in his pockets, his shoulders hunched up. Seeing her with Neal, his mouth quivered, but he didn't say anything as he came over and sat next to them on the couch.

"You okay?" she asked.

He didn't answer, his fists in his lap, arms rigid.

"Steven?" she asked.

He hunched more.

"Don't worry." She touched his shoulder. "It's going to be—"

"Leave me alone!" His voice was low, but definite.

She hesitated, then withdrew her hand after one gentle squeeze. An aide showed up with grape sodas, and to keep Neal occupied, she shared one with him, keeping up a steady monologue about how cold it was, how glad she was that it was Welch's, because that was the only brand she liked and what did he think, and if he maybe wanted a sandwich or a Snickers bar. There was a lot of commotion out in the hall, and whenever there was a flurry of activity—people running in to whisper to aides who would then leave, any kind of shifting of personnel that might mean something bad—she spoke more loudly, so that they wouldn't have to pay attention to it. While the talking was distracting Neal, she could tell it was getting on Steven's nerves, but since he sat back at one point, still rigid, but at least not hunching, she figured it was helping.

No one seemed to know exactly what was happening, and the shouting in the hall was garbled. She would catch occasional phrases, whenever someone opened the door, but many of them seemed contradictory. All she really knew was what her agents had told her on the way over in the car, and that was pretty sketchy. "Shots fired, Shamrock down. Transport Sandpiper." The only things she had found out since then was that her mother *had* been hit, and that her father had been there when it happened. The two of them had been on the way to a luncheon or something, and the shots had been fired from a nearby window when they got out of the car.

Her mother had been hit. And no one knew where. She closed her eyes, trying not to picture the bullet hitting her in the chest, or the head, or—she had to stop, had to pretend that none of this was happening, that—

"Meggie?" Neal asked, sounding scared.

"What?" She realized that she was trembling, and must have unconsciously clutched at his arm. "I mean, don't worry, everything's okay."

Maybe if she kept saying it, it would be true.

"I'm scared." He was crying again. "I want Mommy and Daddy."

"I know. Don't worry, they'll be here soon." She took a deep, shaky breath. Now that she had started thinking, she couldn't stop remembering the things she read about, or seen on film, her whole life, all the people who had been shot, and—except she couldn't let herself think about it. Her mother falling, the blood, her lying in a—but she was going to crack up, if she kept thinking about it, and—Steven and Neal needed her. She had to get a grip.

But, that beautiful grey dress. A dress she had *borrowed* once. Her mother falling, the blood spreading over the grey cloth, agents swarming around, grave newscasters reporting around the clock about—she had to stop. Kennedy, King, Kennedy, Sadat—she couldn't keep—something touched her arm and she stiffened, looking up to see Preston sitting on the table in front of the couch.

"Hey, kids," he said gently, one hand on Meg's shoulder, the other on Steven's, Neal in between them.

Looking at him, Meg thought that she really *might* panic. He was—rumpled. Sleeves rolled up, tie undone, his handkerchief nowhere in sight. And he seemed tired. Very, very tired. She closed her eyes for a second, knowing that her brothers were as afraid to ask him what was happening as she was.

"How are you guys doing?" he asked.

Meg gulped. "Is—I mean, is everything—"

"We're going to have to wait for a little while," he said.

"Is Mom—" Steven's voice was very small. "Is she—"

"There're a lot of people trying to help her. We just have to keep praying, okay?" He glanced at Meg. "We've got some lunch out there for you guys. How about giving me a hand, Meggo?"

She nodded, guessing that he wanted to speak to her privately, having to swallow several times at the thought.

"How come I can't come?" Steven asked. "Can't I—"

"No," Preston said. "Sorry. Hang out here and keep Neal company, Big Guy."

Steven nodded unhappily, and Preston hugged him, then Neal, as Meg stood up, finding her right leg asleep, but trying not to make a big production of stamping on it.

"Be right back," Preston said, and gestured for an aide to come sit with Steven and Neal, a woman by the door responding. Janice, or Janet, or something—Meg couldn't remember.

Meg followed him out to the crowded corridor, walking requiring a conscious, difficult effort.

"Are you okay?" he asked.

She nodded, even though she wasn't.

"Good," he said. "Because you're going to have to keep taking care of them for a while. I don't know when your father's going to be able to get down here."

"Is Mom—" She took a deep breath. "What's happening?"

"They've been operating since noon," he said, automatically checking his watch. "It's—" He stopped, looking very unhappy, then started again. "It's not very good, Meg."

Jesus. But obviously he had to tell her, because she was going to

56

have to be prepared, if anything—her brothers were going to *need* her. So, even though she wanted to collapse, or sob, or maybe even pass out or something, she just nodded.

He nodded, too, and despite the chaos swirling around them, the tiny section of the corridor where they were standing seemed absolutely silent for a few seconds.

"Is she—" Meg tried not to gulp visibly. "I mean, where—"

"The shoulder and the chest. And Bert Travis took one in the leg," he said.

Bert Travis was one of her mother's agents. "So, he'll be all right," Meg said, looking down at her hands.

Preston nodded.

That was good news—and she wished that she cared more. "Mom—" She took a deep breath. "N-not the head?"

"No, kid," he said gently, putting his arm around her. "Not the head."

Meg blinked, not wanting him to see how close she was to crying. "I was mean to her this morning. I wouldn't—"

"Forget it," he said.

How was she supposed to do that? Meg shook her head. "Yeah, but—"

"Forget it." He leaned over to kiss her forehead. "Can you handle your brothers for a while longer?"

She nodded. "When will Dad be able to come see us?"

"He's—" Preston hesitated. "I'm not sure. As soon as he can. He's—in pretty bad shape."

Okay. Jesus Christ. She suddenly felt like a tiny child—and a wizened adult. "Should I—I mean, is there anything I can—"

"You can take care of your brothers," he said.

Walking back into the waiting room, her hands were shaking so much that she put them into her pockets, aware that she was pretty obviously without lunch.

"The sandwiches weren't ready yet," she said.

Her brothers didn't say anything, waiting for older sister answers.

"I guess it's going to be a while," she said and sat on the couch. "Maybe they can bring in a television or something, and we could—"

"I don't think we'll be able to find one," an aide said quickly, and she remembered what almost every single station was going to be covering. How many times had she watched live coverage—or historical footage—of shootings, and bombings, and all sorts of other tragedies. And how many times had she watched without ever *really* thinking about the family that was falling apart somewhere. It was always too easy to forget about the families.

They were in the room for a long time, surrounded by people they barely knew, most of whom kept their distance and spent a lot of time exchanging nervous glances.

Which wasn't at all helpful.

Meg kept her arm around Neal, who cried on and off, finally falling asleep against her. Steven, who had been slouching down with his fists clenched, noticed right away and sat up.

"Okay," he said in a low voice. "What's going on?"

"I told you," she said, just as quietly, trying not to wake Neal up. "Everything's okay."

"Then, how come Dad isn't here?" he asked.

She hesitated, not sure how to answer.

"I'm not a little kid," he said. "What's going on?"

She looked at him, small and stiff, fists tight. "They're operating on her."

"Is she—" He stopped the same way she had when she was talking to Preston. "I mean, where—"

"Not the head." She saw his eyes get very bright. "Steven, they're doing their—"

"Shut up!" he said.

Okay, she'd handled that one completely wrong. Meg sighed. "Steven—"

"Just shut up!" He kicked the table as hard as he could, then stood up and kicked over a chair. "Shut up and leave me alone!"

"Meggie!" Neal woke up, clutching at her as she moved to get Steven. "Meggie, don't leave me!"

"I'm not." She tried to pry his hands off her arm. "Neal, I'm just—" She winced as Steven, who was crying now, kicked over another chair.

"Come on, Steve," an agent said, trying to stop him. "Calm down. Your mother's going to be—"

"Get off me!" Steven punched at him, and the other agent who had come over to help.

"Come on, son," the second agent said. "Let's—"

"I'm not your son!" Steven yelled. "Stupid jerks! You're supposed to protect her, and you let them shoot her! You god-damn—"

"Steven, don't." Meg managed to pull away from Neal, and get in between him and the agents. "Steven—"

"Leave me alone!" He kept swinging, hitting out at anything that came near him, kicking and struggling as an agent gently held him from behind, pinning one of his arms. "Let go of me!" He kept the other arm flailing. "Let go of me, you son of a bitch!" The fist got Meg in the face and she gasped before she could stop herself, her hand going to her mouth. He heard the gasp and went limp, staring at her, tears streaming down his cheeks.

"Meggie, I'm sorry." He stumbled forward against her as the agent let go of him. "I'm sorry, I didn't mean to. I didn't—"

"It's okay." She put her arms around him. "It isn't your fault. I walked into it."

"But, I hit you," he said, crying harder. "I didn't mean to, Meg. I really didn't mean to."

She hugged him more tightly. "I know. It's okay."

"Don't hate me!" he said. "Please don't hate me!"

"I love you," she said, and reached back to pull Neal over, knowing that he must have been terrified by the whole scene. "I love both of you."

"Don't leave us again," Steven whispered, hanging on to her as fiercely as Neal was. "Please?"

"I won't," she promised.

8

ONCE STEVEN STARTED crying, he couldn't seem to stop, and he held her hand as they all sat on the couch. An aide finally *did* bring in sandwiches, but neither of her brothers would eat, and Meg felt too sick at the thought of food herself to try and make them. There was something exhausting about just sitting on a couch for hours and she concentrated on staying awake, the room windowless and stuffy.

"What time is it?" Neal asked sleepily.

Meg squinted at her watch. "Almost six." She kissed the side of his head. "You didn't have any lunch. You want one of those sandwiches, maybe?"

He shook his head, and she didn't push him. There was some noise in the hall, the first sounds she'd heard after hours of ominous silence, and she picked up one of the cans of warm grape soda, drinking some to steady herself. Her mother's aides were looking at one another, and Meg held her breath, perching on the edge of the couch, hearing a lot of voices as someone opened the door.

"What is it?" Steven asked. "Is something happening?"

"I don't know. I'll go find out." She followed the exodus of aides and agents to the hall, so dizzy that she wasn't sure she could walk. She met a grinning Preston on his way in to see them.

"It's okay, Meg," he said. "She came through it okay."

Meg started to speak, then realized that she had to sit down. Quickly. She lowered herself into a chair, while Preston continued over to her brothers. People were talking at her, but she didn't answer, too dizzy to even sit up straight.

"I know how you feel," Preston said, by her chair suddenly.

Meg lifted her face out of her hands, managing to smile. "When can we see them?"

"I'm not sure," he said. "We're going to move the three of you upstairs, though. At least get you on the same floor."

Preston and a bunch of agents led them through some offices, to a back hallway and staircase, up to the floor where the recovery room apparently was. The new waiting room was more comfortable, with easy chairs and an overstuffed couch, and the three of them were finally allowed to be by themselves, away from all of the aides and agents, although the room was heavily guarded.

"Your father will be down later," Preston said, glancing at Meg. "In the meantime, can we get you guys anything?"

"Yeah," Steven said, his grin huge. "You got some food around this place?"

A LOT OF people stopped by to visit them in the next couple of hours—Vice-President Kruger and his wife, the Secretary of State and a bunch of other Cabinet members, the Speaker of the House and *his* wife—both of whom Meg knew pretty well, the Senate Majority and Minority Leaders, all kinds of people. Meg did most of the talking, while her brothers sat around and looked happy.

All she knew now was that her mother was in serious, but stable condition, and still in the recovery room. So, she was probably resting, but not necessarily comfortably. But *resting* at all was enough of a miracle, in and of itself.

Meg was very polite, making small talk with all of the visitors, none of whom stayed long—but most of the time, she kept her eyes on the door, waiting for her father to come.

Right after eight, he did.

"Daddy!" Neal scrambled off the couch, running over to meet him.

Their father hugged him, and Meg noticed that he was wearing a different outfit from the one he'd had on at breakfast. He was smiling, but his eyes were dark and his face looked like newspaper someone had crumpled up and then tried to smooth out again. His hands were shaking, too, in a way that she usually associated with his having too much caffeine.

"I'm sorry," he said, hugging Steven now, as Neal hung onto his jacket. "I had to be with your mother."

"Is she okay?" Steven asked. "She's going to be okay, right?"

Their father nodded, somewhat mechanically.

"Can we see her?" Neal asked.

"Probably in the morning," he said. "She's really not awake yet." He hugged Meg, and she saw how bloodshot his eyes were, from strain probably, but it looked more as if he had been crying—and so, she hugged him extra-hard.

"I'm sorry," she said.

He nodded, and she could hear him swallow before he broke away. Then, he cleared his throat. "What I think you all ought to do, is go back to the house for the night."

"Why can't we stay with you?" Steven asked. "I mean, like, they've got plenty of beds."

"Because there isn't anything you can do here," their father said. "And I'd feel better knowing that the three of you were all safe at home, and I didn't have to worry about you."

Jesus, he couldn't be thinking that someone was going to *shoot* them, could he? Maybe he just meant he'd rather see them sleeping in their own rooms, instead of being cooped up in a hospital waiting room with a bunch of Secret Service agents.

She wanted to stay behind—because, that way, she could at least keep him company, but if she even brought it up, Steven and Neal would have a fit. She looked from her father, to the agents he was giving terse instructions—at length, to her hands. Maybe she could go home with her brothers, and then come back once they were in bed, or—

"Aren't you coming, too?" Neal asked their father.

He shook his head. "I'll be spending the night here. You all can come back in the morning, when your mother's feeling a little better."

When her brothers were distracted for a minute, Meg moved closer to her father. "Do I have to go?" she asked.

"It would be a lot easier," he said, looking at Steven and Neal.

She nodded, careful not to seem reluctant.

He put his hand on her shoulder. "I know how you feel. But right now, the most important thing for you to do is to take care of your brothers. That's what I need right now."

She nodded.

"I'm counting on you," he said.

She nodded again.

THE WHITE HOUSE was somber. Somber and solicitous, everyone looking at them with sad eyes, and waiting on them hand and foot. Meg got her brothers settled in the West Sitting Hall, where the butlers brought them cheeseburgers and French fries and chocolate milkshakes. Meg wasn't at all hungry, but she pretended to eat, so that her brothers would. After their—mostly full—dinner plates were cleared away, and they were served dessert, Meg decided that the two of them seemed to be pretty well occupied by the ice cream and cake, and took advantage of the chance to go down to her room and be *alone* for a few minutes. It felt as though it had been about a year and a half since she'd had any privacy—and she needed some, to decompress, a little.

Or, possibly, cry.

Vanessa was asleep on the bottom of her bed and Meg picked her up, hugging her to her chest. For once, Vanessa just purred, instead of also scratching her, and Meg held her closer, concentrating on not bursting into tears. Felix had told her that there were dozens and dozens of messages, but she didn't feel like looking at them—and she wasn't exactly in the mood to sit down and stare at email, either.

Vanessa flexed her paws, digging them in Meg's chamois shirt, and Meg extricated them, looking at the delicate shape of her cat's leg, soft grey fading into white, with tiny clean claws and barely scarred pads. The white and grey made her think of her mother's dress, that beautiful pinstriped flannel. She pictured her mother getting out of the car: tall, thin, elegant. Smiling at the crowd—there was always a crowd— and then—then—

"Meggie?" Steven asked from the door.

She sat all the way up, releasing Vanessa. "What?"

He shrugged unhappily. "Will you come watch TV with us?"

"What's on?" she asked cautiously.

"I don't know, movies and stuff." He shifted his weight. "Please, Meg?"

She nodded, and they went up to the solarium, Steven and Neal sitting on either side of her on the couch. Sitting very *close* to her. The movie turned out to be a police drama that might have violence, so she put on a situation comedy that they hated. There was a news update right before the show started, and she had to flick away from the channel right away, before her brothers could hear anything more than "Tonight President—"

Since there wasn't likely to be any news coverage there, she turned on the Cartoon Network, and they watched a few cartoons, none of them laughing—even at the parts which were sort of funny.

"I'm tired," Neal said.

Meg nodded. "Yeah, it's late. You should get some sleep."

"Will you come with me?" he asked.

"Sure." She looked at Steven. "Will you be okay up here?"

"I'm coming, too," he said.

So, they went down the small staircase which ended near the Queen's Bedroom and East Sitting Hall, and Meg sent them into their bedrooms to put on their pajamas. Steven didn't argue—which had possibly never happened before in his entire life.

"May we bring you anything?" Felix asked, as she stood in the Center Hall, waiting for them.

Meg shook her head. "I'm fine, but thank you."

"I hope you know how very sorry all of us are," he said.

Meg nodded. "Thank you."

"Would you like me to have your messages brought to your room?" he asked. "There are—"

She didn't want to know how many there were. "No, thank you," she said. "I'll look at them in the morning. I'm too tired to think right now."

Felix nodded. "Of course. I'll have them put on your desk. But Mrs. Donovan wanted us to be sure and tell you that she'll be on the first plane she can get."

Meg looked up. "Really? Do you think she'll be here tonight?"

"I know she's going to try," he said.

Mrs. Donovan was Trudy, and although Meg was pretty sure her parents had hoped that she might want to accompany them to the White House, she had moved to Florida to live near her son, who had four-year-old twins. Meg hadn't seen her since July, when she had visited for two weeks, which had been wonderful. Almost like being home again.

Neal came out of his bedroom, wearing light blue pajamas.

"Did you brush your teeth?" Meg asked.

He shook his head.

"Go brush your teeth," she said. "Then I'll come in and keep you company."

He nodded, leaving just as Steven appeared, wearing old grey sweatpants and a ratty long underwear shirt.

"Did you brush your teeth?" Meg asked.

He made a face, and sat down at the shiny mahogany table where they sometimes had fast, casual meals, and where her parents usually sat, and drank coffee, and read the *Times* on Sundays.

"Felix says Trudy called and she's coming," Meg said.

Steven looked eager. "Tonight?"

Meg shrugged. "I don't know. If she can. It's kind of late."

"Meg?" Neal called from his bedroom.

"Be right there." She glanced at Steven. "I said I'd keep him company for a while."

He nodded, following her.

Neal was on his bed and Meg helped him under the covers, tucking him in and then sitting on the edge of the mattress, as Steven slouched in an armchair across the room. The *huge* room, since, in most Administrations, it had been part of the Presidential Suite—which meant that Neal had the biggest bathroom of anyone in the family, including the Leader of the Free World.

About whom she couldn't bring herself to think right now.

Seeing how tired Neal's eyes were, she turned off his light, then took his hand.

"Will we see Mom tomorrow?" he asked.

She nodded. "In the morning."

"Will she come home then?" he asked.

Hours after major cardio-thoracic surgery? Presumably not. "I don't know," Meg said. "Probably not tomorrow, but soon."

He looked worried. "Is she thinking about us?"

"Of course." She patted his cheek with her free hand. "And Trudy's coming tomorrow."

He immediately sat up. "Is she here now?"

"Not yet," Meg said. "We'll probably see her in the morning, too."

He looked a little tearful for a minute, but she got him to lie back down, retucked him in, and then sat there until she was sure he was asleep. She waited a few extra minutes, just to be sure, then extricated her hand from his and stood up, turning to see what Steven was doing.

He was almost asleep himself, and she very gently shook his shoulder, taking him to his room and doing as much tucking in as his thirteen-year-old pride would allow. Satisfied that he was okay, she went out to the small hallway connecting their bedrooms, so tired herself that she wasn't sure what to do next.

She found Kirby asleep by the fireplace in the Yellow Oval Room, patted him, and then brought him into Steven's room. Kirby wagged his tail, then jumped onto the bed, and settled himself on Steven's legs.

Deciding that Neal needed an animal, too, she wandered around until she found Humphrey, their tiger cat, in the Lincoln Sitting Room and carried him down to Neal's room, depositing him on the bed.

The house was very quiet. The West Wing was probably full of activity—Vice-President Kruger and all of the senior aides and advisors almost certainly working through the night—but, in the West Sitting Hall, she felt as if she were the only person in the entire building. Lonely, but not tired enough to go to bed yet, she sat down on the couch, rubbing her sleeve across her eyes.

"Miss Powers?" a voice said.

She flinched, but then saw that it was only Felix. "Um, yes?"

"There's a call for you," he said. "Miss Shulman, calling from Boston. Would you like to take it?"

Beth. "Very much," Meg said.

"Should I have it transferred to your room?" he asked.

"No." Meg indicated the Presidential Bedroom. "I'll take it in there. Thanks."

The room seemed strange and empty without her parents, and once she was in there, Meg regretted not having gone down to her own room, instead. But, the phone was already ringing, and she would feel stupid asking them to transfer it *again*. She was going to pick up the phone next to her mother's side of the bed, but that seemed wrong, so she sat down to use the one at her desk, instead.

"Hello?" she said automatically.

"Are you all right?" Beth asked.

Hearing her voice, Meg relaxed into the chair, coming as close to bursting into tears as she had all day. "Hi."

"Are you okay?" Beth asked. "I left a couple of messages on your cell, but—are you okay?"

Meg pressed her hand across her eyes, so she wouldn't cry. "Yeah."

"I'm sorry," Beth said. "I mean, I'm *really* sorry."

Meg nodded, forgetting that Beth was hundreds of miles away and couldn't see her.

"How is she?" Beth asked.

Meg swallowed. "Pretty bad. I mean, we weren't allowed to see her or anything. So—I don't know. I think it's bad."

"Is anyone there with you?" Beth asked.

"No, Dad's at the hospital. I mean, Steven and Neal are here, but—" Meg let out her breath, too tired to finish the sentence. "I don't know."

"You sound awful," Beth said. "You should go sleep for a while."

Probably, yeah.

"I really am sorry, Meg," Beth said. "I wish—is there *anything* I can do?"

Meg shook her head. "No. I mean, thanks, but I'm fine. I'm just—you're right; I should get some sleep."

"Yeah," Beth said. "But, if you need to talk, just call me. I mean, even later tonight, if you want. I'll leave my cell on. Okay?"

Meg nodded sleepily.

After they had hung up, she stayed at the desk for a few minutes, resting her head on her arms. It was weird—spooky, almost—to have a conversation with Beth during which neither one of them made jokes. Especially Beth, who took great pride in *never* being serious.

Except that all of this was pretty god-damn serious.

She sat up and looked around at her parents' room. It was large and impressive, but somehow cozy. That is, when her parents were there. Except during the summer, they would almost always have a fire going and the whole family would watch television—mostly movies, or Red Sox games—instead of going to the solarium or to their rooms.

But, tonight, it didn't seem cozy at all. It seemed—abandoned. Scary, even.

Her mother usually sat at the desk, going through paperwork until she was worn out, then moving to the bed, where Neal and Meg's father would be, Meg's father reading, as well as half-watching the television. Steven would be in an easy chair or lying on the carpet, and Meg would sit on the couch, holding homework on her lap so that her parents would think she was doing it. Every now and then, she would even complete a physics problem or translate a paragraph of her latest French reading.

One of the butlers or stewards almost always brought in popcorn, or just-out-of-the-oven cookies, and Steven and Neal would each eat about twice as much as the rest of them put together.

Of course, lots of nights, her parents would be out making appearances, or there would be dinners and receptions downstairs. There were always foreign dignitaries, soldiers, or movie stars to honor. Astronauts, professional athletes, Nobel Peace Prize winners, famous artists and musicians—at this point, she had met so many celebrities that she was no longer even the slightest bit intimidated or impressed by them. She wasn't a big fan of evening gowns, but if interesting guests had been invited, she usually went, with Josh as her escort. Sometimes, directors would come to screen their latest movies in the downstairs theater, and Meg *always* went to those.

Her parents' Siamese cats, Adlai and Sidney, were asleep on the bed, and she went over to pat them. There were books and magazines on both bedside tables; her father's stacked haphazardly, her mother's organized by height and size, the edges perfectly aligned. Her mother always set aside some time, right before going to sleep, to read fiction for a while, and it was one of the few things she ever did just to relax. She wasn't very good at lounging around and doing nothing—although Meg had offered to give her lessons—and when she played tennis or exercised in the third floor workout room, she was usually so competitive and self-demanding that it couldn't really be described as relaxation.

Early one Saturday morning, Meg had walked into her parents' room and found her mother sitting on the couch in a black skirt and silk shirt, her hands folded in her lap. "What are you doing?" Meg had asked, and her mother frowned and said, "Nothing." Meg had looked around at the crowded desk, the morning newspapers and briefing reports everywhere, and the untouched coffee. "Aren't you going to have breakfast?" she asked, very hungry. "I don't really feel like it," her mother said, then frowned again. "I don't really feel like doing anything." "So, don't," Meg said, but her mother reached for her glasses—which meant that she hadn't even bothered to put in her contacts yet, picked up a briefing report, and started reading. Meg wondered if people knew that sometimes her mother wasn't in the mood to be President. Were all Presidents like that? All world leaders? Surely, everyone woke up sometimes and felt like being anything *but* in charge.

Seeing how unhappy her mother looked, Meg sat down and started an inane conversation. Her mother seemed annoyed, then amused, putting her papers down, taking off the glasses, and they sat for about fifteen minutes, talking about nothing in particular, her mother slowly relaxing. Then, a butler arrived with a tray of breakfast—more coffee, juice, hot scones, butter, jams, fresh fruit. Frank began delivering the latest messages and stacks of freshly-generated paperwork, the phone started ringing off the hook with requests from aides, questions from the press staff, and about nine thousand other things—and Meg watched her turn back into the President again. She remembered finding the whole incident depressing, wondering whether her mother enjoyed her life—or just put up with it. There were definitely days when the latter seemed to be true.

Today must be a day that she *hated* the Presidency. Meg sure did. In fact, she kind of hated the entire country. It was impossible not to despise a country where Presidents who were only trying to do good things were shot just for getting out of a car.

She turned the lights out and was going to leave the room, then stared at the blank television screen across the room, a translucent grey. She hadn't seen any coverage at all yet, but it had to be extensive. Christ, various stations had probably already composed *theme music* to accompany it. She didn't want to turn the television on, but which was worse—imagining what had happened, or actually *seeing* it? The shots, the shouts, the blood—maybe imagining was worse.

So, she took a deep breath, and put on the news.

"—doesn't *appear* to be a terrorist attack," a grim-faced pundit was telling the camera, "but it's always possible that—"

She didn't want to hear—or think—about that, so she switched over to CNN.

"—yet another in a long series of violent—" an anchorperson was saying.

Meg closed her eyes. She shouldn't be watching this. Talk about masochistic. She had seen most of the tragedies of the last decade—natural disasters, tragic accidents, shootings, bombings, and, worst of all, terrorist attacks—on instant replay. Sometimes, the endless bad news made it too easy to shrug and say, "Oh, again?" There were probably people all over the country watching this, clicking their tongues, then switching over to see what was on ESPN or HBO. Hell, she had probably done it herself, violence often seeming both distant, and commonplace. Far away from *her* life.

The reporter was describing the scene at the downtown Washington hotel and Meg frowned. When these things happened, it almost always seemed to be a hotel. Why had the Secret Service let her mother go to a damn hotel? They had probably *wanted* her to go in through an underground parking garage or a loading dock or something, but her mother liked to avoid that whenever possible, because she thought it made America look like a furtive, third-world dictatorship, and that it lacked dignity for the President of the

United States to sneak in and out of buildings through back entrances and so forth.

An anchorperson was gesturing towards some film footage of the scene. "At the top left corner of your screen is the window where Bruce Sampson was waiting—"

Meg stared at the harmless, Venetian-blinded window, open about four inches.

"The thirty-six year old unemployed Sampson has a history of—" the anchorperson went on.

Meg flinched as a photograph of a surly, thick-necked, unshaven man came onto the screen.

"His previous convictions include assault with a deadly weapon, assault with intent to kill," the reporter said, "and various sexual—"

Not wanting to hear anything else about *that*, Meg changed to another station, her hand trembling so much that she almost dropped the remote control. This channel was showing film of the presidential motorcade pulling up to the hotel.

"At exactly eleven-thirteen," a solemn reporter was saying, "the President stepped out of her limousine, surrounded by—"

Meg gulped, watching her mother get out of the car, agents everywhere as she smiled at the press and onlookers, and staff members from the other cars began joining the group around her. The film was a little shaky—the cameraperson jostling for position, maybe. Her mother turned slightly as her father got out of the car, and the first shot turned her even more, the sound like a small firecracker. The film was confusing—a blur of blue and grey agents— but the audio stayed on, and Meg heard all of the shouting she had imagined—*worse* than she had imagined—along with three more shots. She couldn't see her parents, but agents were piling into the Presidential limousine, which swerved away from the sidewalk, most of the motorcade right behind it.

She watched the pandemonium of the aftermath, too horrified to move or look away. People were shouting and yelling; agents were clustered around Bert Travis, the agent who had been hit in the leg; still more agents were tearing across the street towards the building from which the shots had come. Her hand was shaking almost convulsively, but she switched the set off, the room instantly dark, and now silent, except for her own breathing.

Someone had shot her mother. Someone had actually—the man had taken a gun, and—Meg leaned back against her mother's desk, her legs feeling weak. But she was supposed to be in charge, so she didn't have the luxury of falling apart right now. Instead of sitting around and being upset, she should go check on her brothers and make sure they were sleeping.

She took one steadying breath and pushed away from the desk, going next door to Neal's room, first. His blankets were crumpled at the bottom of the bed, but he didn't seem to be too restless, so she retucked him in and went to make sure that Steven was okay.

Opening the door to his room, she heard quiet crying. Damn it. She shouldn't have waited so long to check. He was on his stomach, face pressed into his long underwear sleeve, his other arm around Kirby. She sat down on the bed, putting her hand on his back.

"It's okay," she said. "Don't worry, it's okay."

"I'm scared," he said, trying to stop crying.

With good reason. "Don't be," Meg said. "Everything's okay."

"What if," he gulped, "what if she—" He took a shuddering breath. "What if she dies?"

Meg had to gulp, too. "She's not going to."

"But, what if she *does*?" He turned over, his face so flushed that she was afraid he was sick. "What if that's why they sent us home?"

Meg didn't answer right away, the fear sounding very plausible, one that she had been worrying about inside, too. Not that she could tell *him* that. So, instead, she came up with a quick rebuttal. "Look, if they thought something was going to happen, they would have *kept* us there."

"How do you know?" he asked.

She fell back on her most irrefutable answer. "I'm older than you are."

He sat up, his arms going around his knees. "Dad looked like he'd been crying. Do you think he was?"

Yes. "I think it's just because he was tired," she said.

"I've never seen him crying," Steven said uneasily. "Have you?"

Meg shook her head. His parents had been killed by a drunk driver, and she assumed that he had cried a lot about that, but she had only been about a year old, and couldn't remember.

"He looked scared, too." Steven's eyes were huge. "I didn't know he got scared. I didn't think he was *ever* afraid."

Meg moved her jaw. What could she say to that? In very different ways, her parents had both always seemed to be utterly fearless. "I don't know."

Steven pulled his knees even closer. "It makes me scared, too," he said, and she brushed hair—damp from tears, perspiration, or both—away from his forehead.

It was very quiet, except for Kirby, who was snuffling in his sleep.

"If, uh, you want, you can go to bed," Steven said finally. "It's really late and stuff."

"Do you want me to?" she asked.

He shrugged his "I'm thirteen; I'm cool" shrug, even though his eyes were still filled with tears.

"I could have them bring a cot in here," she said.

He shrugged again. "I dunno. If you're lonely or something, you can."

She had to smile. "I'm lonely," she said.

75

9

THEY WENT TO the hospital at nine-thirty, escorted by a veritable phalanx of Secret Service vehicles, and there were dozens and dozens of agents and police officers waiting for them when they arrived— more security than she had ever seen before. It was as though they were all expecting an army of machine-gun-carrying guerillas to appear—which was scary as hell. In fact, Neal almost wouldn't get out of the car, and she had to hold his hand tightly and remind him that their parents were waiting before she could coax him out.

Preston met them in the waiting room.

"Your mother's feeling much better," he said. "You'll be able to go in and see her for a minute."

"When?" Steven asked, very neat in a striped tie and his navy blue blazer. Neal was also wearing a tie, and Meg had put on a skirt.

"In a little while." Preston glanced at Neal, looked worried, and rested his hand on his shoulder. "We're just going to wait for your father."

"Where is he?" Steven asked suspiciously.

"Finishing shaving," Preston said.

Steven frowned, not convinced, and stood by the door to wait.

"Late night?" Meg asked in a low voice.

"*All* night," Preston said, just as low. "Try to get him to eat something with the three of you. If he goes much longer, he's going to collapse."

Meg nodded, feeling her fists tighten nervously—which Preston saw, but she shook her head when he reached out a supportive hand, and stood on her own, with her arms folded.

A few minutes later, her father came in with a crowd of agents and a couple of his aides. He had shaved and changed his clothes, but he looked terrible—grey and exhausted. Drained. Preston was right about them needing to get him to eat.

He hugged each of them, hanging on much longer than usual.

"How's Mommy?" Neal asked.

"Better," their father said. "We're going to go down and see her." He turned to Preston. "Do me a favor, and clear the room, will you? And make sure no one's going to bother us on the way down."

Preston nodded, crossing to the aides standing on the other side of the room, and a moment later, they all left.

"Is she *really* okay?" Steven asked.

"Well," their father spoke carefully, sitting on the couch and pulling Neal onto his lap, "you have to remember that she's hurt. She's not going to be sitting up or walking around."

Steven's eyes were big again. "Will she be awake?"

"Yes. But," he hugged Neal closer, "we all have to be very gentle. We're only going to stay in there for a minute, and then we'll leave so she can get some rest. We don't want to make her talk, either. She has some tubes to help her breathe, and it hurts her throat to talk."

"Does she look like TV?" Neal asked.

"She looks like your mother," their father said. "Don't worry." He reached over to touch Meg's face. "You, too."

Meg nodded. Did Steven want to be young enough to sit on her father's lap and be comforted as much as she did?

Their father stood up, holding Neal's hand. "Come on."

Meg wanted to stay close to him, too, to have him put his hand on her shoulder or back, but since Steven was brave enough to walk by himself, hands jammed into his pockets, then she, as the oldest, should be, too.

Her mother's room was large, and full of doctors and nurses. Meg made herself look again, more calmly, and saw that there were only six.

Only six.

She followed her father and brothers over to the bed, hearing the various hums and bleeps of medical machines, with little colored lights blinking and flashing on each one, afraid to see what her mother looked like.

"Hi, Mom," she heard Steven say, his voice shaking.

"Mommy." Neal's voice was higher, but just as frightened.

Okay, she had to look up. Meg lifted her head and saw her mother, pale and fragile, her right arm full of tubes, more tubes going through her nose and down her throat. The bed had been propped up to make it seem as if she were sitting, but she was obviously very weak. Her left arm was in a sling, tightly bandaged around her shoulder and neck, and there were more bandages visible through the hospital gown, her entire upper body bulky. Incredibly, she was smiling. A tremulous smile, but one that stayed on.

All right, now she had to say something. *Anything*. "Hi." Which didn't come out quite right, so she tried again. "H-hi. How are you feeling?"

"Fine." Her mother's voice also rasped, but that was probably because of the tubes.

"Katie," Meg's father said, gently warning, and Meg saw her mother's eyes glisten for a second as she nodded.

Neal was hanging on to their father's hand, staring at their mother in what appeared to be shock, and Steven still had his fists in his pockets, so expressionless that Meg had to look twice before she realized that he was crying.

No one spoke.

"Um," one of the doctors said, "I think—"

"We just got here!" Meg blinked, surprised by how angry she sounded.

"No, he's right," her father said. "The more rest your mother gets, the sooner she'll be able to come home. Here." He lifted Neal up. "Let's all give your mother a kiss, so she'll be able to sleep better."

"Will it hurt you?" Neal asked anxiously.

Her mother shook her head and tried to snap the fingers of her right hand, Meg's father moving a legal pad over, along with a pen. "It will make me feel *better*," she wrote, in shaky, but distinguishable handwriting.

Neal kissed her cheek, pulling away fast.

"Good job," her mother wrote. "My arm just healed." She winked at him, and Neal laughed, Meg staring at her in frank admiration.

Steven moved in to kiss her, wiping his blazer sleeve across his eyes to get rid of some of the tears. Their mother brought her hand over to his face, holding it there, and he burst into even harder tears.

"I hate him," he said, then ran out of the room.

"Steven," her mother tried to call after him, her voice sounding terrible.

"I'll take care of it," Meg's father said. He bent to kiss her cheek and whispered something, her mother nodding. Then, he straightened up and motioned towards the door. "Come on."

"Can I—" Meg swallowed. "I mean, just for a minute?"

He looked at the doctors, then nodded. "Just for a minute."

When he and Neal were gone, she looked at her mother.

"I, uh, I'm really sorry," she said.

Her mother nodded, and wrote, "I'm sorry for all of us."

"Do you hurt?" Meg asked. Which was a really stupid question.

Her mother shook her head. "How are your brothers?" she wrote.

"Okay," Meg said. "Steven's having a harder time."

Her mother nodded. "What about you?" she wrote.

Meg started to say that she was fine, but instead, began crying. Her mother reached over for her hand, holding on with surprising strength. Meg gripped back, knowing that she had to be a little kid for a few seconds, let someone else be the strong one. But, it didn't seem right to be *taking* strength from someone she should be giving it to, so she let go, getting herself under control with a deep, shaky breath.

"Meg," her mother said hoarsely. "It's okay to—"

"Madam President." One of the doctors indicated his throat.

Her mother looked annoyed, but pulled over her legal pad, turning to a fresh page. "Let yourself get upset," she wrote. "Don't try to hold it in."

"I'm fine," Meg said.

Her mother looked at her, and Meg felt even more power from the concentrated gaze that she had felt from her mother's hand. She wouldn't have looked away, but a nurse tapped her shoulder, gesturing towards the door.

"I have to go," Meg said. "I mean, they want me to."

Her mother nodded, most of the power fading from her eyes, something like vulnerability or loneliness replacing it.

"I'll be back as soon as they let me." Meg bent down, not wanting the doctors and nurses to overhear her. "I really love you," she whispered, kissed her mother's cheek, and swiftly left the room. Remembering that she had been crying, she wiped away the last of the tears with her hand, and four agents accompanied her down to the waiting room where her father and brothers were, all three of them looking up when she came in, Steven's face tear-stained.

"Hi," Meg said, and sat in an empty chair, very tired. She hadn't gotten much sleep. Felix and Gary had helped her move a cot into Steven's room and once she was settled, Steven had fallen asleep, and she was the one lying alone and afraid in the darkness. Even holding Vanessa hadn't helped. It must have been almost dawn by the time she dropped off, because she remembered watching the sky change colors through his window.

She leaned her head against the hard vinyl back of the chair, studying the ceiling. People in the room were talking, maybe even to her, but she concentrated on the ceiling, too tired to follow a conversation. The fluorescent lights hurt her eyes, so she closed them, not wanting to get an even worse headache than the one she already had. It was nice to rest for a minute. Just for a minute.

A hand touched her shoulder and she opened her eyes, startled to see Josh sitting in the chair next to hers. She stared at him in confusion, not sure where they were, or why she had a blanket over her, with just the two of them in the room.

"I'm sorry, I didn't mean to wake you up," he said. "You were having a bad dream."

She squinted at him, still not sure what was going on. "Josh?"

"Hi," he said, with such a nice smile that she decided that this *was* Josh, and she *was* awake. "Are you all right?"

"Um—" Her face felt damp and she realized that she must have been crying in her sleep. She turned away, embarrassed, wiping the tears with her hand. "How did you get here? Don't we have school?"

"Yeah. I, uh," he looked sheepish, "kind of didn't go."

Oh. She shook her head, trying to get rid of the last of the confusion. "What time is it?"

"Going on to two." He stroked her forehead gently, and she was so tired that she sank back against the small pillow on the chair and let him do it.

"Have you been here a long time?" she asked.

He shook his head. "They wouldn't let me in. Then, when Preston got back from the White House, he said it was okay."

Meg frowned, lost again. "Preston left?"

Josh nodded. "Yeah. Trudy got here, and they took Steven and Neal home."

"Oh." She blinked hard, trying to force her eyes to stay open. "Is my father here?"

"Yeah," Josh said. "He's in with your mother."

"Oh." That, at least, made sense, so she let her eyes close.

"You want to sleep some more?" he asked.

She did, but she shook her head.

"You want a hug?" he asked.

Now, she opened her eyes. "Yeah," she said. "I do."

10

SHE STAYED IN his arms for what seemed like a long time.

"You should go home and sleep," he said softly.

Meg shook her head, since she wasn't about to leave without seeing her mother again.

"You'd feel better," he said.

"No," she said. "I wouldn't."

He started to disagree, then nodded. Meg nodded back, too tired to explain.

Preston showed up and sat with them for a while, and her father was in and out, but none of them talked much. Then, right before six, she got to see her mother again, this time for about ten minutes. The doctors had taken the tubes out of her throat and she was able to speak, making small-voiced jokes and being so damn game that Meg had to struggle not to cry, especially when her face would tighten with pain and she would still try to make jokes.

After that, her father made her leave, and a huge clump of agents appeared to take her home.

"You want me to come?" Josh asked.

She really just wanted to be in her room, by herself, and sleep, but couldn't figure out how to say so without being rude, so she nodded. The agents steered them through a side exit, but there was still a crowd outside. Police officers, what looked like a National Guard unit, Secret Service agents, reporters, cameras going like crazy, protestors—*protestors?*—who were pro-NRA, or anti-gun, or—they were yelling for her mother, or against her mother, or waving signs, or—Meg stopped, too scared to go any further. She turned to go back inside, but there seemed to be even more people crowding in behind her, and she stopped again, completely terrified. Josh seemed to be saying something, but her heart was pounding too loudly for her to hear, and suddenly, agents were holding her arms, moving her forcefully through the crowd and into a black car, Josh jumping in behind her. Then, they pulled away from the curb and once she was sure they were out of camera view, she covered her face with her hands.

"You okay?" Josh asked, looking very worried.

She nodded, tears too close to trust her voice. He put his hand on her shoulder, and she brushed it off, trying to get control of herself.

"Meg—" he started.

She shook her head, moving away from him, taking slow, calming breaths. Then, once they were at the White House, she hurried out of the car, heading straight for the elevator to go upstairs, Josh behind her.

As he reached down to take her hand, she pulled away.

"Just—don't, okay?" she said.

He withdrew, putting his hands uncomfortably in his pockets. It was probably only because she was tired and upset, but there was something so annoying about the way he was standing, that she had to concentrate on not looking at him. He must have sensed that, because he shifted his weight, looking even more uncomfortable.

It was very quiet upstairs.

"Meg," he said. "Maybe—"

"I think I hear people in the kitchen," she said, moving past him and towards the West Sitting Hall.

She found Steven and Neal at the table with glasses of milk, while Trudy stood at the stove, stirring things in various pots. Seeing her there, wearing a familiar blue flowered dress with an apron over it and bustling about, Meg leaned against the doorjamb, feeling—for a second—as if they were home, and none of the damn White House stuff had ever happened.

"Meg's here," Steven said, and Trudy turned, crossing the room to hug her.

"Uh, you remember Josh, don't you?" Meg said, before she could do so.

"Of course." Trudy smiled at him. "How are you, Josh?"

"Fine, ma'am," he said, although, mostly, he looked as though he wanted to run away.

Trudy gave Meg a little squeeze that was *almost* a hug, and Meg inhaled a couple of times. Trudy always smelled so good. Like sachets, and Altoids, and talcum powder. As if she had just eaten a gumdrop.

"Why don't you two sit down with the boys?" she said. "I'm just getting dinner ready."

"What are you making?" Meg asked, even though she wasn't hungry.

Trudy went back over to the stove to turn the heat down on one of the burners. "That hamburger casserole you all like."

Meg nodded. It was one of the few casseroles all of them *did* like, even her mother, and they had had it many times over the years. Her head hurt suddenly, and she rubbed her hand across her forehead. All she wanted to do was go to her room, get into bed, and turn off the lights. She should just tell Josh that she wanted to be alone—except that she felt so shaky that she was either going to yell at him or start sobbing.

"Meg?" Trudy said. "Why don't you sit down?"

"No, I—" Control. She didn't want to lose control. But, all of a sudden, she felt— "Um, I'll be right back, okay?" She pushed past Josh and out to the West Sitting Hall, walking quickly—almost running—down to her room.

She was going to cry. She was very definitely going to cry. But, she didn't want—she headed straight into the bathroom, turning on the cold water full blast, washing her face once, and then again. It didn't help and she closed her eyes, gripping the sides of the sink with her hands. Control. She had to—she bit the inside of her cheek, increasing the pressure to try and keep the tears back. The man aiming the gun, the bullets ripping—she hung on to the sink more tightly. If he had aimed a little higher, or two inches to the left, her mother would be lying in the Rotunda at the Capitol Building, and they would all have to be brave and follow the riderless horse to Arlington National Cemetery, while—okay, she had to stop it. Josh was here, and she couldn't fall apart. But, Jesus, she should have told him to go *home*, and not tried to put on an act.

She sat down, pressing her face into the cold washcloth, counting to ten. To thirty. Okay, okay. She was okay. Except she couldn't stop thinking about the man, waiting at the window, while she sat in physics, wishing for something, *anything*, to—she had to stop this. She couldn't keep—*thirty-one, thirty-two*—she stopped at fifty, under control again.

They were all waiting for her in the kitchen—she had to go back there. Slowly, she rewashed her face, then went out to her room, lifting Vanessa up for a quick cuddle. Then, she walked out to the hall, so tired that her arms and legs felt heavy.

Josh was sitting in an antique wooden chair, waiting for her, and she stopped, not sure where the anger had come from, but suddenly furious.

"What are you doing," she asked, "following me?"

He looked surprised. "No, I—"

She scowled at him. "I *said* I'd be *right back*."

"I know. I just"—he blinked—"wanted to be sure you were okay."

"Of course I'm not okay!" she said. "Christ, would you be?"

He shook his head.

"Yeah, well, I just wanted to be alone for a minute," she said. "Jesus, don't you understand *anything*?"

He looked at her nervously. "I'm sorry."

"Sorry? What good is sorry?" She rubbed her forehead, the ache much worse. "Please just leave me alone."

He nodded, edging towards the stairs. "Okay. I'm sorry, I—"

Jesus. "Stop saying that!" she said.

"Okay," he said, looking at her as though she had just turned into a raging demon—which she possibly had. "Y-you want me to call you later?"

She shook her head. "No, I want you to leave me alone. Are you deaf or something?"

"No. I-I hope you feel better," he said.

"I'm not the one's who's sick. I mean, hurt. I mean—" She turned away, walking back to her room. "Just leave me alone. Okay?"

She stood in the middle of her room, fists clenched, trembling and out of breath. Some kind of angry energy came bubbling up and she kicked her desk as hard as she could, several books flying off, her computer sliding precariously close to the edge. Vanessa woke up and ran out of the room. Meg grabbed a book, wanting to throw it after her, but controlled the impulse, throwing it at the fireplace, instead, and knocking over the screen and one of the andirons.

"Stupid cat." She kicked two more books out of her way, walking over to the bed.

"Meg?" Steven asked, behind her.

She whirled around. "Don't you knock? Jesus!"

"Sorry." He took a step backwards. "I was just—"

"Leave me alone, okay?" she said.

He didn't move, staring at her.

"*Okay?*" she said.

"Yeah, sure. Anything you say." He left, slamming the door behind him.

Finally alone, Meg climbed into bed, pausing only to take off her shoes. She turned off the light, then burrowed down under the covers, trembling from anger or fear or—someone knocked on the door.

Christ almighty. She sat up, the anger back, full force. "I said, leave me alone!"

"Meg, it's me," Trudy said.

Oh, God. Meg slumped back down. "I'm sorry. I need to be alone for a while," she said, more quietly.

"Are you all right?" Trudy asked.

Oh, yeah. Totally. "Yeah," she said. "I just need to be alone."

"Call me if you need me," Trudy said.

Meg held her breath until she was sure Trudy was gone, then relaxed. Still shaking, she wrapped the blankets around herself and huddled down. She closed her eyes, fairly sure that she was going to cry, but fell asleep, first.

When she woke up, it was very hot and she wondered if she was sick, or—maybe it was just the blankets. She untwined them, then sat up and looked at her clock, the red numbers blurry in the darkness. Ten-thirty. She slouched back down, staring at the ceiling. Sometimes, when she was upset, sleeping for a while helped—but, not this time. Her stomach hurt, but she wasn't sure if it was hunger or real pain. When was the last time she had eaten? Breakfast. Part of a bowl of Special K. And she hadn't really eaten any dinner the night before, either.

She felt too sick to get up, so she rolled over onto her side, watching the numbers on her clock change. She was just falling asleep when the phone rang. She wasn't going to answer, but what if it was the hospital? Maybe something had—she grabbed the receiver.

"Miss Shulman, for you," the switchboard person said. "Shall I put the call through?"

Good question. Meg sighed. "Yeah, I guess. I mean—yeah. Thanks."

Beth came on. "Meg? How is everything?"

Jesus Christ, she was tired of that question. "Terrible," Meg said, "how do you think?"

"That's what I figured," Beth said.

"What do you mean, 'you figured'?" Meg asked, irritated. "What do *you* know about it?"

There was a long pause.

"In prime asshole mode tonight, hunh?" Beth said.

There were very few people on the planet whom she would allow to get away with saying that—but, Beth was one of them. Possibly the *only* one.

"Look, I was thinking," Beth said. "You want me to come down or something?"

Meg moved the receiver away from her ear, looking at it. "Come *here*?" she asked, bringing the receiver back. "What do you mean?"

"You sound like you need some company," Beth said. "I could hang out with you at the hospital, and—well, whatever you want."

Yeah, because having Josh keep her company had worked out *so well*. "Beth, I really don't—" Meg let out her breath. "This isn't a very good time, know what I mean?"

"Hmm," Beth said. "Not exactly hospitable, are you?"

Meg was going to yell at her, but found her face relaxing, instead. "Has anyone ever told you what a jerk you are?"

"Just about everyone," Beth said.

Something they had in common.

"Okay, I'm going to hang up now," Beth said. "Take it easy, okay?"

"Oh, yeah," Meg said. "Absolutely."

She lay back down in bed, staring up at the ceiling—and the chandelier she really disliked, carefully *not* thinking.

There was a quiet knock on the door. "Meg?"

Trudy. "What." She shook her head. She shouldn't be rude to Trudy. She was never rude to Trudy. "I mean, come in."

Trudy opened the door, carrying a tray into the room. "I thought you might be hungry."

"Oh." Meg sat up, managing to smile instead of saying that her stomach hurt and she would rather be left alone. "I mean, thank you."

Trudy put the tray on her lap: vegetable soup, a grilled cheese sandwich cut in triangles—Trudy was big on bread triangles, a dish of chocolate chip ice cream and a glass of milk.

"Um, thank you," Meg said. "It looks good."

Trudy reached out to touch her forehead. "How do you feel?"

"I don't know," Meg said. "Tired, mostly."

"Well." Trudy withdrew her hand. "I want you to sleep late tomorrow."

"What about the hospital?" Meg asked.

Trudy shrugged. "You can go in the afternoon."

Meg nodded, too tired to argue. She still wasn't hungry, but picked up her spoon to try the soup.

Trudy sat down on the edge of the bed. "Is there anything you want to talk about?"

Meg shook her head.

Trudy might be a nice, nurturing lady—but she also had eyes like laser beams. "What happened with your friend today?"

Meg scowled. "Nothing."

Trudy looked worried, but didn't pursue that.

They sat quietly, Meg moving the spoon around the bowl of soup without eating any.

"This is what you always worried about," Trudy said.

Meg nodded. Even before her mother had run for President and was just a Senator, Meg had worried about security. It had started to get especially scary when she became a serious Presidential candidate and had to be given Secret Service protection very early on—because she had gotten so many threats. But, she had never thought that anything awful would actually *happen*.

She looked up at Trudy, noticing—for the first time—that Trudy was smaller than she was. Kind of weird. When she was little, she had spent a lot of time on Trudy's lap, playing with her pearls or her crocheting, probably being quite annoying. Lots of times, she would try on her glasses, too, draping the chain around her neck.

"Are you sure you don't want to talk about it?" Trudy asked.

"Yeah," Meg said. "Very."

SHE SPENT THE next two days at the hospital, either sitting in her mother's room—or *waiting* to sit in her mother's room. When she was at the White House, she stayed in bed, sometimes reading, but mostly lying down with the lights out, trying to sleep. Being alone was easier than anything else, and she left strict instructions with the switchboard not to take calls from anyone other than her parents or Preston. One good thing about the White House—probably the only thing—was that it was very simple to arrange to stay completely isolated, if one were so inclined. No one could get in, or call, without her permission. And, right now, she just wanted to be alone. Monday, when she would have to go back to school, was more than soon enough to have to deal with people. Even Josh. Especially Josh. She wasn't sure if she was mad at him for not knowing what to do, or mad at herself for being mad at him—but, she was *mad*, and it was easier to avoid him. To avoid everyone.

Sunday night, her father came home for the first time, shaky and exhausted. As Meg passed the Presidential Bedroom on her way to the kitchen for some orange juice, he stopped her.

"Could we talk for a minute?" he asked, an untucked Oxford shirt and grey flannel slacks all that remained of the suit he'd had on all day.

In the room, he indicated the couch and she sat down. Something in his expression suggested that it was bad news, and she swallowed in advance. Maybe her mother had taken a turn for the worse—except, if she had, he would still be over there, but—

"I'm going to ask you to do something that you won't like," he said, "and I'm also going to ask you to please not argue."

Meg nodded.

"I'd like you to drop off the tennis team," he said.

She blinked. "What? There's only two matches left."

He nodded. "I know, and I'm sorry, but I don't want you exposing yourself that way. The Secret Service agrees with me."

Meg stared at him. "How am I exposing myself?"

"With—" He hesitated, and she saw a muscle near his jaw move— "everything that's happened, I don't want any of you in situations where you're unnecessarily vulnerable. Tennis courts are practically impossible to protect, Meg, you know that."

"Yeah, but—" He didn't want her to argue, so she shouldn't argue. "I won't get my letter or anything," she said.

He shrugged that off. "I said I was sorry, Meg, but this is the way it's going to have to be."

It was only two matches, so if he wanted her to quit, she should just do it. Even if tennis was the most important— "I'm captain, Dad," she said quietly. "How can I quit?"

"They won't survive without you?" he asked.

She shook her head. "It's not that. It's just—" Just what? She should shut up already. But, something about having to quit made her feel panicky, made everything seem more real. "Dad, if you want, I'll practice on the court here. It's just two stupid matches and the ISL tournament. Nothing's going to happen."

His expression changed so swiftly to fury that she flinched. "Nothing's going to happen?" he said, his face flushing. "Where the hell have you been for the last week? We're living in a country full of crazies, can't you get that through your head? We get hundreds of threats every day, and you're—Jesus, Meg! You think I like this? You think I like knowing that there's nothing I can do to protect any of you? How do you think that makes me feel?"

Meg hunched into her shirt, feeling too guilty to say anything.

"You think I like having to pen all of you up in this place," he gestured around the room and she could see his arms shaking, "because maybe, *maybe* it's safe? Anyone in the country who wants to hurt you can, and there's nothing I can do about it! I was standing two feet away from your mother, and I still couldn't—I—" He spun away, gripping the footboard of the bed, shaking visibly. "Please leave," he said his voice thick and almost unfamiliar.

She hesitated. "Dad, I'm sorry, I didn't—"

"Please get out!" he said.

Scared and guilty, she hurried out to the hall, hearing the door close behind her. She leaned against the small dining table in the West Sitting Hall, trembling.

"Meg?" Steven asked, just coming down the hall.

She jerked up. "What? What do you want?"

"You okay?" he asked.

No! "Yeah," she said, and ran down to her room, slamming the door. She fell back against it, closing her eyes and trying to calm down. Bruce Sampson probably didn't even know how many people he had hurt with his god-damn bullets. Or maybe he *did* know, and was happy about it. Steven was right to hate him—she hated him, too.

More than anything.

~ 11 ~

SHE STAYED ALONE in her room for the rest of the night, crunched up in bed, reading *Sense and Sensibility*, and holding her cat. Sense and sensibility. Yeah, sure. She threw the book across the room and just held Vanessa.

Would someone really hurt her while she was playing tennis? If it was insane to hurt the President, it was even more insane to go after the President's children. How could anyone be that sick?

Her stomach was killing her, and she held onto it, instead of Vanessa, thinking about the afternoons she and Steven and Neal sometimes spent in the Treaty Room, answering as many of their screened letters as they could, until they were too tired to keep going. Meg tried to get through at least two hundred a week, scrawling quick notes on White House stationary, or just signing her name at the bottom of pregenerated responses—which was less labor-intensive. Some letters were funny, some were sad or lonely, some—*a lot*, actually—criticized the way she talked or dressed or led her life. Other letters asked her to give her mother such and such advice, or wanted to be her pen pal, or requested autographed photos and stuff like that.

She tried not to think about the letters she and her brothers never saw. But now, everything seemed scary, and she had trouble sleeping, dreaming about people with guns firing at her family, people dressed as nurses and orderlies creeping into her mother's room to hurt her—terrible dreams. She would wake up, out of breath, usually crying, and have to turn the light on, holding Vanessa until the fear subsided enough for her to try sleeping again.

And she wasn't the only one who was afraid. Her family was,

naturally, and when she was being taken to the hospital from the car or vice versa, if someone slammed a car door or beeped a horn, she would see her agents tense, ready for action. Everyone seemed to flinch lately, waiting for something to happen, for someone to do something. She covered her face with her arm, trying to will her stomach to stop hurting.

There was a knock on the door and she jumped.

"May I come in?" her father asked.

She lowered her arm. "Uh, yeah. I mean, sure."

He opened the door, and while his expression was composed, he seemed a little shaky and very sad. "I'm sorry I lost control," he said.

"It's okay." Meg blushed, feeling as if she were giving absolution. "I mean, it's probably good for you."

He looked uncomfortable. "In any case, I'm sorry."

"I'm sorry I argued," she said.

"Well, I didn't expect you to be thrilled about the idea." He put his hands in his pockets, looking old and hunched. "I wouldn't do it, if I didn't feel that it was necessary."

"Have they, um, gotten any more threats?" Meg asked. "Like last summer?"

"No. Your mother and I just want to take as many precautions as we can." He sighed. "I really am sorry. The last thing I want to do is hurt my children."

"You aren't hurting us," she said.

"Well." He shrugged dismissively. "I'm not helping very much, either."

It was awkwardly silent.

"Well," he said, and straightened up. "Good-night. Sleep well."

How unlikely was *that*? "Um, yeah," Meg said. "You, too."

SHE SKIPPED BREAKFAST the next morning, staying in her room to fold and refold her tennis uniform, smoothing out all of the wrinkles, hoping that she was going to be able to get through the day.

Right now, she felt like going into her closet, shutting the door, and never coming out.

But, it was getting late, so she went down to the dining room to say good-bye. Her mother's chair was very empty—instead of sitting there, Trudy had been using an extra chair on Meg's side of the table.

"If you hurry," Trudy said, "you have time for some cereal and juice."

Meg shook her head. "No, thanks, I'm not all that hungry."

Trudy frowned and poured her a glass of juice. "Please drink some of this. I really don't want you going off this way."

It was easier to gulp half the juice than to argue about it, even though her stomach rebelled against every swallow. "See you guys later." She glanced at her father. "Tell Mom I said hi, and hope she's feeling better and everything."

He nodded, his eyes almost as tired as they had been the night before. "Have a nice day," he said, either from force of habit, or to make it seem like a normal morning.

As though the matriarch wasn't lying in a hospital bed, torn apart by bullets.

"Meg, wait!" Steven called after her. "Later," he said to the others, his usual tough-kid good-bye.

Meg waited near the private staircase, reflecting briefly and bitterly on the fact that it was probably the first school day all year that she hadn't had to bring her tennis bag. For once, everything would fit in her locker. Big deal.

"Um, look," Steven said, his eyes on his high-tops as they walked downstairs. "I'm sorry."

"About what?" she asked.

"Tennis," he said. "You must feel pretty bad."

Yeah. She shrugged. "It doesn't matter. The season's almost over, anyway. What's the deal on basketball?"

Steven avoided her eyes. "It might be okay, because it's indoors, and they can just, like put on extra guards."

Oh. But she couldn't sound jealous, because there was no point in making him feel lousy, too. "Well, that's good," she said. "I mean, I'm glad."

"Are you, um," he didn't look up, "mad at me?"

Insanely jealous was more like it. She shook her head.

"Well, are you sure? I mean," he blinked several times, "if you want, I'll quit, too, so you'll like, have company."

What a nice guy. "No, don't be dumb," she said. "My season's almost over, anyway. It really doesn't matter."

"You sure?" he asked.

She nodded.

"You don't hate me?" he asked.

Instead of answering, she punched him in the ribs, and he grinned.

"Guess you don't," he said.

She nodded. "Come on, we're late."

There were many more reporters and cameras waiting outside on the South Grounds than usual, and for a second, Meg didn't think she was going to be able to go out there. But, Maureen, her father's deputy press secretary, was—politely—keeping them at bay, so they wouldn't have to answer questions, and she assumed they weren't expected to smile broadly, either. Or even at all.

She could tell that Steven was even more scared that she was, and walking him over to his car before going to hers gave her time to find enough courage to get back to *her* car and inside. Security was tighter than ever, and two extra cars were accompanying her regular detail.

She and her agents rode in complete silence, and she spent the time thinking about her mother. Wondering if she was up yet, what she was doing. If they were letting her eat regular food. If she hurt as much as she had yesterday. If the agents driving her father to the hospital would be able to protect him. If—they were at the school now, and she saw bunches of reporters outside, almost as many as had been there on her first day of school. Seeing the cars, they swarmed over in her direction, still more agents and school security people blocking them back, and Ginette—one of the youngest of Preston's many staffers—trying, and failing, to keep them under control.

Meg gripped her knapsack with her hands, afraid to get out of the car.

"You okay?" Wayne, one of her agents, asked.

She didn't answer, staring at the crowd, the school looking completely unfamiliar. An agent from the car behind them had opened her door, and hesitantly, she climbed out. The cameras were rolling, reporters were shouting and shoving microphones at her—and she froze.

"How do you feel about—" one was saying.

"—afraid for your mother's safety?" another asked.

"—true that you're no longer allowed to play on the—" a third wanted to know.

"Come on," Wayne said, in her ear. "Let's get inside."

"Miss Powers isn't going to be addressing any questions," Ginette was shouting, her voice a little too thin to be effective.

Meg still hung back against the car, and then agents had each of her arms, propelling her almost painfully through the crowd and inside.

The hall was also jammed, with students and a few teachers, all of whom were staring at her. She veered into the main office for a minute, but that seemed to be mobbed, too, so she went back out to the hall, *ordering* herself not to cry.

"Are you all right?" Gary, one of her other agents, asked quietly.

Oh, yeah. She was swell. She nodded, not looking up in case her eyes were red. "I have to see Mrs. Ferris." Her tennis coach.

"We can have someone take care of that for you," Gary said.

She shook her head, walking down the hall, people moving out of her way. No one said anything to her, and she was half-relieved, half-hurt, focusing on the floor.

Her coach, who was also a history teacher, was sitting behind the desk in her classroom. Meg knocked on the door and Mrs. Ferris looked up, and then came out into the hall.

"It's good to have you back," she said. "How is everything?"

Everything sucked. "Fine, thank you." Meg pulled her uniform out of her knapsack. "I, um—I mean, my father—" She stopped. "I'm really sorry, but I'm kind of not allowed to play anymore."

Mrs. Ferris nodded. "Mr. Fielding spoke to me about it."

Thank God, as ever, for Preston.

"I hope the President is okay," Mrs. Ferris said. "We're all praying for her."

Meg nodded. "Thank you." The White House had been releasing photos of the President holding staff meetings, looking vibrant and cheerful—which would have been all well and good, if it hadn't been a complete sham. Make-up, strategically placed pillows to prop her up in the chair, clothes carefully pinned in place, artful and flattering lighting—the whole nine yards. Her mother actually *was* running meetings, but doing it while lying in bed, looking terrifyingly pale and exhausted.

"I'm very sorry about all of this," Mrs. Ferris said. "Is there anything I can do to help?"

Meg shook her head. "Thank you, but it's okay." If walking away from tennis was her biggest problem, she would have counted herself lucky. Probably.

"We're going to miss you on the team," Mrs. Ferris said, "but obviously, everyone understands."

Certainly, they would know that she would never leave the team by *choice*. "Would I, um—" Maybe she shouldn't ask this, but she couldn't help wanting to know. "How do you think I was going to do at the ISL?"

"I would have been stunned if you didn't make the finals," her coach said, without hesitating.

Which would have been nice. Meg swallowed, feeling tears, but suppressing them. "It would have been Kimberly Tseng, probably?"

Against her, in the finals to determine the top singles player in the league.

Mrs. Ferris nodded. "Odds are."

Yeah. She had always considered Kimberly the one genuine threat in the league. "Do you think I could have beaten her?"

Mrs. Ferris nodded again. "As long as you didn't lose patience with the dinking and dunking."

Kimberly was a superb player, but—as opposed to Meg's slashing, attacking, fast-paced game—her style resembled a relentless and infallible ball machine, and she was inclined to beat opponents with sheer, infuriating consistency.

It was too late now, of course, but it was nice to know that she *might* have won.

She made it to her locker, and then homeroom, without breaking down, but could tell from the trembling tension in her arms and legs that it was going to be a very difficult day. Especially since there was an Upper School-wide meeting for silent worship scheduled, which would obviously include a call for prayers for her mother, during which she would have to look game and grateful—and not cry.

As she walked into the room, people stopped whatever they were doing, awkward and uneasy. She saw Alison coming over and abruptly turned her back, making it clear that she didn't want to talk to anyone. *Couldn't* talk to anyone. She heard Alison hesitate, then move away.

No one else even tried to approach her, and when the bell rang, she let everyone else leave first, pretending to fumble through her knapsack. Walking to the door, she saw Josh in the hall, leaning against a locker, his hands nervously in his pockets.

She was barely hanging on right now, and if he hugged her, she was going to fall apart. So, she carefully kept her distance.

Everyone else in the hall was staring at her, as if she had lost a limb or been horribly burned or something, and no one knew how to treat her anymore.

"Uh, hi," he said.

"I need to be alone," she said stiffly. "Okay?"

"Oh." He stopped. "I'm sorry."

"What, is sorry your new word?" she asked.

He stepped back uneasily. "No, I—I mean, I just—"

"Well, quit saying it, okay?" she asked. Did he have to act so damned nervous? He was supposed to be her closest friend, for Christ's sakes. What was he doing being afraid of her?

"Is it okay if I walk with you?" he asked, still keeping his distance.

Jesus Christ. Would it be possible for him to be *more* tone-deaf? She frowned at him. "You have to ask permission?"

"No, I just—I don't know what you want me to do," he said.

It would probably be a mistake to answer that honestly. She frowned at him. "Right now, that might not be such a great question, Josh."

"I'm sorry. I mean—" His expression was very unhappy. "I just don't want to upset you."

"Too bad, because you're doing a hell of a job." She moved past him and down the hall, knowing that he wouldn't come after her. None of this was his fault—why did she keep yelling at him? She couldn't tell if she fell like falling down and crying, or turning around and hitting someone.

People were watching her, and she gave the entire hall a mean look, afraid that if anyone came near her, she might do something irrational.

Because, of course, barking at a sweet, nice—if sometimes infuriatingly tentative—guy made perfect sense.

Her whole French class stopped talking when she walked in and she had to gulp, suddenly very nauseated. There was an empty desk in the back and she took it, praying that no one would come over to her—which people either seemed to sense, or word had gotten around that she wanted to be left the hell alone.

When class started, her teacher's voice sounded like the robot-teacher in the Charlie Brown cartoons, and she looked at her desk, concentrating on not throwing up. If he called on her, she would probably pass out.

Neal was on his way to school now—were his agents taking care of him? He was so small. It was awful to think of a crowd of agents surrounding an eight-year-old. Was he as scared as she had been? As she still was?

When the bell rang, her stomach jumped as much as she did.

"Mademoiselle Powers?" her teacher asked.

Great. She was going to throw up all over Mr. Thénardier. She walked up to the front of the room, gripping her knapsack.

"Ah, Mademoiselle Powers," he said. "I wanted to—"

"Could I talk to you tomorrow, sir?" she asked. "I'm not feeling very well."

"Of course," he said. "Would you like me to take you down to the clinic?"

"No, thank you." She headed for the door, taking deep breaths. She didn't want to throw up. If she did, she would never live it down. No one ever forgot people who threw up at school—or on top of Japanese prime ministers, for that matter. She had a brief flash of Anne-Marie Hammersmith vomiting all over the place in the third grade. During geography. The last she'd heard, Anne-Marie had lost the election for Homecoming Queen. She was incredibly beautiful, so it was probably because of people who remembered her throwing up.

Only, now she had to go to physics. The last time she had gone to physics—and wished for something, *anything*, to get her out of class—how would her mother feel if she knew? *She* felt like King Midas.

She veered over to the nearest water fountain, pretending to take a drink, but really hanging on for support. But before her agents could talk to her, she started walking again, her legs weak. The science lab didn't have any windows—like the waiting room at the hospital, when they were sitting there, wondering whether her mother was—she pulled her sweater sleeve across her face, ordering herself not to be dizzy. Then, she sat in the back of the room and opened her book, the page blurring in front of her eyes.

As her teacher began his lecture, his voice seeming unnaturally loud, she hung on to her book, the corners digging into her hands. She should be taking notes, but she was afraid to move and get a pen, since the motion might make her feel worse.

"Hey," someone next to her—Nathan?—whispered. "You okay?"

She nodded, sucking in a deep, nausea-controlling breath. It didn't work, and she shoved away from her desk, running out of the room and down the hall to the nearest girls' lav, two of her agents right behind her. There were three juniors standing around by the sinks, and they stared at her, then hurried out.

"Meg," one of her agents said, "are you—"

"Leave me alone!" She leaned against the wall, resting her head on her arms, fists tight.

"We just have to make sure you're all right," he said, but she could also hear them checking the room to make sure that there was no one else in there, no potential threats. Oh, yeah, they were *great* at their jobs.

"Okay," Wayne said, "we'll—"

"Jesus Christ!" She whirled around, her face flushing with a sudden hot fury. "Can't I even throw up in private?"

They nodded, both edging towards the door.

"You follow me everywhere," Meg said, hearing her voice shake, "make my stupid life miserable, and then, *then*, when we god-damn need you, no one's around! Mom probably would have been better off without you—all you do is make things worse. *Tempt* people to hurt us!"

"Meg," Wayne said quietly, "calm—"

"Don't tell me what to do!" she said. "You're not my parents—you're not anybody! You're just stupid jerks who can't even do their jobs!"

"Meg," he put his hand on her shoulder, "just—"

She jerked away. "*Touch* me, and I'm getting new agents! I don't have to put up with that."

"Okay." He moved to the door. "We'll be right outside."

She nodded. "Of course. A bunch of professional voyeurs. Professional *cowards*."

Neither man said anything.

"What would you do if someone was in here, anyway?" she asked. "Let them shoot me a couple of times, and *then* react?"

Still, neither of them responded.

"Oh, I forgot—I'm the President's daughter. God forbid any of you talk to me." She shook her head. "I should have figured. If you're scared to *talk* to us, naturally you're going to be too scared to protect us. Jerks." She pushed past them and out to the hall, every muscle trembling, fists clenched to keep from bursting into reaction tears. Then, she stopped. "By the way," she said, "thanks for getting me kicked off tennis."

~ 12 ~

SHE WENT STRAIGHT to the car, not even stopping by the office to let them know that she was leaving. She slouched in the backseat, not speaking—or even putting on her god-damn seat belt—and they drove her home in silence.

At least the stupid reporters were gone. Probably off tormenting Steven and Neal. Sons-of-bitches.

At the White House, she left the car without her usual thank-you, going directly up to her room and putting on a nightgown. Trudy came in with ginger ale and fussed over her for a while—tucking her in, fluffing her pillows, and adjusting the draperies to make the room darker, so that she could maybe get some sleep.

But she was still too upset to even try, so she sat down behind her computer and started looking for film, photos, analysis—anything she could find about the shooting. Except that it was mostly all stuff she had already seen—more than once—and it was exhausting and unpleasant to read the latest conspiracy theories: that the Pentagon was behind it, as a way to remove her from office; that the Trilateral Commission was behind it, for primarily economic reasons; that *her father* was behind it—and so on. Endless, stupid, paranoid theories, with specious, but detailed, "evidence." When she started to come across a stream of misogynistic, practically *gleeful* blogs and comments, she couldn't bring herself to look any further. Instead, she picked up the phone, calling down to the chief usher's office and asking him to send up the latest news magazines. *US News & World Report, Time, Newsweek*—all of the usual suspects. Because, somehow, something she could actually hold in her hand would seem more *real*. Less easy to scroll past.

He was reluctant to do it—her parents had probably asked to have the magazines kept away from the three of them, if possible—but she insisted, and a butler appeared with several issues a few minutes later.

Her mother was on all of the covers, except for one, which had a picture of the Presidential Seal, with a silhouette of a gun in front of it. Two of the covers were close-ups of her mother's expression as the bullets hit: surprised pain. Eyebrows up and startled, mouth tightening in a wince. The fourth cover was a picture of her seconds before; smiling, arm lifting in a wave, framed by dark-suited agents.

She dropped the magazines in her lap, afraid to look inside. The prevalent message on the covers was *"Again?"* And again and again and again.

She opened the first magazine and found the predictable five or six stories associated with assassination attempts: the editorial lament, the minute-by-minute account, the biography and personal profile of the gunman, along with a rehash of other assassins from Lee Harvey Oswald on, the requisite article about the challenges faced by the Secret Service in a dangerous world, and finally, the one describing every detail of the doctors' work. All accompanied by pictures in living color. Terrific. Some enterprising person was always there, taking pictures of leaders crumpling in agony.

There were lots of photographs of the assassin, smirking in most of them, and often dressed in military surplus clothing—or jailhouse jumpsuits. He was also quoted more than once, saying things like "Too bad I missed" and "Guess that showed *her*." It wasn't like there was any doubt that he was insane. Insanity was no excuse.

The post-shooting photos of her mother were only staged ones of the "active meetings" in her hospital room. There weren't any pictures of her walking around, "on the road to recovery," since she still couldn't *sit up* for extended periods of time.

There were shots of the Vice-President, and of senior staff and cabinet members, all working to keep the United States going, without missing a beat. Pictures of her father, very pale, appearing not to have slept in days. There was even one of her, going into the hospital with Neal and Steven the morning after it happened. She had a hand in Neal's, the other on Steven's shoulder, and the three of them looked very grim. The President's children, demonstrating what the caption described was "unsettling gravitas." Preternatural, even. Would the writer have been happier if they had staggered up the sidewalk, sobbing?

The coverage in all of the magazines was pretty much the same. Some of the pictures were duplicates; some were just different angles. She was in all four: with Steven and Neal, the same picture, in two; then, in the third, she was alone, rushing into the hospital that first afternoon, her eyes dark and huge—which was dubbed "controlled terror." The one in the fourth magazine was the worst, because she couldn't remember its being taken, except that she was wearing her black Levi's, so it must have been Saturday. She was sitting by herself on a bench in a hospital corridor, with her elbows on her knees, her face in her hands. The First Daughter, in a moment of private grief, the caption said. And it *was* private. It didn't seem right that they could publish that in a national magazine. She looked small and scared, and as if she were trying as hard as she could to hold herself together. The kind of picture that was going to show up in Year-in-Review issues. Not very fair.

The articles all talked about her mother's courage. The slim, physically fragile woman, and her incredible inner strength. About her gallantry, her unquenchable sense of humor. About an Administration so well managed that "the wheels of government continued turning without a hitch." About Vice-President Kruger's superb clutch leadership, and reactions to the incident from world leaders, all of whom were appalled—her mother was very well-liked.

And the articles talked about the family. "Public composure" was the big phrase. Public composure and private agony. Loving family shattered by gunfire. All of which had apparently led to her mother jumping a good fifteen points in the polls. What a way to do it.

She knocked the magazines onto the floor, sick of reading about it. The thing the magazines ignored was that all of them were real people. The stories were glib, play-by-play analyses, without any emotion. Stories that were, after all, out to sell magazines. Maybe even to entertain.

"That the best you can do for reading material?" Preston asked from the door.

"They're pretty bad," she said.

"I know. That's why the three of you weren't supposed to see them." He was wearing dark brown flannel pants with a brown, tan and white argyle V-neck, a white shirt, and skinny brown tie. His loafers were so pristine that it looked as if people carried him around all the time so that his feet wouldn't touch the floor. "How are you feeling?"

She shrugged.

"Too shiny?" he asked.

She looked up. "What?"

"My shoes," he said.

"Oh." She nodded. "Well, yeah. They look too new."

"They *are* new," he said.

Oh. She frowned.

"I really wonder what goes on in your head, kid," he said.

She shrugged.

"What's going on in it right now?" he asked.

She shrugged again. "Nothing much."

"You've been reading those," he indicated the magazines, "and nothing's going on in your head?"

"Not really," she said stiffly.

"Been all over the Internet, too?" he asked.

Which, the last she'd heard, wasn't against the law.

"Well, I envy you," he said. "I think I'd be going crazy."

Was this the part where she was supposed to dissolve in tears? She didn't say anything.

"Not that it's not upsetting, anyway. Your family is very important to me." He looked right at her, and she nodded self-consciously. "How do you feel?" he asked, his voice gentle.

Christ, how many people were going to ask her that?

"Public composure," he said.

Something like that, yeah. She shrugged.

"Have you had lunch?" he asked.

She shook her head. "I'm not hungry."

"Well, *I* am," he said. "And I missed breakfast, too."

"Why don't you just go down to the Mess," she said. Most White House staffers ate in a special dining room on the ground floor of the West Wing. "Or you could have someone in the kitchen make you something."

"I thought we could cook," he said.

She looked at him suspiciously. "What do you mean, *we*?"

"Get cleaned up," he said, "and I'll go tell Carl we're taking over."

Jesus. Couldn't he figure out that she just wanted to be alone? Why was everyone so god-damn dense?

"Hurry it up, okay?" he said, closing the door behind him as he left.

Not sure what else to do, Meg changed into sweatpants, a blue Lacoste shirt, and her Topsiders. She always wore her Topsiders around the house, because slippers looked stupid. Once, someone had given her a pair of slippers that looked like pink fuzzy rabbits, and she had had to wear them to be polite, in spite of the fact that she felt like an idiot. Slippers were not cool.

Preston was alone in the upstairs kitchen, wearing a white

Presidential Food Services apron—and was, she assumed, devastated that it wasn't color-coordinated.

"Where is everyone?" she asked.

"I gave them a break." He handed her a glass of dark liquid. "Want a Coke?"

"Well, yeah, I guess." She sipped some, watching him rummage through the cupboards and refrigerator. Preston wasn't a person she thought of as being an industrious little chef.

"Do you cook?" she asked.

He laughed. "What do you think—I go home, open cans of ravioli, and eat them cold?"

Probably, yeah—on the rare evenings when he didn't exist on take-out, since she had seen him grabbing a slice of pizza or eating out of take-out containers more times than she could count. She frowned. "I don't know. I never really thought about it."

"Well, think about it," he said, turning on the coffeemaker.

"What's your apartment like?" she asked.

He grinned. "Immaculate. What do you want to make?"

"Um, sandwiches?" she said.

He shook his head. "I was thinking more along the lines of a glutinous pasta concoction."

"Okay," Meg said, suddenly feeling hungry.

"Great." He started wiping off mushrooms with a damp paper towel—which made her suspect that he really *did* know his way around kitchens. "Your job is to create something absolutely wonderful for dessert."

Wait, *she* had to work, too? "Dessert?" she said.

"You have no idea how hungry I am." He opened the cupboard where the baking supplies were kept. "Here. Use your imagination."

At first, the whole thing seemed kind of dumb, but Preston's enthusiasm was contagious and the cooking started being fun. He was sautéing the mushrooms, along with onions and peppers, which he assured her were an integral part of his pasta plan. End quote. She was whipping cream, and when he asked her why, she said that it was an imperative component of her dessert plan—which was a lie. Actually, she had no plans whatsoever, but whipping cream might give her time to think of one. Not that she wouldn't be happy slopping the cream onto graham crackers and eating them without further adornment. But, Preston probably had a more discerning palate. *Most* people probably did.

They ate at the table in the West Sitting Hall. Preston had combined his sautéed vegetables with noodles, fresh dill, cracked pepper, and lots of buffalo mozzarella cheese and butter, and it was one of the better pasta concoctions she had ever eaten. He had also made a salad: spinach, romaine and Boston lettuce, cucumber slivers, purple onions, shaved carrots, and Heirloom tomatoes. She drank Coke, and he had coffee, and they didn't talk about anything difficult—just football, and skiing, and their favorite paintings in the White House, and Great Meals They Had Known. She felt better than she had in days.

"Well." He sat back. "Let's see this dessert of yours."

"Okay, but you have to wait here." She carried their plates towards the kitchen. "I'll just be a minute."

She scraped and rinsed the plates, trying to think. Maybe she would have to go with graham crackers, after all. She took down two nice hefty bowls and broke graham crackers into them. The freezer had homemade chocolate and chocolate-chip ice cream, and she filled the bowls with alternating spoonfuls of the two flavors. Then, she melted chocolate chips in the microwave, with a dash of vanilla, to make a sauce, which she poured over the ice cream, before adding more-than-generous spoonfuls of the whipped cream. But she needed one final—*elle ne savait quoi*—there were some Oreos and she crushed a few, covering the whipped cream with the pieces. Finally, she stuck a spoon in each bowl and carried them out to the table.

Preston grinned. "Way to go, Meg."

"Old family recipe," she said.

He nodded and picked up his spoon. "I could tell at once."

They talked about the best ice cream places in the city—about which they strongly disagreed, Woody Allen movies—before he got weird, and their favorite Robert Parker mysteries, Meg feeling so relaxed that she finished her entire dish of ice cream.

"What a little piglet," Preston said.

She grunted cooperatively. "How come you're not over at the hospital or anything?" Propping up the First Gentleman, presumably.

"Because I wanted to have lunch with you," he said.

She moved her jaw. "Summoned to try and cheer up the fraying-at-the-edges First Daughter?"

He shrugged. "Why not?"

Good to know that no one was talking about her behind her back, or anything.

"Steven's pretty upset with his agents," Preston said.

She looked up sharply. Was that meant for her? "Oh. Did they do something to bother him?"

"I guess he's blaming them for your mother being shot," he said.

Meg flinched at the word "shot." How could he come right out and say it? "Sounds pretty immature," she said, calmly.

He shrugged again. "People do funny things when they're upset."

Meg let out her breath, annoyed. Preston didn't usually play games. "What, did my agents fink on me, or something?"

"They didn't 'fink,'" he said. "They're worried about you, Meg."

She nodded. "They should be, if they have that much trouble protecting people."

"Is that really fair?" he asked.

Like she cared, one way or the other? She played with the sauce and melted ice cream left in her dish. "What difference does it make?"

"I don't know." He drank some coffee. "Bert Travis's family is probably feeling pretty lousy about the whole thing."

"He's not even on crutches," Meg said, irritated.

"He could have been killed," Preston said.

"Yeah, well, so could—" She stopped. "Forget it, I don't want to talk about it."

He nodded, and it was quiet for a minute.

"You know," he said, "sometimes things like this make families even closer."

"What do you do in your free time," she asked, "read Hallmark cards?"

"Everyone needs a hobby," he said.

She frowned, not amused.

"Okay." He finished his coffee. "It's just something to think about. Want another Coke?"

She shook her head.

He made a tennis swing with his arm. "Feel like hitting a few?"

Oh, yeah, right. "Why?" she asked. "I'm not allowed to play anymore."

"You might feel better if you got some exercise," he said.

"Oh," she said, nodding, "so now I'm fat?"

"No. Just thought it might make you feel better." He reached across the table to pat her shoulder, then collected the dishes, carrying them out to the kitchen.

"Are you mad?" Meg asked, when he returned.

He tilted his head. "Should I be?"

"Well," she didn't look at him, "I guess I was pretty rude."

"So, you were rude," he said, shrugging. "No problem. Just be selective. You want to be rude, come find me."

Meg frowned uncertainly. "I don't get it."

"You don't want to take things out on the wrong people, that's all," he said. "Your agents. Your friends. Anyone who isn't directly involved."

Meg folded her arms. Was he bugging her about Josh now? Nothing like having a private life.

"Can't keep these things inside, Meg," he said. "You do, and they come out at all the wrong times, you know?"

She didn't say anything.

"You have to find someone to talk to. It doesn't have to be me, but—" He paused. "If you don't talk about it, you'll drive yourself crazy."

Meg looked at her hands.

"Well," he said. "I guess I've annoyed you enough."

She nodded.

"Then, maybe I'll head back over," he said. "Unless you feel like hitting a few, or checking out ESPN, or something."

She shook her head.

"Okay. Whatever." He stood up. "You know where to find me."

She nodded.

"Good." He bent to kiss the top of her head. "Thanks for letting me have lunch with you."

"*Letting* you?" she said.

He looked sad. "You didn't have a nice time?"

She had to grin. "It was swell."

When he was gone, she sat at the table for a long time, thinking. He was right—she had to talk to *someone*. But, this wasn't exactly a great time to seek Josh out. And if she couldn't talk to Josh, who— she glanced at her watch. Going on to four. That meant that school had been out for—she picked up the nearest telephone.

Beth answered on the third ring.

"Um, hi," Meg said.

"Hi," Beth said. "Everything okay? What's up?"

"Nothing. I mean, things are—I don't know. Pretty bad." She swallowed. "I was wondering, um—do you think you can maybe still come here?"

"Sure," Beth said. "When?"

— 13 —

BETH TOOK AN evening shuttle down, the White House sending a car to the airport to pick her up. Meg was just as happy to stay at home, and avoid her agents. She waited downstairs in the Diplomatic Reception Room, slouching on a yellow sofa. Since she wasn't in the family quarters, her agents *were* around, but at least they weren't making themselves obvious.

"Miss Shulman is arriving, Miss Powers," a Marine guard told her from the door.

"Thank you." She went through the vestibule and outside to the edge of the South Drive.

One of the inevitable black cars pulled up and Beth got out.

"Hi," she said, grinning.

Meg grinned back, especially at her rust felt hat, a small feather in the band. "Nice hat."

"Fall," Beth said, and glanced around. "I was kind of expecting photographers."

"Disappointed?" Meg asked.

"Yeah, actually." She picked up her overnight bag and a Barnes & Noble bag, and they looked at each other. "Never done much hugging, have we?"

God, no. "Not really," Meg said.

Beth nodded. "Well. No point in starting now."

Definitely not.

Beth's grin came back. "Then again, what the hell?" She gave Meg a quick hug, then continued past her into the house.

"You're really weird," Meg said, following her.

"But, *oh* so charming," Beth said.

Depending upon one's definition.

Beth stopped on the red carpet outside the Diplomatic Reception Room, looking up and down the Ground Floor Corridor at the Presidential Seal, and the portraits of First Ladies. "This place could grow on me."

"Oh, yeah," Meg said. "It's terrific."

Beth pointed at the paintings of Jacqueline Kennedy and Eleanor Roosevelt. "Those don't impress you?"

They kind of did, but Meg shook her head.

"That's what I like about you," Beth said, draping her arm over Meg's shoulders. "You're so much fun to be with." She took her arm away. "Your brothers here?"

Meg gestured towards the ceiling. "Yeah, up there somewhere. Dad's still at the hospital."

"How's your mother?" Beth asked.

Meg shook her head, crossing the hall to the main staircase.

They found Steven and Neal in the solarium with Trudy, watching an old *Star Wars* movie.

"Hi, Mrs. Donovan," Beth said cheerfully. "Hi, guys." She hefted the bookstore bag. "Better turn that off—it's present time."

"Candy?" Meg guessed.

Beth laughed. "Can't pull the wool over *your* eyes, can I?"

"How was your flight, Beth?" Trudy asked.

"Well, exhausting," Beth said, "but—"

Meg nodded. "The whole hour and a half."

"Yeah, with a good night's rest, I'll probably be okay," Beth said. "But, my God, I remember my last trip to Zimbabwe—"

Trudy laughed, standing up. "I have some brownies and cocoa downstairs waiting for all of you."

"Not," Beth said, "double chocolate with butterscotch chips."

Trudy nodded, smiling.

"Invite me more often," Beth said to Meg.

"No, don't worry," Trudy said, as Meg moved to help her. "You four just wait up here."

Beth sat down on the couch next to Steven and Neal. "How are you guys? You holding up okay?"

They both shrugged.

"What do you think of the hat, Steven?" she asked.

He shrugged again. "Pretty dumb."

"I agree." Beth put it on Neal's head, and Neal actually laughed— a sound Meg hadn't heard for almost a week. "Now, then." She reached into her bag, pulling out a gift-wrapped present with a red ribbon. "This one's for your mother and," she reached back in, coming out with a blue-ribboned hardcover, "*this* one's for your father."

Meg leaned over to see the title. A very nice edition of Emerson's *Nature and Other Writings*. Which was definitely her father's kind of thing. "Good choice."

"Well, thank you, Meghan," Beth said.

"How come Mom's is wrapped, and Dad's isn't?" Neal asked.

Beth shrugged. "Because your mother always used to say, 'Pretty wrapping makes the experience complete,' and your father would say, 'Oh, for God's sakes.'"

Meg studied her, impressed. "You have a hell of a memory."

"It's a curse," Beth said sadly.

No doubt. "So, where's my present?" Meg asked.

"Well, okay, so I brought *most* of you gifts." Beth pulled out a Hardy Boys book—number eighteen, *The Twisted Claw*. "My personal favorite," she said, and handed it to Neal.

"Hey, wow, thanks!" Neal said, sitting back to check it out.

"And this," Beth took out a biography of Sandy Koufax and gave it to Steven, "is for you. An educational gift," she said to Meg. "Both inspirational and precautionary."

"I don't suppose you have anything in that bag for me," Meg said, being Dorothy in *The Wizard of Oz*.

"Pay no attention to the man behind the curtain," Beth said, and tossed her a thick paperback.

Meg looked at the cover—splashy and trashy, lots of embracing—then turned the book over, feeling the spine. "The binding's broken."

"Well, sure," Beth said. "I had to read it and make sure there was plenty of sex." She grinned. "There is."

Trudy came back in, with Jorge, one of the butlers, carrying a tray of brownies and cups of cocoa, and they watched the rest of the movie, Beth lightening the atmosphere considerably. After saying hello to Meg's father, who finally got home around eleven-thirty, they ended up in Meg's room, Meg stretched out on the bed while Beth examined the music on her computer.

"Your father looks even worse than you do," she said.

Meg nodded. "He's not sleeping much." Possibly not sleeping *at all*.

Beth nodded, then gestured towards the computer. "You have the most embarrassingly dated collection of anyone in the entire country under fifty."

Meg shrugged. "They've got just about every CD in the whole damn world upstairs."

"No, we'll just have to make do," Beth said, her voice long-suffering. Then, she bent over her overnight bag, pulling out a pack of Newports. "Want to get over on the Establishment?"

Smoking was completely forbidden in the White House, but since Trudy had been known to sneak a cigarette here and there, and some of the members of her mother's kitchen cabinet were notoriously fond of cigars, the rule got broken—mostly on the basis of the smoker's status within the Administration's hierarchy.

"You are just too cool," Meg said.

"I'd be cooler if I actually *lit* them," Beth said, sticking a cigarette in her mouth.

Probably, yeah. She had seen Beth hold a cigarette at more than one party over the years, but had possibly *never* seen her take an actual puff.

Beth opened the bedroom door. "Come on."

Christ, she didn't feel like getting up. "Come on *where*?" Meg asked, lying on her bed.

"Just come on," Beth said.

Meg followed her out to the Center Hall, Beth walking as cautiously as a cat burglar.

"Be careful," Beth whispered. "We don't want to be seen."

"Oh, well, lucky we're in the White House," Meg said. "No one's *ever* around."

"Shhh," Beth hissed, and slunk down the hall a few feet.

"You're what," Meg said, "a senior now?"

"Be quiet, you want to blow our cover?" Beth flattened just inside the doors leading to the West Sitting Hall. "You think it's clear?"

Except for butlers, and stewards, and the like. Meg shrugged. "If they're not making Dad a late dinner, I guess so."

"We'll have to chance it," Beth said grimly, and crept down towards the kitchen.

Meg, starting to get amused, jogged after her.

Beth crouched down near the dumbwaiter, just outside the kitchen. "What do you think? Do we go for it?"

"Well, I don't know," Meg said. "What's the primary goal?"

"I call it"—Beth paused, for effect—"Operation Heineken."

Meg laughed.

"Look," Beth said, "if you're scared, just say so. No one will ever have to know."

"No fear here," Meg said.

"Good." Beth took a deep, shuddering breath. "This is a very emotional moment."

"See you on the other side," Meg said.

Beth nodded, then released her breath, darting into the—as it happened, empty—kitchen. She ran her hands across the front of the refrigerator, as though testing for alarms, then opened the door a centimeter at a time. Her arm snaked inside, pulling out one bottle of beer, then another. "Try to find an opener, but *be careful.*"

Meg nodded, easing the silverware drawer open and extricating one.

"All right." Beth wiped her sleeve across her face. "Now, look. Anyone stops us, and you keep going, you hear me? *Just keep going.*"

Meg laughed.

Beth frowned at her. "Damn it, this is no time for levity!"

"Sorry," Meg said.

Beth nodded impatiently. "Let's just get out of here." She stuck her head out into the hall, looking both ways, then motioned for Meg to follow her. They had just gotten back to the Center Hall when Beth stopped dead, Meg, naturally, crashing into her.

"What is it?" Meg asked, uneasy in spite of herself.

"I *tripped the sensors!*" Beth said, her voice horrified.

Which, all things being equal, was entirely possible. "What do we do?" Meg asked.

"Run like crazy!" Beth raced down to Meg's room, closing the door once Meg was inside, and leaning against it, out of breath. Then she looked up, grinning. "Was that fun?"

"Lots," Meg said.

"Good." Beth handed her the beers. "Open these, and *I'll* put on our favorite song." She clicked on a file on the desktop, and the Commodores' "Brick House" started playing.

"Our favorite fantasy, more likely," Meg said—although more in her case, than Beth's.

"For you, maybe," Beth said, dancing slightly and pretending to inhale on her unlit cigarette. Then she stopped, seeing Meg sitting in the rocking chair by the fireplace. "What, you're not having fun?"

"A whole lot," Meg said, and took a sip of beer. "Really."

"Well, we'll have to remedy *that.*" Beth scrolled through the music files. "Jesus, you have a lot of damn musicals on here."

Yeah. So?

Beth put on "Tea for Two," and began dancing—sweetly—to that, instead. But she stopped again when she saw that Meg hadn't gotten up. "You're *still* not having fun?"

Meg shrugged.

"Well, it's not good, if you're not having fun." Beth looked at her for a minute, then sighed deeply. "Oh, *all right*."

"What?" Meg asked.

Beth just sighed, clicking on a different file. "*Now* are you happy?"

Meg grinned, as Joan Jett's "I Love Rock and Roll" blasted out of the desktop speakers. "Yeah," she said. "I am."

BETH WAS SUPPOSED to fly back to Boston the next afternoon, so Meg had permission to stay home from school. They had stayed up very late, listening to music and then strolling down to the kitchen for a second beer, but they got up pretty early, so that they could go over to the hospital for a quick visit. They caught her mother—who was wan and shaky, but trying to seem energetic—between meetings, then were driven back to the White House. They ended up at the table in the West Sitting Hall, while the downstairs chefs prepared brunch.

"Are we the only ones here?" Beth asked.

Meg nodded. "Except for the Cast of Thousands." Which was the nickname she and Steven had given the staff on the very first day they moved in.

"Do they mind fixing us stuff?" Beth asked, uneasily.

Meg shook her head. "They get upset when we *don't* ask."

Few things made the Residence staff's blood run colder than moments when, for example, they caught the President wandering out of the kitchen with a spoon and a cup of yogurt, absentmindedly eating out of the carton as she walked.

After an astonishingly short wait, they were served a huge meal of juice, fresh melon, muffins, doughnuts, eggs, bacon, sausage, and milk.

"I sure would be fat if I lived here," Beth said.

Meg shrugged. "On school days, I mostly just have cereal."

They ate with very little conversation.

"Pretty tough week," Beth said.

Meg nodded.

"She doesn't look like she's well enough to be working," Beth said.

No, but it sure as hell hadn't stopped her. In fact, on the second day, she had overheard Glen, her mother's chief of staff, telling Winnie, the deputy chief of staff, that her mother had been trying to get the 25th Amendment lifted before she even fully came out of her anesthesia, and that she had, officially, submitted her formal written declaration to resume office to the Speaker of the House and the President *pro tempore* of the Senate just after three in the morning— and that her doctors had not been enthusiastic. Since the Speaker was a very close friend of her mother's, he had actually still been at the hospital, presumably trying to lend mostly-ignored moral support to her father, and he had managed to convince her—with some difficulty, and a quite heated conversation, Meg gathered—to wait a few more hours. So, ultimately, she had reassumed the Presidency at about seven AM, approximately nineteen and a half hours after she'd been shot.

Which, as far as Meg could tell, was at least three weeks premature.

"At least she's getting better," Beth said.

Meg shrugged, eating a cube of melon in an attempt to prove that she had something resembling an appetite.

Beth started to say something else, but helped herself to more bacon, instead.

The melon was delicious—at the absolute perfect stage of ripeness—but her stomach hurt, so Meg put her fork down. "I don't feel like talking about what happened. Okay?"

Beth helped herself to some eggs, too. "Then, we won't."

Meg nodded.

"I'm sorry about tennis," Beth said.

Another verboten subject, but Meg nodded, telling herself that she *didn't* feel tears in her eyes. "Thanks. It isn't—well. It's no big deal. Thanks."

It was quiet for a couple of minutes.

"If you want," Beth said, "we could go listen to 'I Love Rock and Roll.'"

Meg shook her head. "I'm sorry, I know I'm being a jerk. I'm just kind of tired."

"Then, let's go watch a movie or something," Beth said.

That seemed like a reasonable enough idea, and they ended up carrying orange juice and a few of the doughnuts up to the solarium, where—after a short debate—they decided to put on a couple of old *Avengers* episodes, which made Meg sad since that was something she usually only did with her parents once in a while, after Steven and Neal had gone to bed. Although she had watched a few of the Cathy Gales, and a single Tara King, she had never particularly seen the point of watching anything other than Emma Peel episodes.

"You sure have a lot of messages in your room," Beth said.

And the stack got bigger every day. Meg shrugged. "To be honest, I haven't really looked at them."

"There are probably some from me in there," Beth said.

No doubt. Meg shifted her position. "I don't know. When I get back from the hospital, I just haven't been—well, you know."

Beth nodded. "What's the deal with Josh?"

Meg scowled into her orange juice glass. "What do you mean?"

"I just kind of figured he'd be around," Beth said. "You haven't even mentioned him."

Meg shrugged, tightly gripping her glass.

"You guys have a fight or something?" Beth asked.

Or something. "Yeah, I guess. I mean—" Meg let out her breath.

"Christ, I don't know. One minute, he was at the hospital and I was really glad he was there, and the next minute, he was bugging the hell out of me, you know?"

Beth shook her head.

Meg glanced at the television where Steed was goofing around about having raced up the stairs in a department store because he'd heard that Mrs. Peel was in Ladies Underwear. "I don't know." She sighed. "It's like, he just stood there and let me yell at him. He didn't do *anything*."

"I'd be mad, too," Beth said.

"No, you don't understand. He was acting like we don't even know each other. Like I was the President's daughter and he was some, I don't know, *peon* or something." She glanced over at Beth, who was frowning. "I'm not explaining it right."

Beth shrugged. "So, explain it."

Which was going to be a challenge, since she didn't completely understand it herself. "I don't know." She rubbed her eyes, since her head was starting to ache even more than her stomach already did. "It was like he didn't know what to do at all. Like, I yelled at him, and he just got all nervous and scared. And then at school, he was doing the same thing. Like he thought I was going to *hit* him or something."

"Maybe he thought you were," Beth said.

Oh, please. Meg just looked at her. "What was he, threatened?"

Beth didn't say anything, looking right back, unblinking.

"Yeah, well, he shouldn't do that. I mean, part of it—*most* of it, even—was that I was mad in general, not at him. I mean—" She shook her head. "We've been seeing each other for a hell of a long time—I should be able to yell at him, you know?"

"What," Beth said, "because you're close, you should be able to abuse him?"

"No, I—" Meg stopped to think that one over. "Is that what I was doing?"

Beth nodded. "Sounds that way, yeah."

Oh. Meg looked at her uneasily. "I wasn't trying to. I mean—you know what I mean. I can yell at *you*, and you don't fall to pieces."

"It's different," Beth said.

Yes, and no. "No, it isn't. I mean, *Christ*, for all I know, we're going to—" She flushed slightly. "Well, you know."

"No." Beth brought her eyebrows together in pretended confusion. "I don't."

Right. "Don't be a jerk," Meg said.

"But," Beth's eyebrows moved even closer, "I really don't—"

"*Sleep* together, for Christ's sakes!" Meg said.

"Oh. That." Beth grinned. "What, you think that's a big deal?"

Meg was about to get mad, but she forced herself to take a slow, deep breath. "Am I the only one who knows that you talk a lot?"

Beth nodded. "Don't spread it around."

Especially since Beth had always preferred passing around rumors of that sort *herself*. Meg slouched down, staring at Steed and Mrs. Peel, without really watching the show. "It *is* a big deal," she said quietly.

Beth nodded. "If you think about it, Meg, you're lucky to be in a position to be considering it."

A fair point. "Still the same old losers at our school, hunh?" Meg said. Jocks and jokes, predominantly. All of whom were absolutely *determined* to attend Ivy League schools.

"Pretty much. Anyway," Beth swung her feet onto the coffee table, "you know me. I've got a thing for older men."

"You don't know any older men," Meg said. At least, not any dating prospects.

"I know." Beth looked sad. "I guess it's my own private hell."

And she was probably only half-kidding. Meg grinned. "You are *such* an asshole."

"I know," Beth said.

They were companionably silent.

"I couldn't say that to anyone in this whole stupid city with them getting all hurt or mad or something—even Josh." Meg sighed. "*Especially* Josh."

Beth nodded.

"It's like, I don't even have *friends* anymore," Meg said.

Beth shrugged. "It changed at home, too. By the convention, even Sarah was treating you funny."

"Yeah," Meg said. As the primary and election season had progressed, people she had known half of her life—like Sarah Weinberger—had been so intimidated, or freaked out, or *something*, that they barely spoke to her anymore. She glanced over. "I was afraid you were going to get weird, too."

"I was *already* weird," Beth said.

True enough, albeit in a different way. Meg shook her head. "You know what I mean."

Beth looked at her as though she were a complete idiot. "My God, Meg, I remember you sitting in first grade, crying."

"My ear actually *ruptured* that day," Meg said defensively.

"Yeah, I know," Beth said. "It's just if I start to get flipped out, I think about things like that."

Meg nodded, her hand automatically cupping her ear from the memory. They were supposed to be writing their sentences while their teacher, Mrs. Stokes, worked with a reading group. Meg had sat in the back of the classroom, crying and holding her ear, too shy to tell her teacher because it was supposed to be quiet time. But Beth had noticed, and had no qualms about interrupting the reading group. Mrs. Stokes had had Beth walk her down to the clinic, where she stayed on a green leather cot, crying, until Trudy came to pick her up.

"Makes me not feel weird about you," Beth said.

She and Beth were—she hoped, inescapably—nothing if not caught up in each other's histories. "My mother flew home that night," Meg said. "Even though it was a Wednesday."

Beth nodded. "She always flew home, when there was something wrong with you guys."

Almost always. But, anyway, she had *that* time. "Yeah." Meg lifted her legs up onto the couch and wrapped her arms around her knees. After an emergency trip to the pediatrician, Trudy had tucked her into bed with soup and toast triangles, but Meg couldn't stop crying, even though her father had come home early from work.

Then, suddenly, her mother was there, smelling of winter wind and perfume, gathering her up in a big warm hug while Meg cried and told her about how much it had hurt. Told her more than once. Trudy brought up a big bowl of mashed potatoes, which was Meg's favorite food in those days, and she and her mother—who still hadn't even taken off her coat—shared it, her mother saying funny things to make her laugh, Meg forgetting that she had ever had an earache.

Feeling self-conscious, she glanced over at Beth. "Uh, sorry."

Beth just shook her head.

"She was such a good Senator," Meg said, then sighed. "I wish she'd stopped there."

14

NEITHER OF THEM spoke for a while, looking at the *Avengers*, as one episode ended, and another one started.

"I don't know what to do," Meg said.

"About what?" Beth asked.

Good question. Meg grinned wryly. "Well, everything—but, I meant Josh."

"I like Josh," Beth said. "I don't think you should blow it over something like this."

Maybe. Then again, it was probably already irretrievably wrecked, anyway, and this entire conversation was moot.

"So, he didn't react exactly the way you wanted," Beth said, "so what? Let him have faults, why don't you?"

It wasn't that easy. Meg frowned at her. "Being afraid of me is a pretty god-damn big one."

"It's a pretty god-damn *normal* one. I mean—" Beth drummed on the arm of the couch with one hand for a minute. "Did it ever occur to you that you'd have a lot of these problems even if she *weren't* President?"

"Sure," Meg said. "She'd still be Senator."

Beth shook her head. "I mean, if she weren't in politics at all. If she was—I don't know—a bus driver or something."

Meg pictured her mother perched elegantly in the driver's seat, taking people to places she thought they would enjoy more than where they had asked to go. "A tight ship, but a happy one," she would say, smiling.

"It'd be *great*, if she were a bus driver," Meg said. And she was sure that every night, her mother would sit at the kitchen table for hours, industriously polishing the badge on her Massachusetts Bay Transit Authority cap, studying the transit code and route books so that she would be able to speak intelligently about every facet of the MBTA, and its probable future development needs, and ways in which the agency could evolve and better serve the public.

"You're missing the point," Beth said, sounding impatient. "I mean—you're doing it right now."

Meg looked up. "Doing what?"

"Do you have any idea how hard you can be to deal with?" Beth asked.

Whoa. Meg leaned away from her. "What do you mean?"

Beth glanced at the television, and then clicked it off entirely. "Well, for one thing, you're always so busy thinking, that people can't tell if you're thirty miles away, or listening to them, or what."

"I listen to people," Meg said uneasily.

"Only sometimes," Beth said.

Hmmm. Meg folded her arms, starting to get very uncomfortable. "What else do I do?"

"You don't talk to people," Beth said without hesitating. "You get all upset about things, but you won't tell anyone about it, and you just walk around looking mean."

"My mother got *shot*," Meg said. "Of course I'm upset."

Beth shook her head. "You do it all the time, Meg. You always have."

Meg looked at her for a minute, then scowled. "So, I don't talk, and I don't listen. Great." She moved her jaw. "That's just great."

"You're also touchy as hell," Beth said, then grinned. "It doesn't mean I don't like you."

"It's not like I'm the only person in the world with faults," Meg said, feeling extremely sulky.

"Right. You have faults, I have faults, Josh has faults—maybe even Preston has faults." Beth paused. "Although I can't think of

130

any." She glanced over. "And don't pretend like you didn't laugh, because I saw you."

"I didn't," Meg said.

Beth just looked at her.

Maybe knowing each other so well wasn't such a terrific thing. "Well, I didn't," Meg said.

Beth nodded. "Good for you. Talk about an iron will."

Meg tightened her arms across her chest, somewhere between being amused—and giving her a smack. "You really make me mad, you know that?"

Beth nodded again. " 'That little Powers girl,' my mother used to say. 'Such a temper.' "

"She did not," Meg said.

"Well—no," Beth conceded, and now Meg *did* laugh. "But, I wouldn't have argued."

"You would have encouraged her, more likely." Meg slumped down into her sweatshirt, pulling the material up to cover the bottom half of her face. "I don't give *you* lectures."

"It's one of the things I like about you," Beth said. "Everyone *else* does."

Meg nodded. What with parents, and step-parents, and a long series of teachers who had never particularly seemed to enjoy having such a sharp, opinionated kid in their classes, Beth had probably gotten more than her share.

"Are you mad at me?" Beth asked.

For being honest? "I don't know, a little." Meg sat up, taking her face out of the sweatshirt. "Not really."

"You should just be—more receptive." Beth gestured around the room, indicating the entire White House in general. "Don't use it as a crutch, you know?"

Yeah, right. Meg shrugged. "Easy for *you* to say."

Beth nodded cheerfully.

"I'm always going to be the President's daughter," Meg said.

"I mean, as long as I live. Me, and Amy Carter, and Chelsea Clinton, and—"

"You're also the only person I know who's ever had lunch at Buckingham Palace," Beth said.

Meg flushed. "It was more like high tea."

"For Christ's sakes," Beth said, and laughed. "Will you listen to yourself?"

"I don't listen to *anyone*," Meg said.

Beth nodded. "Oh, right, sorry. I forgot."

They looked at each other for a minute—a tense minute—and finally, Meg grinned.

"Let's go get some lunch," she said.

Beth glanced at her watch. "It'll be more like high tea."

Once again, slugging her seemed like an excellent idea. But, Meg settled for giving her a fairly hard shove, instead. "You really *are* an asshole."

"I know," Beth said. "Good thing I'm beautiful."

AFTER HIGH TEA, SOMEONE in Preston's office arranged for a car to take Beth to the airport, and Meg went outside with her to say good-bye.

"Feel free to, you know, call me up sometime," Beth said. "Let me know what's happening."

A not-so-gentle reminder to return some of her god-damn messages. "Well, I don't know." Meg looked around to make sure that at least five people were within earshot. "If you can't manage to bring me more than a kilo, what good are you?"

Beth shrugged expansively. "Hey, I did my best. If you start getting greedy, you're going to blow the whole thing."

"Yeah, well, you'd better get it right next month," Meg said.

Beth nodded. "I'll talk to my people in South America."

"Good," Meg said. "Have your people call my people."

They both laughed, and Beth adjusted the tilt of her hat.

"*Still* no photographers," she said sadly.

"Sorry." Meg shifted her weight. "Look, um, I'm really glad you came."

Beth shrugged a "don't mention it" shrug. "Just keep it in mind when you're doing your Christmas list."

Meg laughed. "What a jerk."

"I know," Beth said. "I can't help myself."

After the car was gone, Meg went back upstairs, running into Neal in the Center Hall.

"Hi," she said. "What's up?"

He stopped, looking at her accusingly. "How come me and Steven had to go to school, and you didn't?"

"Because I'm the favorite," Meg said.

He scowled.

"That was a joke," she said.

He just scowled.

"I'm going to go take a shower and change," she said. "You and Steven get cleaned up, too, so we can be over at the hospital by five-thirty. And one of you ask Mr. Collins to get some flowers together, okay?"

He nodded sulkily.

"Okay." She bent down. "Should I hug you, or am I too gross and ugly?"

He squirmed away. "Way too gross."

"Fine. Your loss." She walked to her room, pleased to hear him laugh.

When they arrived at the hospital, their mother was just returning from a brief walk down the hall, surrounded by doctors and aides and agents. Their father had his arm around her waist, and she was leaning heavily on him, exhausted from what had probably only been fifty or sixty feet. But when she saw them, she straightened up, smiling.

"Is it five-thirty already?" she asked.

They nodded.

"How do you feel?" Meg asked.

"Oh, much better." She had stopped leaning on Meg's father. "In fact—"

"Madam President, why don't we go into your room," Dr. Brooks said, "so I can check you over, and then you all can have some privacy."

Her mother nodded, and Meg knew she had to be feeling awful as she sank into the wheelchair a doctor rolled over.

"Don't I look silly?" she asked Neal, who giggled. She looked at the rest of the family, smiling her politician smile—which always made Meg sad, because she would only use her mouth, and her eyes would look terrible. Lonely, angry, depressed—whatever. In this case, fighting pain. "When I come home," her mother motioned towards the wheelchair, "I'll see if I can get two of these, and then, we can have races." Meg's father was the only one who didn't smile, and she lifted an eyebrow at him. "The image doesn't appeal to you?"

"It's a delightful image," he said.

"Thank you." She smiled at Meg and her brothers—which, somehow, wasn't at all reassuring. "This will only take a minute," she said, and let the doctors wheel her into the Presidential Suite.

Their father sat on a low couch. "Come here," he said. "Let's have some hugs."

Neal jumped on his lap, and their father hugged him very tightly, Meg and Steven standing with their hands in their pockets. Their father gestured to the couch and they sat on either side of him.

"Beth get off okay?" he asked Meg, and she nodded. "Good." He turned to Steven. "How about you? How was your math test?"

Steven shrugged. "You know."

Neal pulled on their father's tie, and when he nodded, took it off completely. "Can Mom come home now? 'Cause she's walking around and everything?"

"Well." Their father hesitated. "It may be a few more days."

"This weekend?" Neal asked.

"More like next week, I think. But, we'll see." He shifted Neal so that he could see all three of them. "Your mother's pretty tired today, so let's all be nice and quiet with her."

"What," Steven said, "you mean we have to go home?"

Their father shook his head. "No. I just meant to take it easy. Not to jump around or anything."

"Why would we do a jerky thing like that?" Steven asked. "You think we're that stupid?"

"No, I'm sorry," their father said. "I know you're not."

Steven glared at him. "Then, why the hell do you keep telling us all the time?"

"I'm sorry." He put his arm around Steven's shoulders.

As far as she could tell, Steven always picked fights at the hospital because he was afraid he would burst into tears. When they were in her mother's room, he would slouch in a chair, fists clenched, not saying anything, and more than once over the last week, he had had to run out because he was crying.

"Quit looking at me," he said to Neal.

"I'm not," Neal said, looking at him.

Steven's right fist tightened. "Dad, make him quit looking at me!"

"Shhh," their father said gently. "Everything's okay."

"Oh, yeah." Steven stood up. "So okay she can't even god-damn walk." He hurried down the hall, disappearing into the men's room.

Meg's father sighed, starting to move Neal onto Meg's lap.

"Don't!" Neal grabbed his arm. "Don't leave!"

"I'll go," Meg said, to avert a possibly noisy crisis. She walked down the hall, frowning at the agents by the restroom door. "Don't come in here," she said, then knocked. "Steven? You in there?" Which was a pretty dumb question. "I'm coming in, okay?"

Slowly, she opened the door and saw Steven sitting on the floor, below the paper towel dispenser, arms around his knees.

"You're not allowed in here," he said.

"What are they going to do about it?" She sat next to him. Men's rooms were colder and creepier than ladies' rooms. At least, this one was. She didn't think she had been in any others.

He was trying very hard not to cry, but it didn't work, and he hid his face in his arms.

She rubbed his back. "Come on, it's okay."

"She can't even walk," he said, his voice choking. "She can't even stand up."

Yeah. It was pretty horrifying to see. "It takes a while to get better, that's all," she said.

"Oh, right," he said bitterly. "So she can go outside and have someone else shoot her?"

There wasn't much she could say in response to that, so Meg just rubbed his back.

"It's not fair," he said.

Nope. It wasn't.

"She should quit," he said.

It was impossible, but Christ, if only she could. "She's President," Meg said. "The President can't just quit."

He didn't say anything.

Meg sighed. "She *can't*, Steven."

He nodded grimly. " 'Cause she doesn't care about us. That's why."

It had to be more complicated than that—but sometimes, she wasn't sure, either. "Steven, come on," she said. "You know that's not true."

He stood up, laboriously washing his face with a paper towel. "You gonna stay here and watch me go to the bathroom?"

She shook her head, also getting up. He kept his back to her and as she left, she heard a small sound, which meant that he was crying again. She kept going, not wanting to disturb his privacy, leaning against the wall outside to wait.

After what felt like a very long time, he finally came out, his eyes red and his hair wet from having washed his face. She put her arm around him before he could say anything defensive, leading him down the hall to their mother's room. She released him at the door, and they walked in, Meg with her arms folded across her chest, Steven's hands stuffed in his pockets.

"Hi," Meg said, and Steven nodded.

"We were just talking about what to have for dinner," their mother said, all propped up, her eyes looking too shiny—and probably feverish.

"Whatever," Meg said, and Steven shrugged.

"Here." Their father leaned over with a sparse menu written in ornate calligraphy. "Why don't you guys take a look at this?" He touched Steven's shoulder, but Steven moved away, shrugging his hand off.

Meg pretended to read the menu, which, because her mother's diet was still restricted, was pretty dull, although the hospital was at least making a huge effort to *serve* the food beautifully. She sat back and closed her eyes, her head starting to hurt. If her mother wasn't talking or asking direct questions, no one really said anything during their visits.

Christ, what a mess.

"I thought maybe Killington," her mother said. "Or Sugarbush."

Meg opened her eyes. "Killington?" She must have missed something.

Her mother nodded. "I thought, for a change, we might want to go there at Christmas. Unless you all would rather be at Stowe."

Meg looked at her doubtfully. Skiing? In less than two months? This, from the woman who couldn't even walk down the corridor and back?

"I'll be fine," her mother said. "I thought it might be nice to be in New England for a while."

"You mean, go home," Steven said.

Their mother nodded. "For a few days."

So, they talked about skiing, and every silence, no matter how brief, made Meg very uncomfortable. She'd always thought that the expression about air being thick enough to cut with a knife was stupid—except that, unfortunately, it was also accurate. Everyone talked about bland, meaningless things, while emotions flew around the room and smashed into each other. For a family of people she thought of as non-stop talkers, they sure were having trouble keeping a conversation going. And it was easy—too easy—to let her mother do all of the work.

It was like chess, sort of. Everyone watching everyone else, trying to figure out what moves people were going to make next, so they could set up the proper defenses. For that matter, it was like stupid *politics*. Even her mother, who was famous for her ability to manipulate—and charm—audiences, couldn't make any of them relax or let down.

But, they weren't much good as a family if they could only handle it when things were going *well*. Which seemed like such an appropriate sentiment that she almost said it aloud. But, why make things worse?

"You're awfully quiet tonight," her mother said.

"What?" Meg asked, startled. She looked around and saw that they were the only two in the room. "Where is everyone?"

"They'll be right back." Her mother frowned. "You didn't eat much again."

"I had a big lunch," Meg said. High tea, even.

"It was good for you to have Beth here," her mother said.

Meg nodded, and it was quiet again.

"I'm sorry," her mother said in a low voice.

Meg looked over. "About what?"

"That I can't make it easier. I'm trying, but—" She shook her head, her face the scary light grey color. "It'll be easier when I'm home."

And became a target again.

"You all must be so angry at me," her mother said.

Meg waited for her to go on.

"You must feel as though I—" She swallowed, and Meg watched the tendons in her neck move. "I don't know. Asked for it."

The uncertainty in her expression made Meg feel guilty, and she shifted in her chair. "No, I—I mean, we—I mean, just because you're President—well, you shouldn't have to worry about stuff like this. That's what's wrong."

Her mother touched her bandages unhappily. "I never dreamed it would really happen. I never thought anyone—" She shook her head.

Meg couldn't think of anything to say, so she picked at some cat fur on her sweater cuff.

"I hated my mother for dying," her mother said, softly.

Meg blinked, not having expected that particular remark. It had happened when her mother was five—a riding accident at the Connecticut estate her mother's family used in the summer. A farm Meg's grandfather had, as far as she knew, immediately sold after his wife's death. It had been like something out of *Gone with the Wind*, a case of a person taking a jump that was beyond her abilities.

"I really resented her for it," her mother said, speaking in such a low voice that Meg had to lean forward to hear her. "Leaving me like that."

"Well," Meg twisted a little in her chair, "she couldn't help it."

"I know that *now*," her mother said. "But when I was your age, and younger, I always felt—" She stopped, looking right at Meg. "I guess I thought that if she *really* loved me, she never would have done something that incautious. That, in a sense, she asked for it."

Well, the argument could certainly be made—and convincingly so. Meg avoided her eyes.

"Meg, I would never hurt any of you intentionally," her mother said.

Meg nodded, staring down at her hands.

Her mother sighed. "Well. I guess it's too late for that, though, isn't it?"

Meg looked at the door. Where were her father and brothers? Because—she hated this conversation.

"Meg," her mother said. "It's all right to feel—"

Meg jumped up. "I'm going to see where Dad and those guys are, okay?"

Her mother nodded, seeming to crumple into herself.

"It's not that—" Meg stopped. "I mean—"

The door opened, and her father came in, carrying Neal, who was sobbing.

"It's okay," he was saying soothingly. "You're okay now."

Her mother looked at him and he nodded, her mother's eyes brightening. That meant that Neal had gotten sick to his stomach again—which he had been doing a lot lately. Her mother reached out with her good arm and her father lowered him gently onto the bed. She hugged him close, even though her face had stiffened with pain, whispering to him.

Steven was leaning against the wall, his posture slumped and unhappy, and Meg went over to lean next to him, her mother's low voice and Neal's crying the only sounds in the room.

15

WALKING INTO SCHOOL the next day felt strange—as if she had been away for years. People seemed afraid of her, the same way they had been when she had first started the January before: staring, then muttering comments to each other as she passed. Maybe, if she got *really* lucky, they would start taking sneaky cell phone photos of her, and selling them to the highest tabloid bidders.

There were Homecoming posters all over the place, which was depressing. Josh had been so cute when he asked her to the dance, making a big deal of it—bowing low, giving her a white rose, even though it was pretty well understood that they would be going together. Or, *would* have been.

She looked down the hall, seeing him at his locker. His shoulders looked sad. Slouched. Josh never slouched—he had grown about three inches in the last year, and was pretty pleased about it.

Oh, hell. Beth was right. She started towards him, but now he was going the other way. Because he had seen her? She stopped. Okay, fine. If that was the way he wanted it. She turned and went to her own locker, irritated at him again.

She sat in English first period, looking at her book so she wouldn't have to meet eyes with anyone. She hadn't slept well the night before and felt like resting with her head on her arms, but her teacher, Mrs. Hayes, probably wouldn't be too thrilled about that. Christ, though, it would be nice to take a nap for a minute. She leaned her head on her hand, sliding her elbow until her upper arm was flat on the desk. That was probably as close to lying down as she could go without getting in trouble.

Then, as Mrs. Hayes discussed some of the different journeys serving as metaphors in *Heart of Darkness*, someone knocked on the door. Meg—and everyone else in the class—sat straight up.

Oh, God, not again. Jesus Christ, she couldn't do this again. Had they gotten into the hospital somehow, or—she hung onto her desk with both hands, waiting for the bad news. Her parents, Steven, Neal—Mrs. Hayes crossed to the door, opening it.

"Of course, Carol," she said. "I think you left it in the back."

Meg slumped forward, closing her eyes. It wasn't her family. Thank God it wasn't her family. She felt, rather than saw, the hard looks the rest of the class was giving the little tenth grader, who grabbed her notebook off the back table and hurried out. Meg took deep breaths, her heart feeling as though it was jumping all around her chest, caroming off her ribs.

"Well, now," Mrs. Hayes said. "Where were we?" She returned to the front of the room, passing Meg's desk, squeezing her shoulder so swiftly that Meg almost didn't notice. Now, she *did* rest her head on her arms, trying to calm down. It was just some kid, it wasn't—but maybe something bad was happening, anyway, or—she had to check.

She caught her teacher's eye, indicating the door. Mrs. Hayes nodded and Meg jumped up, almost running out of the room. One of her agents—who was posted in a strategic location in the hall—looked startled.

"Have to make a call," she said briefly, pulling her phone out of her jeans pocket.

He followed her down the hall, and they passed one of the patrolling agents on the way, who looked uneasy and also fell into step behind them. She found a relatively private alcove, speed-dialed the number, and asked for her mother, the aide on the other end telling her that she was in a meeting.

"It's kind of important," Meg said, knowing that she had to hear her mother's voice before she could relax.

She was put on hold, and then, after a couple of minutes, her mother came on.

"Meg?" She sounded worried. "Is everything all right? Where are you?"

"School." Meg let out her breath. Her mother *sounded* okay. Tired, maybe, but her voice was strong. As though she was starting to get better, at least. And she was obviously safe. Right now, anyway. "Are you all right?" she asked, to be sure.

"I'm fine," her mother said.

"Is Dad okay?" she asked.

"He's fine," her mother said. "Meg, what's happening? Are you sure you're—"

"Yeah." She leaned against the side of the alcove, her legs feeling weak from relief. "Steven—" She let out another breath. "Steven and Neal are probably okay, too."

"Yes, they are." Her mother's voice was gentle.

Okay. "And you're *sure* you are?" Meg asked.

"Yes," her mother said. "Meg—"

"I have to go now," Meg said quickly. "Sorry I interrupted you and stuff, I just—I wanted to be sure you guys were okay."

"I love you," her mother said.

"Um, yeah, me, too." Meg shifted her weight. "See you after school." She hung up, resting against the wall until she felt under control. Intense fear was exhausting.

Time to go back to English. She crossed the hall to the water fountain and splashed her face, managing to soak part of her shirt and sweater in the process. Too tired to worry about it, she started down the corridor, stopping abruptly.

Josh was waiting against some lockers, his expression nervous—and concerned, his arms tense across his chest. They looked at each other, neither moving. Then, Meg walked over, leaning in for a hard, silent hug.

"Buy you a drink, sailor?" she asked against his ear.

He laughed, hugging her closer.

"I'm sorry," she said. "I've been a really terrible person lately."

"You've been going through some pretty terrible things," he said.

"Yeah, but—" She shook her head. "It's still no excuse. I'm sorry, Josh. I really am."

He hugged her even closer, not saying anything. For a minute, it was enough to be touching; then, it wasn't, and they were kissing about as hard as they had ever kissed, Meg not caring *who* was around to watch.

Behind them, someone cleared his throat. They broke just barely apart, turning to look. It was Mr. Carlisle, their physics teacher, his face stern, but also amused.

"Shouldn't you two be in class?" he asked.

They nodded, Meg too happy to blush.

"Then, maybe you ought to go," he said.

They nodded again and he nodded back, continuing on his way.

"We probably shouldn't risk him catching us *twice*," Meg said.

"Probably not," he agreed, much more flushed than she was.

She leaned up to kiss his cheek, and they walked down the hall, holding hands.

"Are things any better?" he asked.

"I don't know." She sighed. "Not really."

"Will you let me help you?" he asked.

Something which, apparently, did not come naturally to her. "I'll try," she said.

He nodded, tightening his hand.

When they got to their English classroom, she stopped.

"Don't let me hurt your feelings again," she said, "okay? I mean, if I take stuff out on you."

He flexed his muscles. "I'm tough."

Which might come in handy. She smiled. "Good."

He opened the door, and it wasn't until she stepped inside that it occurred to her that their coming back together was going to be pretty obvious. Indeed, the entire class—including Mrs. Hayes—

grinned, and someone sang the first few bars of "Reunited." This time, Meg blushed, and Josh was the one who looked pleased. She sat in her isolated seat, while Josh returned to his regular seat—since she couldn't really move her books over during the middle of class.

"What, you don't even sit with him?" someone to her left asked.

"Matt," Mrs. Hayes said to him, "tell me what you think about the opening to Chapter Three."

"Uh, yeah, uh—what page is that?" He picked up his book, fumbling through it, and Meg relaxed. That was two she owed Mrs. Hayes.

Having Josh nearby made things much easier and, even though she wasn't hungry, she sat at her normal lunch table—and it was very nice to be with a bunch of people who weren't wearing suits. Also, people who talked about things like homework, dumb gossip they'd seen on the Internet, and the Redskins. Normal things. She didn't really participate, but it was soothing to listen.

After school, she went directly to the hospital. Her mother was in meetings most of the time, and looked even weaker than she had the day before. But, she and Meg's father were pretty cheerful because the doctors had decided that she could come home on Monday. Meg carefully didn't allow herself to think about the prospect of her having to go back out in public—and vulnerable to maniacs again.

Josh was coming over that night, and Meg got home just in time to change. Since she had been so rotten to him, she sort of felt as if she should put out some effort. She wore her one pair of jeans which could never be described as being baggy and a grey cashmere sweater, along with a silver chain and appropriate small hoops. She also put on lip gloss, mascara, some of her mother's Chanel No.5, and even used some blush to highlight her cheekbones. First-date time.

She sat on the stairs leading to the Ground Floor Corridor to wait. Josh was right on time, and when she went to meet him in the Diplomatic Reception Room, she wasn't sure why she felt so shy. He had also taken some care dressing, and was actually wearing a tie underneath his sweater, and his charcoal grey pants—which she personally thought were sexy as hell. His cheeks were red—it had been colder than usual, all week—but instead of a jacket, he had on a maroon tartan scarf. How jaunty.

"Hi," he said.

She smiled nervously, and they walked upstairs, her agents—who, stupidly, had to follow her around the house whenever she left the private quarters—leaving them at the top of the stairs once they got to the second floor.

"Wait a minute," Josh said, after they were gone, and grabbed her in a hug. They kissed until they were out of breath, Meg hoping that neither of her brothers were going to appear unexpectedly—and also hanging onto the railing with one hand, to make sure that they didn't fall down the stairs.

Josh moved back, straightening his glasses. "Hi."

Meg laughed. "Hi."

They ended up on the third floor, where her brothers were playing a subdued game of pool in the Game Room. So, they hung out with them for a little while, until Neal looked more cheerful, and Steven decided he was hungry, and the two of them went downstairs to go find Trudy—or one of the stewards or butlers—and get something to eat.

She wasn't supposed to go into bedrooms alone with Josh—even though there almost a dozen empty ones available, and it was tempting—so, they sat on the couch in the Washington Sitting Room, instead, holding hands.

Meg let out her breath. "This feels kind of like the first time you came over."

He smiled. "I was scared to death that night."

"Yeah, me, too," she said.

He looked surprised. "*You* were?"

Well—yeah. What did he think? "Of course I was." She picked

up his hand, still feeling shy. "I mean, I didn't really know you, and for all I knew, you were—well, I'm not all that great at trusting people." With, granted, on many occasions, good reason.

"Yeah," he said wryly. "I've noticed."

She flushed, and dropped his hand. "Are you mad at me?"

"You were mad at *me*," he said.

"No, I wasn't. I was just—" She sighed. "Mad, in general."

"It didn't *seem* that way. I don't know. Sometimes I wish—" He stopped.

Was he about to break up with her? It sounded that way. She moved slightly away from him. "What?"

"I kind of wish I'd had a bunch of other girlfriends," he said. "Before you, I mean."

"To see if I measured up?" Meg asked stiffly.

Josh just sighed. "Meg."

"Yeah, well—" She heard Beth's voice saying, "You're doing it right now," and stopped. "What do you mean?" she asked, more pleasantly.

"Thank you," he said. "What I *mean*, is—well, going out with you is kind of like—I don't know—running a marathon before you can *walk* or something."

Meg frowned. "I don't get it."

"Think hard," he said.

Josh was rarely snarky—but, he'd probably earned the right during the past week or so. "It's not my fault," she said, making an effort to sound less defensive than she felt. "I mean, I'm just normal."

He shrugged. "I just sometimes wish I'd started off with someone more my speed."

"What," she said, "you mean, I'm fast?"

He laughed. "Well, that's not *quite* what I meant."

She sat back, also grinning. "Do I detect a note of irony there?"

"Let's just say 'fast' isn't the word I would have used," he said.

"Oh, yeah?" She thought about that, then pushed him down, kissing him. "What word would you have used, Josh?"

He leaned up to kiss her back. "Out of my league."

"That's four words." She lifted herself onto her elbow so she could look at him. "It's also stupid."

"Well, maybe." He took off his glasses, and put them on the end table, blinking to focus. "Reporters bug me a lot. They call my house, even."

Meg frowned. "I thought that guy from the *Post* was the only one."

He shook his head. "It happens a lot."

And she knew there was all sorts of stuff on the Internet—because she had seen some of it herself. "You should have told me," she said. "Preston could probably do something." Not with the paparazzi, probably, but maybe with the mainstream media.

Josh shrugged. "I just say no comment, mostly, or that they have the wrong number. Anyway, the thing is, they usually ask what someone like me is doing dating someone like you, and it's not all that dumb a question."

The hell it wasn't. "Yes, it is," Meg said. "And it's really rude, too."

He just shrugged.

"Well, I'm sorry," Meg said. "I'll tell Preston to—"

"It's not that big a deal. I only brought it up because—" He paused. "Actually, I kind of forget why I brought it up."

"You were failing to make a point," she said.

"Oh. Right." He laughed suddenly. "You just said what I think you said, right?"

Probably.

He laughed again. "Mmm," he said, moving to kiss her neck.

Which felt good, but they weren't done yet. She leaned away from him. "I thought we were having a conversation."

"Later," he said, kissing her ear now.

She moved away again. "The thing is—"

"I bet you want to do *this* later," he said.

She nodded.

"Okay." He put his hands behind his head, smiling up at her. "Go ahead."

"The thing is, I *need* you to think that I'm normal," she said. "I mean, if you feel funny around me, it's like—I don't know. I need to know that I can be cranky, or sad—" or yell at him—"without everything falling apart."

"I didn't know what to do." He sat up, looking worried. "I *still* don't."

That made two of them. "You know what it is?" she asked. "Part of it—a lot of it, even—is *me*, not trusting you, but *you* need to trust *me*, too. I mean, you need to feel more secure about the whole thing. It's not like if we have a fight, I'm going to run out and find some other guy." Even if the tabloids insisted otherwise, constantly. "I mean, you have to trust me. All that matter is what I *actually* think, not what people try to make you *think* I think."

He nodded.

"Does that make sense, or is it stupid?" she asked.

"Both," he said.

She smiled. "That's what I figured."

"Mostly, it makes sense," he said.

She nodded, and they were quiet for a minute.

"Well." He put his arms around you. "Enough conversation."

More than enough.

He left at around twelve-thirty, and once Meg was back on the second floor, she couldn't hear any noise at all. Was it this quiet when her mother was home? It couldn't be.

She assumed her brothers and Trudy were asleep, but where was her father? It was late enough so that he had to be home by now. Maybe he had gone to bed, too, or—but her parents' bedroom door was open, and he wasn't in there. Maybe he was spending the night at the hospital again? Something he'd done more than once during the past week or so.

She walked down the hall towards her own room, but paused by the Yellow Oval Room and peeked inside, even though it was dark.

Her father was sitting on the couch, staring at the low, banked fire in the fireplace. Embarrassed by the idea of watching someone who didn't know she was there, she stepped away and sat down in a nineteenth-century chair to think.

She couldn't just go to bed and leave him there. But, if he wanted to be by himself, she shouldn't interfere with that, either. Maybe—she walked down to the West Sitting Hall, then came back again, whistling aimlessly and calling Vanessa in a loudly hushed whisper that he would have to hear. Indeed, a small light went on in the room. She stuck her head through the open doorway.

"Hi, Dad," she said. "I'm going to bed now."

He turned with a composed expression. Too composed. "Okay. Good-night."

"Yeah." She put her hands in her pockets. "How was Mom?"

"Tired," he said.

Meg nodded.

"Josh was here tonight?" he asked.

She nodded.

"Good," he said.

It was quiet.

"Well." Meg took a couple of steps towards the door. "Um, good-night."

He nodded.

— 16 —

MEG SPENT MOST of the night before her mother came home in her room. Worrying. The media, and the blogosphere, kept talking about how important it was for a President to be completely strong and unafraid in a first, post-shooting appearance. To give the country confidence and all. But, that meant taking risks—smiling and waving longer than necessary, that sort of thing.

She and her brothers were going to stay home from school, so they could be there as soon as she got home, but her father wasn't letting them go to the hospital because, he said, the car would be too crowded. But she knew damned well that it was really because he didn't want to have to worry about them being exposed to danger, too.

Around nine, she put her book down, deciding to go see what her brothers were doing. She found them in the solarium with Kirby, looking subdued and sad, only half-watching the television. Trudy—who had brought over several different outfits, so her mother could choose—and her father were still at the hospital.

"Hi," she said.

They nodded.

Okay, they needed some serious cheering up. "I came to see how my little peasants were doing." She tilted Neal's chin, studying his face. "Although I had no idea they were going to be such *ugly* little peasants."

Neal giggled, pulling his head away.

"I mean, good Lord." She patted Kirby. "This is the only decent-looking one in the bunch."

Her brothers laughed.

"You look just like us, Queenie," Steven said.

"Oh, God, no." She pretended to search for a mirror. "I can't possibly be *that* ugly."

"Don't kid yourself," Steven said.

"Well." Meg sat in between them, even though there wasn't enough room. "I'm the Queen. I can get away with being ugly."

"Lucky for you," Steven said, and Neal laughed.

"Are you going to watch TV with us, Meggie?" he asked.

"If you're not watching anything too stupid." She squinted at the television, recognizing *Airplane*, which her brothers usually found reliably hilarious. "Looks pretty stupid."

"How come you always laugh when you see it?" Steven asked.

"Well," she put a benevolent arm around each of them, "I like to keep my little peasants happy."

Neal laughed and Steven snorted, shrugging her arm off.

"Ah, yes." She slung her arm back around him. "Happy peasants. That's what I like to see. Lots of happy, little—"

"If you want to make us happy, how about shutting up, so we can watch the movie?" Steven said, pleasantly.

"When I can make you happier by sitting here and telling you swell jokes?" Meg asked.

"You tell *dumb* jokes," Neal said.

Meg narrowed her eyes. "What do you know about it? You're just a peasant."

"He got some book larnin', though," Steven said, staring at the movie.

Meg laughed, and gave him a quick hug.

"Do that again, chick, and you eat this." He showed her his fist.

"Oh, yeah, I'm real scared," she said.

He nodded. "You best be, girl."

"Don't worry, munchkin," she said. "I am."

Their father came in. "I should have known you all would be up here," he said, putting on a parent smile, his eyes very tired.

"If it ain't the First Gentleman." Steven nudged Meg. "He's got lots of book larnin'. Why don't you try some of your jokes on him?"

Meg hung her head shyly. "Well, if you really think so." She adjusted her position with some theatricality. "See, like, this funny thing happened to me on the way upstairs, right? I was like, walking by the Lincoln Bedroom, right? And this man comes out and says, 'Hey.' So I says, 'Hey what?'"

"Real quick of you," Steven said.

She nodded. "Yeah, that's what I thought. Anyway, so he says to me, 'Meg,' he says—" She stopped, looking at her father. "What's the matter, don't you like my joke?"

"I love your joke," he said, his smile genuine. "Go on."

"Actually." She frowned. "I don't really know any jokes." Tragically enough.

"At least you tried, Queenie," Steven said.

Their father looked both confused and amused. "You all seem pretty cheerful."

"Happy little peasants," Meg said. "How's Mom?"

Her father nodded, instead of answering—which didn't seem encouraging. "We'll be leaving the hospital at ten." He bent to be at Neal's level. "It's getting kind of late, pal. Why don't you come down and have a snack with me and Trudy, and then we'll see about some bedtime, okay?"

"But, the movie!" Neal pointed at the television. "Can't I watch the movie?"

"The sooner you go to bed, the sooner you'll wake up and your mother will be here," their father said.

Neal thought about that, then yawned.

"Thought so." Their father stood up. "Do you want to give your brother and sister a kiss?"

Steven held out his fist. "Kiss me, and you eat this."

Neal giggled. "Night, ugly Queen," he said to Meg.

"Good-night, ugly worm," she said.

It wasn't until later—much later—when she was in bed, that she let herself worry again. She had two extra quilts on the bed and Vanessa was asleep on her chest, but Meg was still cold. She kept picturing the scene: her mother leaving the hospital, arm strapped up in the sling, smiling bravely and confidently at the crowd—and there *would* be a crowd. There was always a crowd. A huge crowd that the stupid Secret Service wouldn't be able to handle. And in that crowd, there might be a person who—the phone rang, and she flinched, but since it was the direct line and not the switchboard, she knew it was her mother, so she picked up.

"Hi," her mother said. "I'm sorry, did I wake you up?"

Not by a long shot. "No," Meg said, "I couldn't—I mean, I was awake. Is anything wrong?"

"No, I just—" Her mother paused. "Not right now, please, okay?" she said, to someone who must have just walked into her room. "Anyway," she came back on, "Steven called me a little while ago."

Not surprising. "Yeah, he's kind of uptight about tomorrow," Meg said.

"Well," her mother said. "I guess we all are."

Could Superwoman's armor have just cracked ever so slightly? "*You* are?" Meg said.

"My God, Meg, what do you think?" her mother asked.

"I don't know, I—" Meg swallowed. "You aren't going to do anything—risky, are you?"

"Kiddo, I'm going to smile, wave, and dive into the car," her mother said.

"Dive?" Meg asked, the image almost amusing.

"In a manner of speaking." Her mother let out her breath. "Nothing's going to happen, Meg. We're all on edge because this is my first time back out there, that's all."

"We're all on *edge* because you're important to us," Meg said through her teeth.

154

"I know," her mother said quickly. "I'm sorry."

"Sorry you're important to us?" Meg asked.

"No, I just—it really will be okay." Her tone changed abruptly. "So, what are we going to eat tomorrow night? Pizza? Chinese food? Mexican, maybe?"

In other words, things that would make her brothers happy. "Are you allowed to have stuff like that?" Meg asked.

"I'm the President," her mother said. "I can do anything I want."

Meg smiled. A line her mother always enjoyed using—although, sometimes, she wasn't kidding. "I'm serious. Wouldn't it be better for us to have custard and scrambled eggs and stuff like that?" She laughed at the gagging sound her mother made. "I'm only being helpful."

"Let me put it this way," her mother said. "I'm not eating any more meals that don't require teeth."

"Hmm," Meg said. "What an interesting way to describe it."

"Let's just say I refuse." Her mother paused. "I really miss you. All of you."

That kind of went without saying, didn't it? But, wow, there had been *a lot* of open expressions of emotion and affection in her family lately—which was not exactly their norm. "Um yeah," Meg said. "We do, too."

"Well." Her mother coughed. "I have some people I need to talk to, but—I'll see you in the morning?"

Christ, she hoped so.

THE PLAN WAS for her parents to arrive at the South Grounds, where the press would be waiting to "capture" the reunion. So, in order to look like proper Presidential children, Meg wore a red plaid kilt with a V-neck sweater and white shirt, and her brothers put on ties, khakis, and their tweed jackets.

Preston came upstairs to inspect them.

"Very nice," he said. "How about some smiles? You all look like you've forgotten how."

They smiled obediently.

"You've definitely forgotten how." He glanced around with exaggerated caution. "Okay." He reached into the inside breast pocket of his jacket. "If you all promise not to laugh, I'll show you something." He hesitated. "Do you promise?"

"We promise," Meg said, already grinning.

"How about you two?" He looked at Steven and Neal. "I mean, if this leaks, it could be very embarrassing. Can you keep a secret?"

Steven shrugged. "For a price."

"How about I catch bounce passes for a whole half-hour?" Preston said. "And we'll work on your spin dribble."

"Sold," Steven said.

"Will you play pool with me?" Neal asked.

Preston nodded. "Half an hour."

"Okay, I promise," Neal said.

"Remember," Preston said, "you are the only three people in Washington, except for my optometrist, who know about this."

Meg laughed. "Optometrist, hunh?"

Preston nodded, very grim. "Optometrist." He sat on a yellow couch, taking an eyeglass case out of his pocket. "I went in for my check-up a couple of weeks ago, and look what I ended up with." He put on the stylish, dark brown framed glasses, looking very sad.

"Talk about *wimpy*," Steven said.

Preston nodded. "I guess it's the end of my swinging bachelor days."

Although much to Beth's—and, for that matter, *Meg's*—dismay, he actually had a girlfriend who was an assistant undersecretary in the State Department.

"Can I try them on?" Neal asked.

Steven decided that he wanted to wear them, too, and Preston let them, standing up and smiling at Meg. "What do you think?" he asked.

She watched Neal strut around, the glasses slipping off his nose. "Do you need them for reading?"

Preston nodded. "And it isn't bad enough for me to get contacts, or go for laser surgery or anything."

"I bet Dad'll fire you," Steven said, taking the glasses from Neal and putting them on. "He doesn't want any lame four-eyes working for him."

"Can't have any eggheads," Preston agreed. His cell phone rang and he picked it up, listening for a minute, then nodding. "Great, thank you." He hung up. "Let's get ready to head downstairs—they've just left the hospital."

"Um, without incident?" Meg asked, slipping into an automatic media cliché.

Preston smiled. "Without incident."

There was a very large and telegenic "Welcome Home, Madam President!" banner hanging from the Truman Balcony, and about a hundred aides and staffers had gathered to greet Their Leader.

When the motorcade pulled up, agents jumped out, surrounding her mother's car. Her mother stepped out with a wide smile, her cheeks flushed with healthy color. Flushed with rouge, more likely, but she still looked good. She was wearing a sweeping grey cape—to minimize the sling, Meg figured—and the press and staff broke into what seemed to be spontaneous applause.

"Thank you," her mother said, her voice sounding effortlessly powerful—so, all of those hours she'd spent using the breathing and lung expansion tube the respiratory therapists had provided her must have helped. "It's great to be home."

"Can we go hug her now?" Neal whispered, trying to twist away from the hand Meg had on his arm. "Come on, Meg, let go."

"Okay, but be careful," Meg whispered back. "Don't hurt her side."

Neal nodded impatiently, and she released him.

"Mom!" He ran over. "Hi!"

"Hello, darling." Their mother bent awkwardly, and Meg saw her father move closer, his hand on her back.

Her mother kissed Neal, hugging him with one arm, then kissed and hugged Steven. Meg moved in for her turn, hearing cameras all around her, feeling like part of a five-member amoeba clump.

After the stagy reunion, her mother gave a short statement, and then her press secretary, Linda, nodded to indicate that the reporters could ask her mother a few quick questions, most of which focused on her health, her confidence level, and her positions on gun control and the insanity plea. Her mother was light and relaxed—witty, even, except on gun control, where she was very serious—although, actually, her positions had *always* been strongly in favor of strengthening the current policies and eliminating as many loopholes as possible. Only maybe now, they meant more. Maybe.

She noticed that her mother seemed to be trembling slightly, and Linda must have picked up on that, too, because suddenly, the news conference was over and the President was striding cheerfully inside. There was a wheelchair waiting for her in the Diplomatic Reception Room, along with several members of the White House Medical Unit, but Meg was pretty sure that the press didn't know that.

She and her brothers took the stairs, meeting their parents outside the elevator on the second floor where Trudy, along with most of the house staff, was welcoming their mother back. Dr. Brooks was quietly steering her towards the bedroom suite, which had been carefully set up to maximize her convalescence.

Her mother was trembling more, even as she smiled and chatted with people.

"Madam President, I think it might be in your best interests to rest for a while," Dr. Brooks said.

"Yes, I think so, too," her mother said, and the staff instantly faded away, returning to whatever they had all been doing.

"In fact," Dr. Brooks said, "why don't I check your—"

Her mother's good hand was gripping the arm of the wheelchair, the skin white. "I think I need to be by myself for a while," she said, her voice low.

"Okay," Dr. Brooks said. "First, why don't we—"

"I'm sorry, please excuse me." Her mother pushed out of the wheelchair and walked shakily into her bedroom, shutting the door behind her.

Meg glanced at Steven and Neal, wondering if she looked as scared as they did.

"Your mother's been under a great deal of stress this morning," their father said, patting Steven—who was standing right next to him—on the back. "Don't worry." He turned to Dr. Brooks. "Give us a while, will you, Bob?"

Dr. Brooks nodded, sitting on one of the couches, his medical bag on the floor next to him. The few aides who remained walked down the hall as though they had just remembered very important things they had to do, although a nurse stayed behind.

Meg's father moved to the bedroom door, rapping gently. "It's only me, Katie," he said, and went inside, closing the door.

"What's wrong with her?" Neal asked, anxiously. "Is she crying?"

"Now, don't you worry about a thing." Trudy took his hand. "She just needs a little privacy. Come on." She led him to the mahogany table. "You sit down with your brother and sister, and I'll bring you all some hot chocolate." Trudy's panacea. That, and Vicks VapoRub.

Trudy returned with hot Danishes and cocoa for the three of them, while Jorge served Dr. Brooks and the military nurse coffee. The cocoa and Danishes were long gone before the bedroom door opened and Meg's father came out, nodding at Dr. Brooks, who stood up, lifting his bag with him.

"Here, Russell." Trudy poured him some coffee. "They're warming some milk for Katharine."

He smiled gratefully. "Thank you."

"Gross," Steven said.

Meg elbowed him. "Shut up, you little brat."

"It's all right, Meg," their father said. "He has a point."

"Can we see Mommy?" Neal asked.

Their father pulled out his handkerchief to wipe off his chocolate mustache. "As soon as Bob's finished." He slipped the hanky back into his pocket. "But, remember, you still have to be very careful. Especially if you get on the bed."

"We know, Dad," Steven said, sounding irritated.

"It's just a reminder." Their father indicated Neal with his eyes. "And watch Kirby."

Kirby, lying on the floor, wagged his tail.

Trudy bent to straighten the red Welcome Home ribbon he was wearing on his collar. "You know, I believe I'll go upstairs for a while."

Neal looked worried. "Are you sick?"

"Of course not." She smoothed his hair with the same motions she had used to fix Kirby's ribbon. "I just think you all ought to have some time alone together." She winked at Meg's father, gave them each a hug, and left.

When Dr. Brooks and Lieutenant Hamlin, the nurse, came out, they went in, Meg feeling very formal. Their mother was propped up by pillows, and even though it was obvious that she had washed her face and reapplied her make-up, Meg could tell that she had been crying. Now, however, she was smiling, and Adlai and Sidney were curled around her legs. Kirby came in, tail wagging furiously, and Steven grabbed him before he could bound onto the bed.

"Hello, Kirby," their mother said cheerfully. "Steven, don't worry about him. Come on." She patted the bedspread, and Kirby climbed up onto the bed, large and clumsy.

"Kate." Meg's father was immediately at her side.

"I'm fine. I won't break." She smiled at Neal. "Come sit with me. I'm lonely."

Neal beamed, scrambling across the blankets to sit next to her, larger than Kirby, and only slightly less clumsy.

Meg looked at Steven, who had his arms across his chest, and one of his unreadable expressions that she was pretty sure meant worry.

Jorge came in with a tray, including some hot milk, and her mother frowned as though confronted by a particularly challenging puzzle, her good arm around Neal, and unavailable to accept the mug.

"Thank you, Jorge," she said. "Just put it there," she inclined her head towards her bedside table, "and I'll have some in a moment."

Problem solved. No wonder she was the President. Meg sat on the sofa by the fireplace, wondering why none of them seemed to know how to act. She sure didn't. It would have been easier if Trudy had stayed. Her father was jittery—sipping coffee, putting the cup down, picking it back up again. Steven was rocking on his heels, not saying anything, and Neal was just smiling and playing with their mother's hand.

"Well," their mother said. "This is rather like a wake."

Meg jumped, Steven rocked, their father frowned.

It was quiet again.

Meg stared at her hands, twisting her fingers into different contortions. What was everyone else thinking? She had envisioned the President in bed, in her lounging gown, the family gathered around her, everyone being very loving. Instead, silent tension.

"Have we all had breakfast?" her mother asked.

"Twice," Steven said.

More silence. Meg made her hands into a church with a steeple, then opened them to see all the people. Why didn't someone make a joke? If only she could think of one.

"Well," her mother said, "I'm sure all of you would rather—"

"What, you don't want us in here?" Meg asked, surprised by the hostility in her own voice.

"Of course I want you in here," her mother said patiently. "It's just—well, I don't know. You all seem so uncomfortable." She blinked a few times, lifting her arm away from Neal long enough to pick up her mug and drink some milk.

"Are you tired?" Meg's father asked. "Would you like to rest for a while?"

"I just got *up*, Russ." Her mother sounded testy, and the waves from this parental exchange moved—unpleasantly—through the room.

"Well, hell." Steven jammed his hands into his pockets, his voice grumpier than either parent's. "You wanna play Monopoly or something?"

Meg laughed, relieved that someone had finally said something funny, and her parents smiled.

"I like Monopoly," Neal said happily. "Can I be the car?"

"*I'm* being the car," Steven said.

"What if I want to be the car?" their mother asked. "I get tired of being the shoe all the time."

"I assume that's a joke," their father said, "since I'm the one who's always the shoe."

Their mother nodded, rather tightly. "Yes, Russell, it's a joke."

"Well, good." He smiled. "Because I'm the biggest, and this time, *I'm* being the car."

Steven shrugged. "I don't care. I call being the dog."

Meg stood up. "Where's the set? In the solarium, or what?"

"Meg, don't bother," her mother said. "Someone can bring it."

Whatever. Meg sat back down.

"What's Meg, anyway?" Neal asked. "The thimble?"

Steven nodded. "Yeah. She's always the thimble."

"I'm always the dog, jerkhead," Meg said from the couch. "You're lucky I'm giving you a turn."

"Oh, yeah," Steven said. "Real lucky."

"Will you all stop bickering?" their father asked, already on the phone.

"So speaketh the proverbial pot," their mother said.

"Look, if being the car means that much to you, I'll—" He returned to the telephone. "Thank you. Just bring it to our bedroom, please." He hung up, smiling at all of them. "Okay. Who's going to be banker?"

~ 17 ~

MEG GOT TO be banker. She was always the banker. They played for about two hours, everyone being much better sports than usual, and the game didn't break up until lunch was served—which, Meg noticed, was vegetable soup and easily digestible pasta. So much for pizza and Chinese food.

Politically speaking, it was amusing to watch her mother play. Her technique was to buy up all of the low-income land, like Baltic and Mediterranean Avenues, cover them with expensive housing, and make a killing. Kind of like what they did in Boston some years back, and Meg remembered the Senator regularly speaking out against this practice. Luckily, her mother never played Monopoly in public.

Neal was annoying to play with—he would buy St. James Place and Ventnor Avenue, and then refuse to give up the pretty colored cards, spoiling anyone else's chances for monopoly. In her family, whenever anyone landed on the income tax square, they would automatically give up the two hundred dollars without bothering to figure out their assets, since her father got such gleeful joy out of totaling them up and assigning debts. Once a tax attorney, always a tax attorney. Steven spent his time trying to get the dice to fall just right so he would land on Free Parking, and get to take all the money from the middle of the board.

Meg, on the other hand, was a very subdued player. She would buy every single piece of land that she could, and then, hoard them, waiting for someone to say, "Hey, who has Kentucky Avenue?" As banker, she was able to keep mental track of how much money everyone else had, and she would ask incredibly high prices for the desired property, which the greedy land buyer—often her mother—would pay, and then be too bankrupt to put any housing on it. Her mother was always having to cash in hotels and spread her wealth more sensibly. Meg would take half of whatever she earned from sales and collecting two hundred dollars as she passed Go, and put it under the board where she wouldn't spend it. Then, at key moments of the game, when a member of her family was about to go under financially, she would pull out some of the hoard and offer outrageous sums for the person's property. Little knowing how much money she still had hidden, the person would accept the overwhelmingly generous offer; Meg would acquire another monopoly, and by investing more of her savings in housing, win back the fortune she had paid for the land in no time.

She liked playing Monopoly.

"Well, let's see," their father said, figuring out their scores as the rest of the family finished lunch. "It looks as if Meg has just nudged you out, Katharine."

Her mother frowned. "How much?"

"Four thousand, six hundred, and eighty-six dollars," he said.

"It's because of the damn money she hides under the board," Steven said, his mouth full of garlic bread.

"It's 'cause she steals from the bank," Neal said. "I see her do it."

Meg put down her fork, offended. "I don't steal. I just plan ahead more carefully."

He shook his head. "You just *cheat* more carefully."

"What's this you're saying?" Meg lowered an eyebrow at him. "You cheat?"

"I do not!" Neal said.

"Well, wait." Meg pretended to be perplexed. "If I cheat *more* carefully, the only conclusion I can make is that *you* cheat *less*—"

"Meg, leave him alone," their mother said. "I'm sure that neither one of you cheats." She frowned. "Although that money trick of yours *is* a little sneaky."

"Don't knock it," Meg's father said. "Every Administration needs a fiscal wizard."

"Yeah," Meg's mother said wryly, "and I'm stuck with one who's underage."

Meg grinned. Winning was nice. Winning was *fun*.

Her mother glanced at her watch. "Well, if you'll all excuse me, I think it's time for me to get some work done."

"You're not going downstairs," Meg's father said quickly.

"Not today," her mother said. "That, however, does not preclude work." She reached awkwardly onto her bedside table, moving the phone onto the bed.

As she spoke to members of her staff, setting up afternoon meetings, Meg watched her turn into the President, a change she hadn't seen very often lately—and was now aware that she hadn't missed.

Her mother paused, glancing at Meg's father, who didn't look very happy, either. "I have to. You know that."

He sighed, but nodded. "Come on, guys," he said. "Let's go do something athletic."

"Don't you have to be the First Gentleman?" Steven asked, checking before he got excited.

"Not today, I don't," their father said firmly, and Meg wondered if that was meant to be a criticism of her mother. Probably not a conscious one. "Let's go shoot some baskets, and Brannigan can get some nice pictures out of it."

Mike Brannigan was one of the primary White House photographers, who was supposed to follow them around and take informal pictures of the First Family. Once, he caught Meg leaving her bedroom on her way to get the book she had left in the West Sitting Hall, her face covered with Noxzema. He had also taken pictures of her swimming at Camp David, and trying to find a place to sunbathe on the White House roof in early March, during an unexpected heat wave. Meg had complained to her parents, who decided that rather than having evil intentions, Brannigan was simply in the habit of taking photos of *everything* the First Family did. Her mother had given him the firm suggestion that he exercise a little more decorum, particularly in the presence of adolescent women.

It was Meg's opinion that he was a closet lecher, given to constant secret fantasies. When she broached this to Steven, he said, "Yeah, you only wish," and since then, Meg had kept this opinion to herself. She also spent a few months checking around corners and behind doors, much to the amusement of the staff. But, after her mother's warning, Brannigan had confined himself to appropriately chaste shots of her walking Kirby on the South Lawn, studying at the black walnut table in the Treaty Room, and making popcorn with Steven and Neal. Meg still didn't trust him, and if her father coerced her to play basketball, would be certain to wear something shapeless like one of her most ill-fitting Red Sox t-shirts, old grey sweatpants, and—in all probability—an ancient terry-cloth hat. The hat was the epitome of tacky, and by no means flattering, but it practically covered her eyes, and she would far rather be frumpy than self-conscious.

"You going to play with us?" Steven asked.

"Why don't you," her mother said, before Meg could answer. "Get some color in your cheeks."

Meg was going to sigh long-sufferingly and say, "All right, if I *have* to," the way she normally would, but rather than start trouble, she smiled brightly and said that she would be delighted. Enchanted. Overjoyed.

She played for almost an hour at the small court—it only extended a few feet past the top of the key—down near the Lyndon Johnson Children's Garden. Another narrow and secluded section of the South Grounds had been converted to a baseball pitching area, where Steven had convinced the gardeners to make him a regular mound and home plate. Probably not a permanent addition to the White House grounds. The Camp David staff had gone all-out, making him a perfect place to practice, including a batting cage—and Meg was pretty sure that the Marines and Navy people stationed up there used it regularly themselves when no one was visiting. Which made perfect sense to her—she thought it was pretty damn fun to goof around in the batting cage herself, even though her skills were such that Mendoza seemed like the Splendid Splinter in comparison.

Outdoor activity felt good, but Meg found that she got tired pretty quickly. Frightening how easy it was to get out of shape—and how little time it took. She was going to have to start playing tennis again, even if she could only do it here on the White House court.

And no, it *didn't* bother her that Melissa Kramer had somehow managed to upset Kimberly Tseng in the ISL finals, and gone home with the No. 1 singles championship. It didn't necessarily mean that, if things had been different, *she* would be the current title holder.

Maybe.

Steven and her father gave every indication that they were going to play all afternoon, as they scrimmaged against a few off-duty Secret Service agents, a White House electrician with an amazing jump shot, and an uncoordinated, but very tall guy who was on her mother's speechwriting staff—and Neal was doing his stubborn best to keep up with all of them. Meg, tired of playing—and being elbowed by scrambling opponents—and having her picture taken, moved to a picnic table on the sidelines and sat down to drink some of the fresh lemonade a steward had brought out for everyone. The steward was a pretty fair player in his own right, and—at her father's behest—had joined in for a few minutes, until he fouled one of the

Secret Service agents so hard that the guy swore at him, and if she and her brothers hadn't been there, Meg had a feeling that a fist-fight might have broken out. In any case, the steward quickly returned to the Residence, and a National Park Service guy took his place, until he twisted his knee trying to block the electrician, and also had to retire from the game.

Her father was easily the oldest player out there, but he was *very* competitive, and spent regular time up in the third floor workout room—unlike certain world leaders—so, he was more than holding his own. Steven was, literally and figuratively, in over his head, but that didn't stop him from driving down the lane repeatedly, and boxing out everyone in sight. Neal was plucky, but left the court a couple of times to eat cookies at the picnic table.

Starting to get bored—and a little chilly, Meg decided to go inside and either start answering her backlog of email, or maybe bang on the piano in the East Room for a while. To call her musical repertoire limited was a considerable understatement, although Josh sometimes taught her simple tunes. Very simple. She wanted to learn things like *Rhapsody in Blue* or the *1812 Overture*, but mostly he only showed her stuff like basic Christmas carols and the Pink Panther theme.

"How about one more?" Mike Brannigan said, pointing his camera from the far end of the court. "Why don't I take one of you wiping your face with that towel?"

"Why would I wipe my face?" Meg asked. "I'm not perspiring." Much.

"Meghan doesn't perspire," Steven said solemnly. "She glows."

"Right." The ball came flying out-of-bounds in her direction, and she caught it. "You, on the other hand," she snapped a hard pass at him, "sweat."

"Yup," he agreed, trying a hook shot that just barely grazed the backboard. "You only wish you were a guy, so you could, too."

Meg nodded. "I confess." She picked up the towel without thinking, blotting her face, and heard the camera click.

"Thanks, Meg," Brannigan said. "Good shot."

She blushed, putting her terry-cloth bucket hat back on. "See you guys later," she said, nodding politely at everyone before wandering away, her agents behind her. *God forbid* they let her walk across the backyard by herself.

Preston, who had been come out a few minutes earlier to watch them play, joined her. Ordinarily, he definitely would have jumped right into the game—he was a fast, smooth, and sleek player—but he was wearing a suit and tie and dress shoes, so he had mostly stayed on the sidelines.

"Heading for the house?" he asked, when he caught up to her.

No, she was going to race to the Southwest gate, and make her escape into the city, eluding anyone and everyone who attempted to follow her. Then, she would have extensive, appearance-altering plastic surgery, and start life anew in a faraway land.

They walked around the cement circular drive surrounding the central part of the South Grounds, passing the Herbert Hoover White Oak and the Bill Clinton and Franklin D. Roosevelt Small-leaved Lindens. Her mother didn't have a tree yet. She had some roses, though.

"How're you feeling?" Preston said.

Meg shrugged. "Kind of tired. I guess I'm out of shape."

"No, I meant about today," he said. "Having your mother home."

Weird question. How did he *think* she felt? "Oh," Meg said. "Well—I mean, you know. I'm *glad*."

He nodded. "Me, too. Things okay with old Joshua?"

She blushed. "Yeah."

"Good," he said.

They walked along, and he kicked a dried leaf that gardeners had somehow missed raking up. Off with their heads.

"I've had some phone calls from *People*," he said.

Meg scuffed her Adidas Barricades along the cement, looking for a leaf of her own to kick. "How come?"

"Because of everything, they want to extend your interview, or at least, change the focus a bit. I told them it would be up to you and your parents." He glanced at her. "What do you think?"

Meg scuffed harder. "What did Dad say?"

"I thought, in this case, that it might be better to find out your opinion, first," he said.

Meg looked over at the putting green—which the current occupant of the Oval Office never used, although she *had* once caught the President idly, and quite happily, swaying back and forth on the old-fashioned swing nearby. "What do they mean, 'extend the interview'?"

"It means that you'd have to answer a lot of difficult, and potentially very painful, questions," he said.

Right. "Oh," Meg said, her face tightening. "You mean like, 'How does it feel to have some maniac blast away at your mother with a rifle he bought illegally at a damn gun show'?"

Preston nodded. "Phrased somewhat more delicately."

Swell. Absolutely swell. She moved her jaw. "What if I don't feel like talking about it?"

"That's your prerogative," he said.

She sighed and walked over to sit down on the white cast-iron bench underneath the treasured Andrew Jackson Southern Magnolia trees, since it was slightly more secluded than the benches right by the South Portico. "What do *you* think?"

He sat next to her. "That you should think it over, then discuss it with your parents."

Who would almost certainly say that it was her choice. "What would you do?" she asked.

"I think I'd extend the interview," he said.

Not the answer she would have expected. Meg frowned. "Why?"

He looked tired. "Meg, they're going to write about it, anyway—the article won't make much sense, otherwise. This would give you a chance to say what *you* think, in your own words, instead of them putting together their version."

Like they weren't going to put their own spin on her quotes, anyway? "What if it had happened the day the issue closed?" she asked. "Would they have stopped the presses?"

"It *didn't* happen then," he said.

Granted, but— "What if—" she started.

He shook his head. "Don't talk 'what ifs.' They're never worth much, but in the White House, they're pointless. Let's deal with where we *are*, Meg, not where we wish we were."

Preston was rarely testy, so he must be really worn-out today. Which meant that she probably shouldn't give him any more grief than necessary. Her head hurt, and she took off her—very stupid— terry-cloth hat, rubbing it against her eyes.

"They're not about to ignore the situation," he said. "Wouldn't you feel better having some control over it?"

Meg shrugged.

"I'm sure you would." He grinned. "Seeing as I know how much you hate having people put words in your mouth."

Well, a stilted joke was better than *no* joke at all, so she half-smiled.

"In the long run, I think it might make things easier for you," he said. "The more you talk about it, the faster you're going to be able to get over it."

Had he, perhaps, not noticed that the Leader of the Free World was still having trouble *sitting up*? "Get over it," Meg said. Flatly.

He looked even more tired. "Get past it. Get through it. Get beyond it. Take your pick."

Every response that came to mind was snappish, so she just shrugged.

"You want to talk about it?" he asked.

God, no. She shook her head.

"Want to come hang out in my office for a while?" he asked.

Normally, yes—but, in this case, no. "No, thanks," she said. "I think I'm going to go play the piano."

"Still trying to learn some Gershwin?" he asked.

Trying, and failing. She nodded.

"Keep up the good fight," he said.

~ 18 ~

THEY HAD THICK corn chowder for dinner—Trudy's familiar recipe, although the chefs prepared it—and dessert was a choice of puddings: chocolate, butterscotch, and rice. No tapioca. Downer.

Trudy took Steven and Neal up to the solarium to watch television, and Meg kept them company for a while. But then, she got bored—her brothers loved reality shows, which she did not—and went downstairs to see what her parents were doing.

Glen and the National Security Advisor were on their way down the hall, presumably having just met with her mother, and they were clearly very distracted, but nodded at her without breaking stride.

When she knocked on her parents' door, there was no answer, and just as she turned to go to her room, her father said, "Come in." Meg opened the door cautiously, not sure what she might have interrupted. But, if her mother was holding a high-level meeting, Glen wouldn't have left—and her father probably wouldn't be in the room at all.

Her parents were alone, and her father was sitting on the couch, watching the Celtics and glancing through the *New York Times*, while her mother was in bed, going through papers and reports, the telephone on her lap.

Even though it was quiet, the room seemed—tense. Very tense. "I, uh—" Meg put her hands in her pockets. "I'm about to go check my email and all, but I thought I'd say hi."

Her parents nodded.

"What are your brothers doing?" her mother asked.

"Still watching junk." Meg looked at each of them in turn, wondering if she'd walked in on the aftermath of an argument. There was definitely a weird energy in the room. "Well. I'll probably say good-night now, in case I fall asleep or something."

"You look tired," her mother said.

And how. Meg nodded. "Kind of. Does, um, Kirby need to go out?"

"Frank just took him," her father said. "And I'll run him out again before I go to bed."

"Oh. Okay." Meg backed up. "Well, good-night."

It occurred to her that she should have hugged her mother, so she went over there, hugging her clumsily, trying not to jar her shoulder or side. Then, she crossed the room to hug her father, not wanting to play favorites.

"Preston tells me *People* is agitating to come back," he said, and her mother, who had just been lifting the telephone receiver, put it back down.

"They, um, want to change it," Meg said.

"Update it?" her mother asked.

Not to put too fine a point on it. "I guess so." Meg didn't look at her, afraid to see her reaction. "Preston said it's up to me. And, um, you guys, too, of course."

"Do you want to do it?" her father asked.

Hell, no. Meg shrugged. "Well, I don't really think it's necessary."

"I rather expect it is," her mother said. "It will seem ridiculous, otherwise."

Meg checked her expression before answering—it was more blank than anything else. Her face was tight, but it had been that way ever since it happened. She sure looked older, though. For the first time—probably ever—her mother actually looked her age. Looked *older* than her age.

"I think it's a good idea," her mother said.

In what universe? Meg sighed. "You mean, I have to?"

"You don't *have* to. It just seems sensible to me." She glanced at Meg's father. "Don't you think so?"

"No," he said.

As far as she could tell, most of the country thought—inaccurately—that her father was nothing more than an easygoing, bland man, probably because, in public, he went out of his way to be pleasant and avoid anything controversial. In private, it was a whole other ballgame, and she was pretty sure that he was the only person in the world—literally—whom her mother occasionally found daunting. Or, anyway, equally tough.

"And why would that be?" her mother asked stiffly.

"That woman gave her a terrible time," her father said. "Why put her through it again? My God, Kate, things are rough enough as it is. Why make things worse?"

Meg drifted towards the door, not wanting to witness—or be part of—an argument. She was pretty sure that her parents fought a lot, but almost never directly in front of her. This was a lousy time to start.

"I'm *trying* to make it easier," her mother said through clenched teeth.

Her father started to say something, looked at Meg, and then abruptly left the room. Meg kept her eyes down, embarrassed.

"I *have* to get back to work full-time," her mother said defensively.

Meg tilted her head, confused, then caught on to the fact her possible interview really had nothing to do with why her parents were angry at each other. "Well, sure," she said. "I mean, if you're well enough."

"I'm fine," her mother said, and it sounded so familiar—and so false—that Meg didn't respond, concentrating on the way her Topsiders curled up in the front. Like elf shoes. She leaned back on her heels, making them curl even more.

"Would you mind leaving me alone?" her mother asked, her voice oddly blurred.

Meg looked up. "Alone?"

Her mother nodded, face turned away, good hand up at her eyes.

Jesus, was she *crying*? Her mother never cried. Not even when her father had died. "Mom?" She approached the bed. "Wouldn't you rather that I—"

"No!" her mother said. "Just leave me alone."

Meg backed up towards the door, feeling guilty—and worried. "I'm sorry," she said, and hurried out.

Too rattled to go into her room, she headed for the East Sitting Hall, planning to go lie on the bed in the Queen's Bedroom, and stare up at the damn canopy, or something. But, it was getting late, and with her luck, Lincoln's ghost would show up. She veered towards the Yellow Oval Room, instead, so she could go stand out on the Truman Balcony, and look at the Washington Monument. But her father was already at the window, arms folded, his back to her.

She was going to say something, thought better of the idea, and closed the door very quietly. Maybe, just this once, she would risk Lincoln's ghost.

"WHAT DO YOU expect?" Josh asked, as they sat in the school library the next day. "When people are upset, they get in fights."

She blushed. "Not everyone's that much of a jerk."

"It doesn't make you a jerk," he said. "It's normal."

Maybe.

Josh reached out to move some hair away from her face, Meg leaning her cheek against his hand. "He's worried about her. Of course he's upset."

"But, she's hurt," Meg said. "You can't yell at someone who's hurt."

"What, you're going to wait until she's better?" he asked.

"No, I—" Meg frowned. Where had *that* come from? "Aren't you listening to me? I'm talking about my father."

He nodded.

What, was he looking for some damn Freudian slip or something? If so, she had absolutely no intention of cooperating.

"I just get the feeling you're mad at her," he said.

Meg shrugged, even though he was right.

After her parents' argument, and lying in the Queen's Bedroom for an hour, staring at the canopy and the chandelier, she had gone to her room, climbing into bed to watch the news. Naturally, her mother was the main story, and the station showed film of the President leaving the hospital. She came out, the grey cape swinging in the wind, and instead of the quick wave and jump into the car she had promised, she stood there—without moving or smiling—as if daring someone to shoot her. Meg had watched, both angry and proud—mostly angry—as agents swarmed closer, and her mother still didn't move, studying the crowd. Then, with a brief nod to the press, and an even briefer wave, she strode to the car, relieved agents crowding her inside. Meg had turned off the television after that, lying in the darkness, so furious at her mother for taking stupid chances that her fists clenched under the blankets. How many people would have the courage to walk outside after being shot, and give someone a perfect opportunity to do it again? Only, why did it have to be *her* mother? Why couldn't it be someone else's mother? *Anyone* else's mother.

"Meg?" Josh said.

She looked up.

"Would you rather talk about something else?" he asked.

Yes. And yes. And yes *again*. "I don't know." She sighed. "Did you see what she did when she left the hospital?"

He nodded.

"That was really selfish," Meg said. "Pulling a stunt like that."

"It was *brave*," he said.

Meg shook her head. "With three kids at home, afraid someone's going to hurt her, and they'll never see her again?" And an expressionless husband who must have had to fight every instinct he had to grab her—but just stood off to her left, watching the crowd in the same alert, silent way the Secret Service was.

Josh folded his arms on the table, leaning towards her. "Would you rather she had come out, burst into tears, and run to the car?"

Meg looked at him, both amused and irritated. "No."

"So, it could have been worse," he said.

It could have been *unspeakably* worse—but there was no point in going into the various possibilities.

"Do you want to talk about something else?" he asked.

God, yes.

"Well." He blinked a few times. "Okay. Then, we will."

Christ, she was turning the poor guy into a basket-case. "I'm sorry," she said. "I just—that conversation would go *way* downhill." Speaking of which. She looked around at the crowded, but reasonably quiet, library. "And you're really the only one who's talking to me lately."

"It's a weird situation," he said. "People don't know how to handle it."

All things being equal, she should probably be appointed the chairperson of that particular club. She slouched forward, putting her head on her arms. "Do you mind if I rest?"

He squeezed her shoulder, keeping his hand there. "No."

Good. She closed her eyes, very much wanting to sleep. Another hand came onto her back, this one clumsier.

"You, uh, okay?" Nathan asked, sounding very unsure of himself.

Meg lifted her head. "Yeah. I'm fine. How are you doing?"

He shrugged, moving his hands into his pockets. "This private?" he asked, indicating the two of them.

Meg shook her head.

"Not until we start making out," Josh said—and she very much appreciated his effort to *act* as though everything was completely normal.

Nathan turned. "Zack, man," he said across the library, and Zachary came slouching over from one of the computers, his pen hanging out of his mouth like a cigarette. They stood there uncomfortably, not sitting down, both the same height, but Nathan at least fifty pounds heavier. Kind of an amusing contrast.

"You going to hang out with us, or what?" Josh asked.

They both nodded, and took seats at the table with them.

"What's with Alison?" Meg asked, scanning the library and locating her at a table near the windows, doing homework.

Zack and Nathan exchanged glances.

"Feels bad," Zack said. "About tennis, and all."

And maybe about the fact that her supposed friend at 1600 Pennsylvania Avenue hadn't been returning phone calls or responding to emails lately. Meg sighed. "Back in a minute."

She walked across the library, her own hands automatically sliding into her pockets. Awkwardness seemed to be the name of the game. "Um, you busy?"

Alison looked up, distinctive in her oversized shirt, skinny leather belt, and scarf made out of two bandannas braided together, one blue, one pink. "No," she said, closing her book.

Meg nodded, pulling a chair over, sitting with one knee up, arms wrapped around it. "I'm sorry. I've really been a slime lately."

Alison shook her head—but didn't meet her eyes. "No, you haven't—"

"Beth says I'm a jerk, and always have been," Meg said.

Alison hesitated for a few seconds, and then grinned. "Well, she's known you longer than I have."

Therefore, making her less susceptible to barks, and snarls, and general surliness. Or, at any rate, more *accustomed* to it. And, being Beth, mostly immune to it, anyway. "I'm sorry," Meg said. "I'm probably going to keep being a jerk sometimes"—or even, *often*—"but, from now on, I'll at least try to *notice* when I do it. Or you guys should, you know, point it out to me."

Alison just grinned.

"The ISL didn't go very well?" Meg asked. The league tennis

championships, about which she knew only a few details, because she hadn't had the heart to bother finding out any more than that.

Alison looked guilty.

"It was just my stupid agents overreacting," Meg said. "It's no one else's fault. Did Renee take my place?" The second-ranked player on the team.

Alison nodded. "Yeah, but that freshman from Bullis pretty much blew her off the court."

Meg had been able to handle that pesky freshman pretty easily during their regular season match, but she was a solid player, who was so intense that she was hard to rattle. But, she hadn't adjusted well to changes of pace, and was prone to unforced errors—and Meg had found it quite simple to capitalize upon these two things. "What about you?" Meg asked. Alison normally played in the No. 4 slot, but also would have moved up, too, and gone into the No. 3 position.

Alison sighed. "Remember that baseliner from Holton-Arms who never stops grunting? She got me 6-2, 6-1."

Another decent athlete, but the grunts had such a piercing quality that it was unpleasant to be anywhere within one hundred yards of her. If Meg had had to play her, she probably would have worn ear plugs—in lieu of hitting her over the head with her racket. "I'm sorry," Meg said. "She's a pain to play."

Alison nodded. "Literally. I had a killer headache, afterwards."

No doubt.

Then, Alison looked at her seriously. "Meg, is there anything I can *do*?"

"No. I mean, thanks, but—I don't know. It seems like my family's just going to have to"—She was going to say "fight," but changed her mind— "figure it out. I don't know."

"Okay," Alison said, "but if there is—"

Meg nodded, studying her for a minute. For some reason, she had always attracted snappily dressed friends. Then, she glanced over at

Josh and Nathan and Zack, all of whom were visibly restless. "Want to go over there, and—I don't know—be rowdy or something?"

Alison grinned. "You mean, try to get kicked out?"

"Yeah." Meg grinned, too. "What the hell."

TALKING TO PEOPLE made things easier at school, but they still weren't so great at home. Her mother didn't seem to be getting better, but was still doggedly making her way down to the Oval Office—in a wheelchair, whenever it could be used discreetly—to work, and every night, when she finally got back upstairs, she would practically collapse. Actually, behind closed doors, Meg suspected that she *literally* did so, more often than not. Her father was tense and worried, drinking far too much coffee, and either angry at her mother for pushing herself, or fiercely protective. Trudy was trying to do everything at once—be there for Meg and her brothers, take care of her mother, comfort her father. Steven slouched a lot, and Neal sat anxiously next to whichever parent happened to be in the room, panicking if neither of them was available.

Meg spent most of her time trying to stay out of the way. When her mother was in the family quarters, Trudy spent hours with her, and Meg would see the two of them walking very slowly up and down the second floor halls, her mother leaning a little less each day. Sometimes, they would be sitting on a couch, Trudy talking in a low voice, her mother nodding unhappily. Sometimes, they weren't talking at all, and Trudy would just be rubbing her mother's good shoulder. Whenever Meg saw them, she would go in the other direction, not wanting to disturb their privacy. A number of her parents' friends had been coming for short visits, including Mrs. Peterson, her mother's closest friend, but as far as Meg could tell, Trudy was the only person around whom her mother wasn't putting on an act.

Coming back upstairs one night after saying good-bye to Josh, she noticed that the door to the Presidential Bedroom was ajar, and checked to see what was going on before entering. Trudy was straightening her mother's blankets and fluffing her pillows while her mother, surprisingly docile, watched her do it. Her father was nowhere in sight, but that wasn't unusual lately.

"Here, drink some of this," Trudy said, handing her mother a mug from the bedside table. "It will make you feel better."

As her mother sipped some of whatever the liquid was, Meg knocked tentatively on the door.

"Um, can I come in?" she asked.

"Of course," her mother said. "How was school?"

Because the very stubborn President hadn't even come upstairs for dinner, so this was the first time they had seen each other since breakfast.

"Okay," Meg said. "How do you feel?"

Her mother smiled a little politician smile, which meant lousy. Meg walked all the way into the room, curious enough to lean over to see what was in the mug. It looked like tea. Very pale, yellow tea.

"Lemonade," her mother said.

"*Hot* lemonade?" Meg asked. Talk about a disgusting concept.

"There are those who find it delightful," her mother said.

"Apparently so," Meg said, adopting the same tone of voice. "Want me to go put on a Victorian dress?"

Her mother just sipped the lemonade, which actually smelled pretty good.

"Can I try some?" Meg asked.

"Ha," her mother said.

Always generous, the Leader of the Free World. Meg stepped back. "So, you, uh, feel better?"

"I think so," her mother said, sounding doubtful. "I was mostly able to work straight through."

"She's *much* better," Trudy said. "We walked for a good half-hour this evening."

Which was definitely progress, so Meg nodded a "You, go!" nod at them. "Outside?"

"Well, let's not get carried away," her mother said.

Trudy touched her shoulder. "It's going to be gradual, Katharine. Recovering from any injury is."

Her mother nodded, suddenly looking so miserable that Meg backed towards the door.

"I, uh, I guess I'll be in my room," she said. "I mean, if anyone wants me."

She had some homework left to do, but decided to read, instead, pulling *In This House of Brede* by Rumer Godden out of her bookcase, and getting into bed, pausing only long enough to pat Vanessa.

"So, what's up?" she asked, rubbing her under the chin, which her cat adored. "Anything good on C-Span today? Oh, yeah? Well, what did I miss?" She kissed the top of Vanessa's head, then opened her book. Nothing like a little private whimsy. Especially with cats. Vanessa had a fine appreciation of whimsy.

"Hi," Neal said, standing just beyond her threshold. He was very respectful of other people's rooms, probably because Steven was a big one for personal space and terrorized anyone who came into his room without express permission.

Meg lowered her book. "Hi. You okay?"

His shrug was a blatant imitation of Steven's "I'm thirteen, I'm cool" shrug. Neal was hitting a macho period and, looking at him in old sneakers, rumpled jeans and blue sweater, with his shirt untucked and half of his collar sticking out, she smiled. He was even starting to *dress* like Steven.

"You want to talk to me," she asked, "or are you too cool to hang out with girls?"

He laughed. "You're my *sister*."

"Sorry," Meg said. "I forgot."

He came over to the bed, climbing up next to her. "Mom's still sick in their room."

Meg nodded. "Yeah, I know."

"Will she be okay soon?" he asked.

"I hope so." Meg ruffled her hand through his hair. He needed a haircut. That was one easy way to see how awful her mother was feeling—normally, she would never let him walk around looking shaggy. It was funny, though—there were White House cosmetologists and everything, but unless they were going somewhere really important, her mother usually cut his hair herself, because they both got a kick out of it. Quality time—if not necessarily quality hairdressing.

"I have to go eat," he said.

Words Steven lived by, too. Meg nodded. "Have a nice time."

"Will you play pool with me?" he asked, not quite looking at her, since she had always made it pretty vocally clear that she hated pool.

She grinned. "Not a chance, pal."

~ 19 ~

THE NEXT NIGHT, Trudy came into her room at about eleven-thirty—which was quite late for Trudy.

"Am I interrupting anything?" she asked, carrying her crocheting. She was making a coat for Kirby.

Desultory emailing. "No," Meg said, pushing away from her computer.

Trudy sat in the old rocking chair by the fireplace, settling herself comfortably. She put on her glasses and squinted at the collection of yarn in her bag. "Time to add some green?"

"Yeah," Meg said. "He looks good in green."

Trudy nodded, taking out her crochet hook. Then, she fumbled in the pocket of her cardigan, pulling out—with a big smile—what was left of a package of gumdrops. "Look what I have."

"Can I have some?" Meg asked.

"I think that could be arranged." Trudy leaned over to hand her the package and Meg helped herself to a licorice one, two yellows, and an orange, then handed the package back, Trudy selecting a pink one before tucking the bag away. "When you three were little, all I had to do to make you happy was give you a gumdrop, and maybe hold you in my lap for a minute."

She was now taller than Trudy, so lap-sitting was no longer practical. Unfortunately. "And Vicks VapoRub."

Trudy nodded. "For nightmares."

Meg thought back, remembering many nights of waking up crying, and having Trudy be the one to come, because her mother was down in Washington. Trudy, or her father.

"I feel very lucky," Trudy said. "Being blessed with *two* wonderful families. A lot of people don't even have one."

Meg nodded.

"I'm going back to Florida in a couple of days," Trudy said.

Which might be bad news, since her son—who was in his late thirties—had been battling kidney failure for quite some time. "Is Jimmy okay?" Meg asked.

Trudy nodded. "The dialysis is helping, although I *do* need to see him. But, I also think it's time for all of you to be alone. I'm starting to be in the way."

Meg stared at her. "But—I mean, you could never—"

"I just think it's time," Trudy said. "You need to work things out together."

"We need *you*," Meg said.

"You need me to go away for a while. But, I'll be back before Christmas." She smiled a very loving smile. "Would I neglect my grandchildren?"

Meg tried to smile back, but swallowed, instead, afraid that she was going to cry.

"You'll be all right," Trudy said. "I have great faith in you."

For no legitimate reason. "It's hard," Meg said.

"It always is." She picked up her crochet hook, starting a green row. "But, don't worry. You can do it."

Meg watched the row get longer, seeming to grow magically. "Trudy?"

Trudy glanced up.

"Can I have another gumdrop?" Meg asked.

ON WEDNESDAY, JOSH had jazz band practice and Meg decided to stay after and wait for him.

"You going to come watch me?" he asked.

She shook her head. "I'll distract you."

"No, you won't," he said. "It'll make me play better."

It would make him show off, more likely—and, therefore, annoy the band director. "Look, I'm still kind of behind, so I'll just hang out in the library," Meg said. "Come get me when you're finished."

In spite of good intentions, once she was in the library, she wasn't really in the mood to do homework, even though it would be at least another hour before Josh showed up. So, she wandered over in the direction of the fiction section, but ended up looking at the political science collection, instead.

There were a lot of Kennedy books. Books about assassinations. Martin Luther King. Books like that. It was always the likable Presidents who seemed to be the biggest targets—never the divisive ones. People like Ford, and Reagan—and now, her mother. There had to be some kind of lesson there, but whatever it was, Meg didn't like it.

She took down a book she had read before, a scary book called *Four Days*. November 22nd, 1963 through November 25th, 1963. Decades ago, long before she had been born—but, it was still a part of her life. Of every American's life.

The book was full of photographs: the window where Lee Harvey Oswald had been waiting; Kennedy, as one of the bullets actually struck him; Jack Ruby shooting Oswald; the funeral—horrible pictures. The worst of all was the famous view of Jackie Kennedy leaving the plane, her pink suit bloodstained.

Meg shuddered, closing the book. The day it happened, when she finally saw her father, he had been wearing a different outfit. The old one must have been—Jesus. She shivered, feeling very cold.

"Meg?" a voice said.

She looked up to see her English teacher, Mrs. Hayes. "Oh, um," she stood up to be polite, "hello."

"I saw you from up there," Mrs. Hayes indicated the checkout desk, where Meg could see a stack of books, "and I wanted to be sure you were all right."

Meg nodded. "Yes. Thank you."

Mrs. Hayes glanced at the Kennedy book. "You should stay away from things like that."

"Yes, ma'am, I should." Meg looked at her in her casual wool skirt and light blue sweater, highlighted by a single silver chain, wondering what it would be like to have a mother who was an English teacher. A mother who sometimes overslept, a mother who got angry when people didn't pitch in around the house, a mother who would run down to the store in jeans and a sweatshirt. A normal mother.

Mrs. Hayes put the book back where it belonged, and Meg thought about mothers who were in the house, mothers who worked in banks, mothers who were doctors and nurses.

"I recommend Anne Tyler," her teacher said, smiling.

"Yes, ma'am, I've read a couple," Meg said, wondering how many children Mrs. Hayes had. Did she have to cook dinner when she finished school, or did her husband do it? Looking at her, Meg had the feeling that she was going to go home and make spaghetti and meatballs.

"I hope you'll feel well enough to come back to the newspaper soon," Mrs. Hayes said. "We miss you."

Meg flushed. She had sort of been neglecting extracurricular activities lately—to say nothing of *curricular* ones. "Yeah. Next week, maybe?"

"Whenever you feel ready," Mrs. Hayes said.

"Thank you." Meg shifted her weight, starting to feel embarrassed. She had never been one to talk to teachers much.

Mrs. Hayes patted her on the shoulder, very normal-motherish.

"Can I ask you a stupid question?" Meg put her hands in her pockets, then took them out. "I mean, may I?"

Mrs. Hayes nodded, her expression amused.

"Do you live in a house?" Meg asked.

Her teacher looked startled.

"I mean, as opposed to an apartment, or Crystal City, or whatever," Meg said.

Her teacher smiled. "Yes, I live in a house."

"Where—" Meg smiled back shyly. "I don't know. Where you have to rake leaves and everything? And carry the trash cans down to the driveway? And a little twerpy kid delivers the papers?"

Mrs. Hayes laughed. "My son."

"Oh," Meg said, self-consciously. "I'm sorry. I didn't mean to—"

"I know," Mrs. Hayes said. "Did you live in a neighborhood like that in Massachusetts?"

Meg nodded. "Yeah. I mean, pretty much. I mean, Mom was the Senator and stuff, but it was still like that. Trick-or-treating, and Christmas caroling, and all of that."

"You have a very close family, don't you," Mrs. Hayes said.

Meg thought about that. "Yeah. I'm pretty sure we do. I mean, lots of times, we fight and stuff, but—" She looked at her teacher uncertainly. "That's normal, isn't it?"

"Very normal," Mrs. Hayes said.

Meg looked up at the clock. "I bet you have to go pick someone up from ballet."

Her teacher also checked the clock. "Soccer, actually."

Same difference. Her brothers had always played soccer. And T-ball, and baseball—and now, Steven was on his basketball kick.

When Mrs. Hayes was gone, she sat back down, thinking about Massachusetts. Like about the garden they had had. Sort of an ugly garden, in Meg's opinion, but her father was really into the idea. On weekends, sometimes, he would make the whole family go out and work in it. He always ran the show, drinking Molson and wearing sweatshirts with the sleeves cut off and all. Her mother would tie her hair back, sip iced tea, and talk about "cultivating the rich brown earth," although mostly, she would just stand around. The President was nothing, if not a city slicker. Meg and Steven would always get in trouble for spraying the hose around, and Neal would get yelled at for weeding biennials. They weren't exactly peaceful afternoons, but still. In spite of making constant disparaging comments, Meg had always enjoyed them.

"Hey," Josh said.

"Oh, hi." She stood up, swinging her knapsack onto her shoulder. "How was band?"

"Pretty good," he said, bouncing a little, which meant that he still had a rhythm in his head. "Get any work done?"

Oh, yeah. Nothing but.

They walked out of the library, Josh still bouncing. Kind of annoying, but also endearing.

"Hey." She put her arm around his shoulders. "Buy you an ice cream, sailor?"

He stopped bouncing. "I'm still waiting to collect on that drink."

"I'll buy you ice cream, instead," she said.

"Are you allowed? I mean," he gestured over his shoulder towards her agents, "don't you have to ask them?"

Meg scowled. Like she cared what her agents thought—about *anything*? Nothing like having a bunch of authoritative little shadows. "You ask them, okay?"

He sighed, but nodded, going back to talk to Gary.

They ended up in a place on Wisconsin Avenue, where they ordered sundaes. People recognized her—the Secret Service cars outside didn't help—but, Josh had a baseball cap in his gym bag and she put it on, which made things a little better. Even the slightest disguise usually helped discourage people. Lots of times, although she felt sort of arrogant, she would wear sunglasses. Her parents always suggested hats, and Preston had given her a Patrick Henry College sweatshirt, which seemed to work the best of all.

"Pretty quiet," Josh said.

She nodded. "Yeah, I know. I'm sorry."

He glanced over at the table where Wayne and Joe were sitting. "You're still not speaking to them?"

Not any more than absolutely necessary. "They bug me," she said.

He nodded, obviously refraining from comment.

"I'm sorry," she said. "We're supposed to be having a good time."

He shrugged. "We can go eat these in the car."

She shook her head, not in the mood to sit in the backseat, with her agents in the front. "Here's better."

"Whatever." He looked around. "They're probably just staring at you because you're so beautiful."

She relaxed. "I'm not beautiful." In fact, she rarely even got past *raffish*.

"Oh, yeah?" He started to stand up. "You want me to ask them?"

"No!" She grabbed the pocket of his hoodie to pull him down. "Don't be a jerk."

He pretended to be crushed. "You think I'm a jerk?"

She nodded. "Yes."

They sat, holding hands, Josh looking so interested in the half a sundae she had left that she gave it to him.

"I was looking at a book about President Kennedy in the library," she said.

He stopped eating. "Not so bright."

"Not really, no." She picked up her cup of water, swallowing some. "I guess things could be a lot worse."

"Things could always be worse," he said.

Was that a sage observation—or unbridled negativity?

"I always figure you should be happy with the problems you have," he said.

Meg put her cup down. "*Happy?*"

"Sure," he said. "Happy that they're not any worse."

Jesus. Meg frowned. "I can't tell if that's optimistic or not."

"What," he said, "you never read *Candide?*"

"I read *Candide*," she said, offended. In *French*, even.

"Okay, then." He went back to eating what was left of her sundae. "Consider yourself lucky."

She watched him eat, imagining worse scenarios. The bullet two inches to the right, or hitting her in the spine, or—or hitting her father, too, or—she shuddered. Enough of exploring the possibilities.

"Things could be worse," he said.

Indeed. She looked at his free hand in hers, feeling the bones and piano-strengthened tendons. "Could I ask you something personal?"

He shrugged. "Go for it."

"What's the worst thing that ever happened to you?" she asked.

He grinned at her. "Other than you not speaking to me for a week?"

She nodded, very serious.

"Oh." His grin left. "I don't know. The divorce was pretty bad."

She nodded again, having expected that.

"And, uh," his hand tightened, "when my mother had the mastectomy."

Meg looked up, startled. "She did? You never—I mean—"

"Tenth grade," he said, and she could hear him swallow. "It was—well—pretty bad."

"I'm sorry," Meg said, and then looked at him uneasily. "Is she—okay now?"

"Far as we know," he said, his voice stiff.

"I'm really sorry." She lifted his hand to hold it to her lips for a second. "How come you never told me about it?"

"I don't like to think about it," he said.

No, she wouldn't, either. "I'm sorry," she said.

"Well." He straightened his glasses. "At this point, we just go through a few bad days every time she goes in for her check-up."

Which had to be fairly frequently. "And you never mentioned it?" she asked.

He shrugged. "It just would have made you paranoid about your mother."

"No, it—" She stopped. Of course, it would have. Incredibly paranoid.

"I don't mean that in a bad way," he said. "I just—well, even before all of this, you were pretty hung up. I mean, about something bad happening to her."

"I always have been," Meg said quietly.

He nodded. "Well, yeah, I know. Because of her not being around much, and all."

And the fact that her *mother's* mother had died young, and— well, lots of things. "I'm still sorry," she said. "I *want* you to tell me about things. Especially if I can maybe help."

"It's not like I haven't had to pry things out of *you*," he said.

She had to grin. "What, I'm not candid?"

He laughed. "No, you're not candid."

"I'm trying," she said. "With you, I mean."

"I know." He smiled at her. "So am I, actually."

She nodded, and they held hands more tightly.

"Things aren't supposed to happen to parents," she said.

"Yeah," he agreed. "It's a lot worse when it's parents."

They didn't speak, Meg thinking about her mother, back at the White House, trying as hard as she could to get better; Josh presumably thinking about his.

"Well," he said. "Enough of this banter. Can I buy you a Coke, scullery maid?"

"*Scullery maid?*" she said.

"Can I buy you a Coke, wench?" he asked.

She grinned at him. "Go for it, sailor."

20

"WELL, THIS IS good," Beth said, on the phone that night. "This is all very good. I like your checking in like this."

Meg laughed. "I suppose I can expect a bill for your services."

"You bet," Beth said. "I've decided that terribly garish and expensive holiday gifts isn't enough."

"Yeah, well, garish you can count on," Meg said. "Don't hold your breath on expensive."

"After all these years, I've grown to expect that," Beth said sadly. "Hey, speaking of presents, your mother's pretty funny—she sent me a thank-you note for the book and everything."

Meg nodded. "She really liked it. I heard her laughing when she was reading it, even."

"Well, it's a funny book," Beth said. "Over *your* head, of course, but—"

"I read it," Meg said. "I got a couple of the jokes."

Beth laughed kindly. "I know, dear. You do try hard."

What a putz. "Just can't quite measure up, right?" Meg asked.

"No," Beth said, sounding regretful now. "I'm sorry." Then, her voice changed back to normal. "Hey, want to hear the Scoop of the Month? Guess who asked me out."

"Oh—Rick Hamilton," Meg said. From fourth grade on, when Rick had moved to Chestnut Hill, just about every girl in their grade had had a crush on him. Too cocky for his own damn good, but still la crème de la crème.

"Yeah, actually," Beth said, sounding slightly disappointed that she'd gotten it right on her first try.

Meg couldn't help being impressed. "My God, really? He's never gone out with anyone who has brown hair before."

"I know." Beth sighed extra-deeply. "I guess it's my lot in life to be successful."

"Oh, yeah," Meg said. "Absolutely."

Beth laughed. "Well—maybe. What do you think I should wear?"

"A hat," Meg said. "Definitely a hat."

ALTHOUGH MEG STILL had a lot of makeup work to do, she managed to make time to hang out with Josh on Thursday night, play tennis on the White House court with Alison after school on Friday, and go to the movies with everyone on Saturday night. She didn't exactly feel normal yet—but it was definitely an improvement.

Late Sunday afternoon, as she worked on calculus, her mother came into her room, walking slowly. She looked very tired, and because she wasn't being the President, was hunched over her side, favoring her injuries.

"My goodness," she said. "I thought *I* was a workaholic."

Meg glanced up at her, feeling cross-eyed. Let *s* equals *f(t)* be the position versus time curve for a particle moving in the positive direction along—

"Why don't you take a break," her mother said.

—a coordinate line. Solve for—Meg shook her head. "I have to finish."

"Take a break," her mother said, more firmly.

Bow to the authority figure. Meg put her pen down. Relative extremum be damned.

"What are you doing?" her mother asked.

Meg shook her head, waving the question away. The Mean Value Theorem, Rolle's Theorem, exponential and logarithmic functions—it was all just too awful to discuss.

Her mother lowered herself carefully into the rocking chair. "One thing I'd suggest. When you're doing a lot of close work, you should look up every twenty minutes or so, and focus on something far away. Exercise your eyes a bit. That way, you won't tire as quickly."

Professional advice. Hmmm. Meg got up to focus out the window.

"See anything interesting?" her mother asked.

It depended upon one's definition. Meg shrugged. "Lafayette Park."

Her mother nodded, rocking in the chair.

"Gets dark early these days," Meg said.

Her mother nodded again. "Winter."

Meg listened to the rockers squeaking softly against the carpet, a sad little sound. What an odd sight they must be: Meg, standing by the window, staring out at the city in the dusk, her mother rocking. The President and the First Daughter audition for a Berman movie.

"Quiet without Trudy," her mother said.

No question about that.

"What do you think about Camp David for Thanksgiving?" her mother asked.

Meg turned away from the window. "Will you be well enough?"

"Yes," her mother said, sounding very determined. "We need to get away from here for a while."

Christ, did they ever.

"No reporters, no one cooking for us—with luck, no *anything*," her mother said.

It sounded great—but, implausible. "Are we allowed?" Meg asked.

Her mother laughed. "I'm going to be extremely assertive."

Camp David was always nice and quiet and peaceful. Rustic. As close as they ever got to having something resembling privacy. Trees, and grass, and lots of hiking trails. An outdoor heated pool, a tennis court, and a huge game-room where she and Steven and Neal usually wasted *hours* goofing off. Of course, it would be a major production—the Secret Service and Marines all over the place, Dr. Brooks and other medical people, aides and advisors galore—but, even so. "Sounds really good," she said.

Her mother nodded. "I think so, too."

"Uh, Mom?" Steven said, at the door.

She smiled at him. "What?"

"Dad wants to know if you're ready for dinner now, or want to wait, or what," he said.

She looked at Meg. "What do you think?"

"I'm kind of hungry," Meg said. Starving, in fact.

"Well, then, my goodness." Her mother stood, surreptitiously cautious with her side. "Let's go."

"Are we having anything gross and soft tonight?" Steven asked.

"Well, I don't know," their mother said. "We've certainly been eating our share of dull food lately, haven't we?" She put her good arm around him. "I *did* request that we be given some nice hard rocks and minerals tonight, but we'll have to see what happens."

"Nuts and bolts," Meg said.

Steven grinned, and moved closer to their mother, allowing himself to be somewhat less cool than usual. "How come everyone's in, like, such a good mood?"

"Oh, I don't know." Their mother fixed his collar, tucking it into his sweatshirt. "Because we're happy to see you."

"No way," he said, but looked very pleased.

Meg smiled at no one and nothing in particular—well, Vanessa, maybe, feeling an unexpected goodness in the air as she followed them down to the West Sitting Hall, where her father was sitting on the couch, reading the Book Reviews, while Neal was bent over a notebook, drawing something with intense concentration. He usually spent a fair amount of time making surprisingly good, and very detailed, diagrams of things like helicopters and military vehicles—although her parents had a pretty strict policy that he *not* draw pictures of weapons and, most of the time, Neal followed that rule.

Meg's father looked worried, seeing how slowly her mother was walking, but she winked at him and his expression relaxed. A little.

The good feeling continued through dinner, everyone careful not to destroy it, although Steven made cracks about the baked macaroni and cheese which was, indeed, pretty soft. Her mother requested that all non-essential calls be held—which meant that they only got interrupted three times. After dinner, they went to her parents' room to watch one of her mother's favorite movies, *The Philadelphia Story*. Katharine Hepburn, Cary Grant, Jimmy Stewart, really funny. Felix brought in popcorn, and warm cookies, and milk and juice—and even her mother seemed to eat a normal, and healthy, amount.

After the movie, her brothers went to bed, and Meg hung out to watch a cable news show with her parents. It was sort of silly to watch the news with the President of the United States—especially during stories when a small grin would cross her mother's face, and Meg would know that the media had gotten more than a few of the details wrong, or possibly even missed something major entirely.

She cheerfully ate popcorn and drank Coke, while her mother skimmed papers and made calls, and her father read. Then, a report came on about Sampson, the would-be assassin, because the mental hospital was about to release a psychiatric evaluation, probably the next day. Meg gulped her mouthful of soda, almost choking, and her parents both stiffened. The story was mostly speculative, although it included a clip from some pundit psychiatrist who opined that the suspect was psychotic and narcissistic, with possible schizophrenia, manifesting itself in violent criminal—Meg closed her eyes, trying not to listen. Why hadn't they just put on another movie? Should she change the channel? Or just wait for it to end, or—the anchorperson moved on to a different subject, and Meg held her breath, afraid to see her parents' expressions. Finally, she glanced over and saw her father looking at her mother, who was looking at her sling.

"Well," her mother said, very quietly. "I hope he gets help."

SCHOOL WENT WELL on Monday. In fact, she knew things were better, because she was having a terrible time paying attention, but now, it was for normal reasons. Like, because it was more fun to draw pictures of Vanessa, or pass notes to people, or stare at Josh. She loved to stare at him when he didn't know she wasn't doing it. Particularly in their French class. French was his favorite subject, so he usually concentrated and volunteered answers and everything. She could watch him all period long, and he would wouldn't even notice. Sometimes Mr. Thénardier did, but Josh would remain oblivious.

He was cute to watch. He would frown when he was listening, and adjust his glasses about every five seconds. He also drummed his pen in soft, staccato rhythms—which kind of made her wonder what unconscious, idiotic habits *she* had, other than the fact that lots of times, she pretended that she had ski boots on, which completely changed the way she walked and stood. No one ever commented on it. Obviously, one didn't question the President's daughter's motor coordination.

So, what with staring, and passing notes, and drawing Vanessa, the day passed pretty pleasantly. They had a great time in their Political and Philosophical Thought class, because Alison was selling M&M's for the choir, and they spent most of the period throwing them at various targets around the room whenever Mr. Murphy turned his back.

Meg's hand slipped with an orange M&M and she bounced it off Mr. Murphy's file cabinet, instead of the "If You See Something, Say Something" poster. Mr. Murphy was not amused. Meg and her friends were. He threatened that if he caught anyone in the act, they would have to stay after school and spend an hour crawling around on their hands and knees, picking up scraps of paper and other improperly discarded trash. Sounded like a fun time.

"The pencil sharpener," Nathan whispered, when Mr. Murphy was standing up at the board, and they threw yellow M&M's, all of which missed, clattering on the floor. Mr. Murphy decided to stop writing on the board and gave his "This is a class of seniors and I don't expect this sort of infantile behavior" speech. They were infantile enough to laugh.

After school, she drifted to a Student Senate meeting, the first one she'd attended since the shooting. The advisor just smiled and said, "Good to have you back," and she ended up being put in charge of decorations for the Christmas dance. Snowflake city. When the meeting was over, since Josh had already left for his piano lesson, she hung out on some benches outside with Alison and Zack and a few other seniors—as well as, of course, a bunch of damn agents posted nearby. Nathan, who had been playing pick-up basketball in one of the gyms, came out and joined them, and they spent another twenty minutes lounging around—and giving very superior looks to any underclassmen who dared to approach the benches. Unless, of course, they were fond of the underclassman in question, in which case, the person—usually a junior—was permitted to join them.

And, for the most part, they *didn't* talk about college applications. At least, not the entire time.

Matt, who was on the football team with Nathan and Zack, came jogging past them.

"Big party!" he yelled. "My house! Friday night!"

She had once been to a party at Matt's house—which had been somewhat out of control and drunken, but she had stuck to bottled water, and no pictures had leaked to the tabloids, so she had every intention of going to *this* one, too.

Even if she had to be really boring, and just drink soda and stuff like that.

Finally, everyone started saying good-bye, and drifting off towards their cars or the Metro, and she followed her agents to the exit location they were using today. Her departures and arrivals were always varied, and even though she—mostly—thought it was overkill, she just did what she was told without arguing, even though she often resented every single second of it.

Today, they were going to deploy from the end of the parking garage, and as she walked in that direction, Zachary and Nathan—and Nathan's on-and-off girlfriend, Phyllis—drove by, Zachary beeping his horn. She waved at them, and then put her hands in her pockets, as she walked over to her cars.

November usually wasn't that cold in Washington, but this year seemed to be an exception. She was going to have to break down and start wearing a jacket to school soon. On the positive side, winter meant skiing, and maybe, if her mother was well enough, they would be able to—there was a loud bang from somewhere, kind of like a gun or a firecracker, and before Meg had a chance to react, she found herself flat on her face on the cement.

One of her agents was on top of her, shielding her with his body, while another crouched above them in a combat shooting position, his body a wide target, facing the direction from which the sound had come, his gun out and leveled. She heard two other agents run over, and tires squealing towards them, as the rest of her detail responded.

"Is it a car?" Wayne shouted, on top of her. "I think it was a car!"

After some tense seconds—a minute, maybe—Gary and the others established that it had, indeed, been a car backfiring, and Wayne lifted Meg up, briskly brushing her off and hustling her to the car, with Joe flanking them.

"You okay?" Wayne asked, out of breath, sliding in next to her on the back seat, as Benjamin, who was behind the wheel, put the car into gear.

"Y-yeah," Meg said, trembling. "I mean—" Her hands were shaking so hard that she clenched her fists. "I'm fine."

"Chuck, get her knapsack!" Wayne said through the window to

one of her back-up agents, and then, the cars were speeding away, all kinds of people staring after them.

Meg closed her eyes and leaned back, not wanting anyone to know how scared she had been.

"I'm sorry," Wayne was saying. "We're—overcautious—lately. Are you okay?"

She nodded, the inside of her head jangling.

"I'm sorry." He leaned over and dabbed her cheek with his handkerchief. "You've got a little cut there."

Meg opened her eyes, still dazed, aware that her cheek was stinging.

"Let me see your hands," he said, trying to open her right fist.

With an effort, she unclenched her hands and saw that her palms were gravel-scraped, and bleeding slightly, like when she was six, and used to fall off her bike all the time.

Wayne frowned. "Sorry about that. We'll take you right to the WHMU, and have them fix you up."

White House Medical Unit. "I'm fine," Meg said, which was a lie. She took a few deep breaths, still shaking, her nerves so jarred that it was hard not to cry. She rested her face in her hands, listening to Joe, who was in the passenger's seat, call the incident in. "Um, I mean, thank you."

They all nodded, and she could tell that they were almost as spooked as she was. She covered her face with her hands again, trying to calm down. If it had been a gun, and the person had good aim, she might be—she closed her eyes more tightly.

When they finally drove on to the South Grounds, she stayed in the car for a minute, wanting to be under complete control before getting out in front of the reporters who had gathered.

With an effort, she straightened up, looking at her agents. "Y-you guys didn't have to do that."

Wayne's expression tightened. "I'm very sorry. We overreacted."

Meg shook her head. "I meant, protect me. I've been so—I mean, lately—I mean, you didn't have to—"

"Come on." Wayne put his hand on her back. "Let's take you inside."

"Yeah," she said, "but—"

"Just come on," he said.

Dr. Brooks was waiting inside, and she was rushed right into his office to have the scrapes cleaned and bandaged. As he waited for the antiseptic to dry, he lifted her wrist to check her pulse.

"Pretty scary stuff," he said, unwrapping a roll of gauze.

Meg was going to be cool and cavalier, but since she was still trembling, didn't bother. "Yeah."

He patted her knee, then indicated the various rips. "Any of those new?"

She looked down at her jeans, then pointed to a wide tear below her right knee. "Um, that one."

He separated the cloth to check. "Unh-hunh, you've got another one there."

She protested against all of the gauze, but no one ever took chances with the First Family.

"You're sure you're okay?" he said. "Do you feel dizzy, or—"

She shook her head. "I'm fine, thank you." She looked at her hands, clumsy with the thick layers of gauze. When she was little, no one ever gave her gauze. She would run into the house crying, and Trudy would wash her off, make her laugh—and send her back out again.

Her father hurried in—he had been off making a First Gentleman appearance somewhere or other, when the word came in, apparently—looking very worried, and when Meg saw him, she had to grip the sides of her chair to keep herself from bursting into tears. He bent to hug her, and then she *knew* she was going to cry.

"Okay," he said gently. "Don't worry, it's okay."

"Just a few scrapes, Russ," Dr. Brooks said. "She's more shaken up than anything else."

Her father nodded, and she was able to keep the tears back until they were getting off the elevator, and he led her across the hall to the Presidential Bedroom, sitting her down on the couch.

"It's okay." He hugged her even more tightly than he had down in the Medical Unit. "Go ahead."

"They were really fast," she said weakly. "Knocking me down."

He nodded.

"I thought it was—I mean, it could have been—" She gulped down another deep breath, unexpectedly close to falling apart.

"Go ahead," he said. "You'll feel better."

Meg shook her head, struggling not to cry. "I can't. I shouldn't be upset because something *could* have happened, when Mom—I mean, it wasn't anything, I shouldn't—"

"I think you should," her father said. "To my knowledge, you haven't yet."

"But—" She tried to stop the tears, and they came harder. "I mean, Steven and Neal don't—"

"At least one of them has come to our room every night," he said.

She stared at him. "Really?"

He nodded.

"What about you?" she asked. "Have you—?"

"Yes," he said. "More than once."

She looked at him, tears running down her cheeks.

"It's good for you," he said. "You invariably feel better afterwards."

She shook her head. "But—"

"Relax," he said.

His arm was comforting on her shoulders, and she cried until she was too tired to keep going, except for an occasional weak gulp.

"Better?" he asked.

"I guess so." She wiped her sleeve slowly across her eyes, a few stray tears still coming out. "I don't understand why he would hurt her."

Her father sighed. "It's the position, Meg. Not the person. You know that."

No, she had been told that; she didn't *know* it. "It's not fair," she said.

"No, it isn't," he said. "I just—I don't know what to tell you, Meg."

No, there weren't any logical answers for this one. She was too tired to lean forward and take any Kleenex from the box on the table, and her father handed her several tissues. "She has three more years," she said. Or, maybe, *seven*.

Her father nodded.

"Well, what if—" She stopped, guiltily.

He sighed again. "You can't spend the rest of her term worrying about it. I mean, in many ways, that would be equally destructive."

She looked up at him, feeling like Neal. "So, you think everything's going to be okay?"

"Well," he said, "insofar as things can be controlled."

Which wasn't very far.

"The Secret Service does a damn good job," he said. "People only hear about it on the few occasions when they *can't* prevent something."

"You mean, things have *almost* happened?" she asked.

Her father hesitated.

"Like if she's going to speak somewhere," Meg said, already knowing the answer, "and they switch locations. They must do that for a reason."

Her father nodded reluctantly. "She gets a lot of threats, Meg. Unfortunately, it comes with the job."

What kind of person would *want* a job like that? "Have there been—attempts?" she asked.

He moved his jaw. "Foiled ones, yes."

Jesus. "Like what?" she asked.

He looked tired. "I don't know. A man on a roof in Chicago. Someone carrying a homemade bomb in Denver. That kind of thing."

The near-misses. Of which, there had been God only knew how many. If she wasn't already worn out, she might have started crying again.

"Usually, your mother hasn't even known about them, until afterwards," her father said. "The Secret Service does a very good, very quiet job. But—they can't always prevent things. No one could."

No. Perfection—even when it came to something so incredibly important—probably wasn't humanly possible. Which sucked, but there was no getting around it. She slouched down. "I've been really mean to them lately. Not speaking to them, or anything."

"I imagine you feel differently now," he said.

She nodded.

"Don't worry," he said. "They understand how you've been feeling, and they're smart enough not to take it personally."

"I hope so." She looked at her gauze-wrapped hands. "Can I redo the *People* interview?"

He nodded. "I think your mother's probably right, and that it's a good idea. I'll have Preston set it up."

They sat for a moment in silence.

Then, she let out her breath. "Dad? Can I ask you something?"

"You may," he said. Her parents were heavily into correcting their children's grammar.

"If you were in a room with him," she said, "and you had a gun, would you hurt him?"

He didn't answer right away.

"Like, remember when she broke her leg?" she asked. "And you like, tried to take that guy apart?"

"I tried to slug him," her father said defensively. "Not take him apart."

That's not how it had seemed at the time, but okay. "Yeah, but all he did was ski in front of her," she said. "This is a lot worse."

He nodded.

"So, would you hurt him?" she asked.

"I don't think it would really solve anything," he said, then smiled slightly. "That's not to say that I wouldn't mind punching him pretty hard."

She wouldn't mind hitting him herself.

"However," her father said, his smile so wry that it was almost a grin.

"Yeah." Meg frowned down at her gauze. "Can I take this junk off? I mean, it's only a couple of scrapes."

He glanced around—at the White House, in general, it seemed—and this time, he did grin. "Sure," he said. "Just put on a Band-Aid, if you need one."

～ 21 ～

SHE HAD BARELY gotten to her bedroom when the telephone next to her bed rang—which was when she remembered that her cell phone was in her knapsack, and that she had no idea where *that* was. Still down in the Medical Unit, maybe?

She picked the receiver up. "Hello?"

"Hey, kid," Preston said, sounding amused. "I just got a call from the Southeast Gate—seems your friend Josh is practically breaking it down, trying to get in here. You want me to have him sent up?"

Meg smiled. "Yeah. And ask them not to give him too hard a time, okay?"

She went downstairs to wait for him, and after a few minutes, he was finally escorted in, driving an unfamiliar car.

He jumped out, looking very upset. "My God, you *are* hurt!"

"I'm fine," she said. "It's just a scrape." Or two, or three, or four.

"What happened? Nick Goldstein called and said he saw your agents knock you down, then drive away about a hundred miles an hour—" He stopped, not waiting for an answer. "My God, your poor face! Are you all right? What happened?"

"I'm fine." She put her hands on his shoulders, seeing that he was literally shaking with worry. "A car backfired, that's all."

"Don't *worry?*" he said. "Jesus, I called your cell about ten times in a row, and you never picked up, and then—I mean, I thought— Meg, you might have been—"

"I'm fine. Come on." She sat him down on the steps leading up to the South Portico. "Everything's okay."

"Jesus Christ. I thought—I mean, I about had a heart attack. I really thought—" He shook his head. "Are you *sure* you're all right?"

"Yes." She put her arms around him, feeling his heart pound against her chest. "Shhh," she said softly. "It's okay."

They kept hugging, Meg feeling his heartbeat and breathing gradually slow down.

"Okay?" she asked, her mouth next to his ear.

He nodded, turning his face to kiss her, a *long* kiss that left both of them breathing harder than was probably a wise idea, right there on the stairs, with plenty of witnesses.

"Whose car is that?" she asked.

He grinned sheepishly. "My piano teacher's. I guess I kind of freaked."

Clearly. Meg looked at him dubiously. "And he trusted you to drive?"

"If he hadn't, I swear to God I would have smacked him," he said.

Meg laughed. "You, and my father."

He raised an eyebrow. "Your father wants to smack my piano teacher?"

"No, he—" She stopped, seeing his grin. "You jerk." She leaned forward to hug him some more. "Can you come upstairs, or do you have to get the car back?"

Josh frowned. "I don't know. I mean, I should probably—I'd rather come upstairs."

"Look, take the car back before *he* has a heart attack," she said.

"Yeah. I guess." He looked worried again. "Are you *sure* you're all right? I mean, all those bandages—"

"You know how they are around here," she said.

"Yeah." He kissed each of her hands, her cheek, and then her mouth, staying at her mouth the longest. "I'm going to call you as soon as I get home, okay? More than once, probably."

Meg smiled, hugging him tightly. "It's okay with me."

SHE GOT SEVERAL other phone calls, including one from Beth, who had seen a news headline on the Internet. Apparently, the story was being reported in more than a few places, even though there wasn't any film or anything. Meg assured everyone that she was fine, and that it was no big deal—but, getting the phone calls felt nice.

Her mother didn't hear about it until she came upstairs for dinner, and she was very concerned. This spread to Steven and Neal, who bent over backwards being kind to her. Steven even held her chair for her. Meg felt like a fool, and escaped to her room shortly after the meal to work on her college essays. In theory.

Instead, she picked up *A Moveable Feast*, pushing Vanessa off her pillow, so she could lie down. It was a book by Ernest Hemingway, about his days in Paris, hanging around with people like Gertrude Stein and F. Scott Fitzgerald, and—one assumed—spending every free moment drinking and carousing. It must have been kind of fun to be a lost generation. Maybe someday, she and Beth should spend some time being officially disaffected.

After a while, Neal showed up, holding a mug of cocoa.

"Meggie?" he said, from the hallway.

"Don't be dumb," she said. "You know you can come in."

He carried the mug over, smiling and setting it down on her night table. "It's to help you work on your essays."

Meg flushed and pointed at her book. "I was just sort of *reading* essays, first. Like, to warm up."

He nodded, believing her.

"Thanks for the cocoa," she said. "Aren't you going to have some, too?"

He smiled, and she noticed the chocolate mustache. "We did."

"Yeah, I see," she said.

He stood there, smiling at her, and he was so cute that she smiled back.

"I have to go to bed now," he said. "But, will you play pool tomorrow?"

She laughed. "Sure. Why not?"

He reached up to hug her. "I'm glad you aren't hurt," he said, his voice muffled against her shoulder.

A sentiment she shared. "Me, too." She ruffled up his hair, which was freshly trimmed. "I like you, even though you're an ugly peasant."

He giggled. "You're the ugly Queen."

"I'm the *beautiful* Queen," she said.

He made a face, and then giggled again. "Blech."

"Come on." She started to lift him up, but he was too heavy. "You're a *fat* peasant."

"I'm not fat," he said.

"Well, you're getting big, then." She headed for the door. "Let's go get me some Oreos, so I can work, and you some Oreos, so you can sleep."

Once they had eaten a few cookies, and her father showed up to haul Neal off to brush his teeth, she went to see what Steven was doing, and found him on his bed, reading. Definitely a member of her family.

"You busy?" she asked.

He didn't look up. "Don't you knock?"

"No," she said. "Just wanted to tell you good-night."

He shrugged. "Good-night."

Since he probably wouldn't hit her while she was already bruised, she decided to take a chance and walk all the way into his room.

"I kind of want to be alone," he said.

"Want a cookie?" she asked.

He glanced over and took two from her, leaving her with one.

"That was singular," she said.

He stopped chewing. "You want it back?"

"No, thanks." She sat on the bottom of his bed. "Today was kind of scary."

"*Kind of?*" he said.

Yeah. "Remember when Trevor died?" she asked. Trevor was the German shepherd mix they had had before Kirby. "You know how it was really bad at first, and then, it was only bad sometimes? Like if you remembered it all of a sudden, and you would feel like crying all over again?"

"I *still* remember it pretty often," he said.

So did she, actually. Trevor had been one great dog.

"What," he said, "and all of this is going to be like that?"

She shrugged. "Makes sense, doesn't it?"

"Swell," he said.

"Swell?" she asked. "What is this, 1950?"

He sort of smiled—and sort of scowled. "You always say it."

"That's different," she said. "*I* am the Queen."

He groaned. "Oh, Christ. Not that again."

"You're just jealous," she said.

"Yeah, right." He took her last Oreo, then stopped when the cookie was already in his mouth. "Did you want this or anything?"

She shook her head. "Not now that it has peasant germs."

"You only *wish* you had some of my germs," he said.

She nodded. "Every time I see the first star."

"Bet you wish on your birthday, too," he said.

"Yup, every year." She punched him lightly on the shoulder and then stood up to go work on her essays.

"You look fine," he said.

"Fine?" she asked, confused.

He gestured towards his own cheek. "Your face. In case you thought you looked ugly or something."

"Oh." Self-consciously, she touched the scrape. "Thank you."

He shrugged and picked up his book again. "Wasn't lying or anything."

With luck.

She crossed the hallway to her room, where her cocoa was quite cold. It still tasted perfectly good, though. She brought it and Vanessa over to her desk, and pulled up the Universal College Application on her computer. Yeah, most of the schools where she was planning to apply had additional essay questions of their own, but she should probably tackle the main one, first.

A life-changing event? Hmmm. A person she admired? Double hmmm. Her viewpoint on a particular current event? *Triple* hmmm.

Christ. Admissions officers had to get extremely tired of reading about other people's significant experiences. But, it was even *more* boring to write about them. She held her hands above her keyboard, and waited for profound inspiration—but, nothing happened.

Maybe she needed to write this in—God forbid—*longhand*. Maybe she would be able to think more clearly, that way. So, she took out a legal pad, and a pen with the Presidential Seal on it—and waited for inspiration.

"I have had a lot of significant experiences. This makes it very difficult to choose one." Oh, yeah, real original. A grabber. She was going to have to try again.

"On January 21ˢᵗ of this year, my mother was sworn in as the President of the United States." Just in case they hadn't noticed that 1600 Pennsylvania Avenue was her home address.

Page three. *"Call me Meghan."* That is, if they really wanted to get on her nerves.

Page four. *"If you really want to hear about it, the first thing you'll probably want to know is where I was born, and what my lousy childhood was like, and—"* Very original. With just a little help from J.D. Salinger.

Page five. Christ, this was wasting a lot of paper. The potential environmental implications were disturbing. Maybe she should give up, and go back to reading. *"I don't know if I really want to go to college. It just kind of seems like the thing to do."* "Then, why are you applying, dear?" they would ask, and promptly reach for the next application.

She looked at her telephone for a minute. Maybe she should call Josh and talk to him. Again.

"Nothing significant has ever happened to me," she wrote. *"I lead a*

very dull life and can't imagine why any college anywhere would want me, or even if I want them—" Garbage, garbage, garbage.

She slouched down in her chair, lifting Vanessa onto her lap. "You want to do this for me?" she asked. "I'll give you speechwriter rate."

Vanessa kneaded her paws on the front of her sweatshirt.

"This is a major drag," Meg said. "I'm really not into this."

Vanessa purred.

One more try, and then she really would quit for the night. *"The thing about most of my significant experiences is that they happened to my mother. I've never run for President. I've never been a world leader. I've never walked into gunfire. But, even though I've never done any of those things, they've affected me."* She paused. Maybe this wasn't such a great idea. *"In my family, small things end up being so large-scale that you kind of feel like stepping back and observing them, instead of participating. Not experiencing. Like this photo I saw recently."*

She hesitated. Heading for dangerous territory there. Oh, well. Damn the torpedoes. *"There was a girl sitting on a bench with her head in her hands, and you could tell that she was trying as hard as she could not to fall apart. And the caption said: 'The First Daughter, in a moment of private grief.' And I looked at it, and all I could think was that it belonged in some Year-in-Review issue. I mean, it was a really disturbing, thought-provoking picture, a horrible image, caught on film. Except, it was me."*

Meg lowered her pen, skimming what she had written so far. Sentimental tripe. Emotionally manipulating. But, accurate. She walked over to her dresser, taking that particular magazine out of the drawer where she had hidden it underneath some t-shirts. She looked at the First Daughter's private grief—which was pretty god-damn *public* grief. She looked at the black Levi's, and the shoulders hunched into the blue Oxford shirt, then closed the magazine and returned to her desk.

"When I came home that night, there was chicken soup. Very yellow,

*with big chunks of chicken and thick noodles. I think Carl makes the pasta himself. There were also grilled cheese sandwiches, with Neal's crusts cut off to make him happy. But my stomach hurt, and I went down to my room to pat my cat. I patted her most of the night. There was some dumb rerun on, and Steven talked me into watching it with him. We did, but I don't remember the plot or anything. I do remember a McDonald's commercial being on, because it was one we liked, but neither of us laughed. I guess it didn't seem very funny. Under the circumstances. So, I looked out the window at the Washington Monument. All bright, and lit-up, and brave-looking. When we were still living in Massachusetts, I remember someone threatened to dynamite the monument, and a SWAT team blew **him** away, instead. You really have to wonder. Not that I know the answer. It seems like there might not be one. I don't know."*

She stopped writing. Could she put "I don't know" in a college essay? Was *any* of this like a college essay? Maybe it wasn't allowed.

"Working hard?" her mother said.

"What?" Meg turned to see her just inside the door, a bathrobe draped over her shoulders, covering the sling. "Yeah, kind of."

Her mother nodded. "Are you getting much accomplished?"

"Probably not." Meg turned the legal pad over, too embarrassed to let her read it.

"Is there anything I can help you with?" her mother asked.

"No, thanks." Meg leaned forward, weight on her left foot, pretending she had on a ski boot.

"Are you sure you're all right?" her mother asked.

Meg stopped leaning on her foot. "Yeah, I was just—oh." Her mother probably hadn't even noticed the Ski Foot. "I mean, yeah."

Her mother bent to examine her cheek, then straightened, apparently satisfied. "As long as you're sure."

"I'm fine." Meg looked at her mother, who was only somewhat hunched now, and less so every day. And it had been quite a while since she had seen her face go white with pain. "Are *you* better?"

Her mother nodded. "Much."

Meg wasn't sure "much" was the right word, but she *did* seem to be improving. Then, she coughed. "Are you, um, mad at me?"

Her mother looked confused. "*Mad* at you? Of course not, Meg—why would I be?"

"Because—" Meg couldn't look at her. "I was such a jerk that day. About the sweatpants, I mean."

Her mother still looked puzzled for a minute, but then she smiled. "Don't tell me you're worried about *that*."

"Well, yeah," Meg said. "I mean—yeah."

Her mother laughed. "Really not to worry, Meg. I'd completely forgotten."

Oh. Meg shifted her position, still feeling uncomfortable. "I didn't mean to be such a jerk to you, I—"

"Yeah, you did," her mother said. "You just didn't mean for anything *bad* to happen."

Maybe. "Yeah, but—" Meg swallowed, her throat hurting. "I was in physics, and I hadn't studied for the test, and—I was wishing for a fire drill or something, to get me out of there."

Her mother smiled, putting her hand on Meg's shoulder. "It doesn't mean you wanted anything bad to happen to *me*." Her smile expanded into a grin. "Although we may need to discuss the part about you being unprepared for your exam."

Hmmm. Maybe she shouldn't have mentioned that. "Yeah," Meg said, "but—"

"Just forget it," her mother said. "Worrying about things like that is a waste of energy."

Energy she should, presumably, apply to schoolwork. Meg let out her breath. "Okay. But—really?"

Her mother nodded.

She should probably just leave it at that, but— "Are you—scared?"

Her mother studied her sling, not answering right away. "To some degree. It's not going to be debilitating, though."

Meg looked at her thoughtfully. "Can I ask you something else?"

"You *may*," her mother said.

Yeah, yeah, yeah. "Something, um, sort of unfriendly?" Meg asked.

Her mother nodded uneasily.

Okay, then. Meg very carefully made direct eye contact. "How come you were such a jerk when you left the hospital? You were like, *waiting* for someone to shoot you."

A muscle in her mother's cheek twitched. "I gather you saw a film clip."

Meg nodded.

"Well." She sat on Meg's bed, hunching again.

"What if something bad had happened?" Meg asked.

"I suppose the hospital would have checked me right back in," her mother said.

Meg shook her head. "It's not funny."

"No," her mother said. "It isn't."

When she didn't elaborate, Meg couldn't help getting annoyed. "Yeah, well, something could have happened. I mean, weren't you thinking about *us*?"

"No," her mother said, and Meg blinked. "I was thinking about how scared I was, and how I wasn't going to let anyone in the whole god-damn country know that."

Her mother never swore.

"Yeah, but—" What a frustrating conversation. Meg frowned at her. "Something could have happened."

Her mother shrugged, wincing almost simultaneously. "Then, I suppose it would have."

"Yeah, but—" Meg shook her head impatiently. "You don't have to go *looking* for it."

"Yes," her mother said. "Sometimes, I do."

It was quiet, as Meg thought about that. "Terrific," she said. "That's—that's just terrific."

218

Her mother sighed. "It's part of my job, Meg."

"Great," Meg said. "And we all just sit around, waiting for the next bad thing to happen."

"If that's the way you want to live," her mother said.

Jesus Christ, was she even a tiny bit human? Meg stared at her. "I don't get it. Don't you care at all?"

"For the rest of my life, every time I get dressed, I'm going to have to think about it. Every time—" Her mother shook her head. "Let's put it this way. Off-the-shoulder dresses are a thing of my past."

Meg looked at her, for the first time thinking about physical scars. The ones that *did* show.

"When you're trying to save the President's life," her mother said, "the cosmetic aspects of it all are certainly not on your list of priorities."

The mood in the room was so unhappy that Meg decided to risk a joke.

She sat taller, even being a little sultry. "Well, it looks like I'm in line for a lot of nice clothes."

"Over my dead body," her mother said, and Meg winced. It was briefly silent; then, unexpectedly, her mother grinned. "A rather unfortunate witticism."

"Yeah," Meg said. Flatly.

"And yet," her mother's voice was solemn, "appropriate in its way."

"That's sick," Meg said. "That's just plain sick."

"Yes," her mother agreed. "Rather." She looked at Meg, her eyes bright with amusement, and Meg had to laugh, her mother relaxing and joining in. It was loud laughing, and Meg felt out of practice.

"The—" She tried to get her breath. "The blue dress. You know, the one you wore for the astronaut thing. Can I have that?"

Her mother stopped laughing instantly. "My blue dress? I love that dress."

"Well, yeah," Meg said. "But, if you're not going to be using it—"

"No. I'm not giving you that dress." Her mother's grin was self-amused. "It's *mine*."

Meg nodded. "Said the dog, from her manger."

Her mother laughed. "Damn straight."

"Ah," Meg said. "You seem to have acquired quite the gutter mouth."

"Yes, indeed," her mother said, using *her* formal voice. "That appears to be the case."

They looked at each other, grinning.

"No way do you get that dress," her mother said.

Meg nodded. "Thank you. I applaud your generosity."

Her mother laughed again, coming over to hug her with her good arm. "I suppose I'm taking you from your work," she said, not straightening up right away.

"Yes," Meg said. "Rather."

$\backsim$ 22 $\backsim$

THANKSGIVING WAS WONDERFUL. Peaceful. Quiet. Relaxed. Meg did a lot of hiking around with Kirby, and once, he even fetched a stick. Agents and soldiers and staff people were lurking everywhere, but her parents had prepared a list of supplies, and the kitchen in their cabin had been stocked with Thanksgiving food, which her parents—alarmingly—were planning to cook themselves. As usual, her father did most of the work, with her mother being a backseat driver about it, and Meg heard a lot of laughing coming out of the kitchen. Steven shot baskets, and played one-on-one with Marines, while Neal spent almost all of his time on the Internet, playing some dumb game with which he was obsessed.

They left Washington on Wednesday, flying up in Marine One, and returned to the White House on Sunday. Josh came over that night, and they went down to the projection room to watch a new comedy, which was going to be released in a couple of weeks. It was fun to be able to sit in a movie theater in the *house*, especially since the easy chairs in the front row were so comfortable, and there was a popcorn machine and everything. But, the theater was for lounging, rather than being romantic. When Josh was around, Meg generally felt like being romantic. The easy chairs were far enough apart so that they could really only hold hands—which they would never do in front of Steven and Neal, anyway. Sometimes, when they were alone, they would sit in the same chair, Meg mostly on Josh's lap, but that would end up being too distracting for serious film-watching.

After the movie—which Steven and Neal decided to watch again, Meg and Josh walked around, ending up in the solarium.

They put on *The Sound of Music*—which was Meg's favorite movie in life—and sat together on the couch to watch. But, once it started, Meg felt unexpectedly restless.

"What's with you?" Josh asked. "I thought this was your favorite movie in life."

"It is," she said. "I just—I don't know."

He put his arm around her and she moved closer, running her hand along the side of his jaw, which felt smooth, but solid. That was good—men were supposed to have nice, strong jaws. Actually, it was probably a good idea for *everyone* to have a solid jaw, but she only noticed it, one way or the other, with men.

"When was the last time you shaved?" she asked.

He shrugged. "I don't know. About two weeks ago."

Golly. "That must be pretty potent after-shave then," she said.

He grinned, but didn't elaborate.

"You have hair on your chest, though," she said. Just enough to enjoy, but not so much that he seemed *furry*—which she thought was an ideal compromise. "That means there's still hope."

He nodded.

"You want me to shut up and watch the movie?" she asked.

He nodded again.

"Okay." She was quiet for a scene or two, watching the nuns, but then—once they were off-screen—she turned her head to kiss his neck, working her way up to his mouth. His attention abruptly left the movie, and his other arm came around her.

"I've seen this movie about six hundred times," he said.

And she had seen it at least twice as many times as he had.

They kept kissing.

"Oh, wait." Meg tried to sit up. "I want to watch this part." She grinned at his expression. "Of course, it's not *imperative*."

"Jerk," he said, and started tickling her, which made both of them laugh.

She was really never ticklish—except around the opposite sex.

And doctors. For some reason, doctors always set her off. Her pediatrician had once said that he loved to treat her, because she made him feel like such an amusing person.

"Cut it out," she said, laughing weakly.

He stopped right away, which she thought was nice. When it came to tickling, some people just didn't know when to quit.

"Of course, if you'd rather watch the movie," he said, kissing her.

She kissed back. "No, thanks. Unless you'd rather."

He shook his head, and for a few minutes, things started getting pretty intense—enough so that she began to worry that one of her brothers, or—even worse—her father or Trudy, might come in without thinking to knock first.

"Hey, wouldn't this be a good time to hear some jokes?" she asked. "I know some really good jokes."

"Can I hear them after?" he asked, concentrating on what he was doing.

And, quite frankly, she *liked* what he was doing. "After what?" she said.

He started tickling her again, and she agreed to stop being a pain. But suddenly, all of this seemed terribly funny, and after another minute or so, she pulled away.

"Do you mind if I wear your glasses for a while?" she asked.

He lifted himself onto one elbow to look at her. "Are you getting in a weird mood?"

She nodded.

"Your weird moods drive me crazy," he said.

She shrugged. "I don't have them that often."

"Often enough," he said.

"Boy, what a grump." She hugged him, pulling him back down.

He moved so that he was mostly on top of her. "I'm not a grump."

"Yeah, you are. Grump, grump, grump, grump—" She decided to stop talking. Funny to think she had gone through a period when the concept of French kissing was too gross to be believed. Ah, the wisdom of ten-year-olds. Or like that song Lauren Bacall sang in *To Have and Have Not*: "How Little We Know." She loved *To Have and Have Not*. In fact, maybe she would be Lauren Bacall for a while. "Steve?" she asked, her voice low and sexy.

Josh frowned down at her. "Steve?"

"Aw, come on, Steve," She pushed his cheek playfully. "Don't be mad, Steve."

"I'm not," he said.

She pushed his other cheek. "You're mad. Admit it, Steve." She folded her hands behind his head. "Kiss me, Steve."

He grinned. "Are you doing *To Have and Have Not*, or *What's Up, Doc?*"

Clever question. "Surely," she said, "my deep, seductive rasp answers that all by itself?"

"Go down another half-octave," he said.

People with relative pitch were so very picky. "Whatever you want, Steve," she said, deepening her voice.

He nodded. "Much better."

She tried to kiss him the way Lauren Bacall would. Only now that she thought about it, Lauren Bacall—and anyone else—would probably be wise to stay away from Josh.

Not that she was possessive or anything.

"Got a match, Slim?" Josh asked, being Humphrey Bogart.

She almost said, "Us," but that would sound so stupid that she might not ever live it down. It was the kind of remark she might *think* to her heart's content, but was much too cool to *say*.

Sort of like "I love you."

"Was you ever bit by a dead bee?" Josh asked, still playing *To Have and Have Not*.

Meg didn't answer, touching his face, moving her hands back through his hair. People talked about "I love you" being really trite, but if that was true, why was saying it such a big deal? Or—more accurately—how come *she* was such a coward about saying it?

"Hey." Josh tapped her cheek. "Wake up. You missed your cue."

"Yeah." She shook her head. "Sorry."

"What are you thinking about?" he asked.

She shrugged. "I don't know. Nothing, I guess."

He shifted onto his side, and she adjusted her position accordingly, her arm trapped under his weight.

"You think a lot," he said.

"Not really," she said. "It just takes me longer."

He laughed, brushing her hair away from her face. Long hair had a tendency to get in the way of amorous encounters, she'd found. "You're cute."

"Thank you," she said. "So are you."

"Thank you." He raised himself slightly. "Your arm must be falling asleep."

"Kind of, yeah." She extricated it, then looked at his eyes, every dot of the light brown pigment familiar. "I love you."

He blinked. "Because I saved your arm?" he asked, sounding as if he were only half-kidding.

"No." Although she liked her arm. "I mean, not *just* that. I mean—well, for lots of reasons. I mean—I don't know. I just love you." She closed her eyes. "I have to rest now."

He laughed, and she smelled after-shave as he bent his head to kiss her. "I love you, too," he said. "Very much."

THE LAST HURDLE, Meg figured, was the *People Magazine* article. Preston had set the new one up for Thursday, when she didn't have play rehearsal—she was helping run lights, which had turned out to be more fun, and less geeky, than she would have predicted—so she could come home right after school and prepare. Get psyched, as Nathan would say.

She woke up in an excellent mood that morning, so cheerful that she wore the Williams sweatshirt she had gotten when she and her father had visited colleges back in September.

"Oh," her mother said, when she walked into the Presidential Dining Room for breakfast.

Meg grinned at her. "Nice shirt, hunh?"

Her mother seemed to be amused, but didn't actually smile. "Perhaps, if it's really necessary to wear a slovenly outfit to school, it would be preferable if it said *Harvard*?"

Yeah, right. Good luck to her and the Boston Red Sox. Meg sat down, taking the Cheerios box away from Neal, pouring herself some, and reading the back.

"Dad!" Neal protested.

"Meg, give him the box," her father said patiently.

Meg sighed the deepest sigh she could manage, and handed it across the table.

"Yeah, thanks," Neal said, scowling.

Meg smiled very graciously at him. "You're welcome. *Il n'est rien.*"

Steven snorted. "French. How totally dumb."

"*Tu es un chien laid,*" Meg said. Ever so graciously.

Her parents looked at her.

"What?" Steven asked. "What did she call me?"

"A handsome and talented basketball player," their mother said. What a diplomat. Her sling had been off for about three days now, and she could use her left arm, albeit gingerly.

Meg helped herself to some toast. "*Il est un grostesque—*"

"Is she calling me gross?" Steven demanded, looking from one parent to the other.

Meg nodded. "*Mais oui. Tu es un—*"

"All right," her father said, laughing. "Enough already. Eat your breakfasts."

"*Forse, è la figlia che non è bella,*" her mother said.

They all looked at her.

"*Francamente, es embarazoso ser visto con ella,*" she said.

"My God, she's speaking in tongues," Meg said. "Call a priest!"

"*Je suis le Président,*" her mother said pleasantly, and winked at Meg's father. "*Je peux n'importe quoi je veux.*"

"Mom, what are you saying?" Neal asked, Cheerios box forgotten.

Their mother shrugged. "That you are one of my two favorite sons."

"But *I'm* the very favorite child," Meg said.

Steven shook his head. "No way. You're too ugly."

"You're about ten times uglier," Meg said.

"Yeah, you wish, chick," he said. "Your whole room's full of broken mirrors."

Whoa, good one. Meg saw that he was going to try to help himself to the last English muffin, and carefully timed her movements so that she could snatch it right out from underneath him. "Because you sneak in there when I'm not around."

"No way," Steven said—and grabbed the English muffin from her hand. "You're *so* ugly—" He paused for effect.

"How ugly is she?" Neal asked, already laughing.

"So ugly," Steven said, "that the Queen was like, throwing up the whole time she was here."

Their father put down his fork. "Steven, the Queen hasn't been here."

"That's 'cause she's scared she might throw up," Steven said without hesitating, and even Meg had to laugh.

Their mother nodded. "I'm afraid it's true. I've invited her several times."

Meg stopped eating her cereal. "How come everyone's picking on me all of a sudden?"

"Because you're so ugly," Steven said.

Meg considered that, then took a bite of toast and jam, following it with a bite of cereal, then chewing to make a very unpleasant mess and opening her mouth to show it to him.

"Stop right there," her father said, but he didn't sound very irritated. "You know I don't like that game."

Meg closed her mouth and nodded sadly. From across the table, Steven showed her an equally disgusting mouthful, and she laughed so hard that she had to gulp half her orange juice to stop choking.

"Now, just stop it," her father said. "I really don't like that."

"Stop choking?" Meg asked, laughing. "I don't like it much, either."

He frowned at her, but she could tell that he wasn't at all mad. "Try to behave like a mature young woman."

Steven laughed raucously, chewing his purloined English muffin.

"I notice he didn't call *you* mature," Meg said.

Steven shrugged. "That's 'cause he didn't feel like he had to. He knows I'm a man."

"*Munchkin* man," Meg said.

Their mother sighed. "Isn't it about time for all of you to go to school?"

"Not me!" Neal said.

"No, not you," their mother agreed. "But, it seems to me that it's time for your brother and sister to leave."

"Boy," Meg said. "Can tell when *we're* not wanted."

Steven nodded. "Yeah, really. *Neal's* the favorite."

"I am not!" Neal said.

Meg pushed her unfinished cereal away. "Boy, let's go find an audience who will appreciate us, Steven."

"Try the zoo," their father said.

"Wow, they don't even love us." Steven clapped Neal on the shoulder. "Take notes on what they say about us, son. We'll quiz you later."

"You know, I bet you would," their mother said thoughtfully.

Meg and Steven laughed evil laughs.

At school, her good mood got better, and she had so much trouble sitting still—and keeping quiet—in her classes that she got yelled at three times. This amused her even more. The choir was selling Christmas, Hanukkah, and Kwanzaa cards now, which weren't as much fun to throw, but they made do with crumpled pieces of paper.

None of their teachers enjoyed this.

At lunch, they were even rowdier, throwing around French fries and Zachary's olives. They got yelled at some more, and spent the rest of lunch being as dignified and elegant as possible—except when they were laughing like hell. Mr. Murphy got so mad during their Political and Philosophical Thought class that he almost kept them after school, but luckily, he didn't. Having to call Preston and tell him that she would be late to the interview because she had detention would be kind of embarrassing.

After her agents dropped her off at the private elevator, Meg making jokes with them, she went to change into conservative clothing, and was ready twenty minutes early. She paced up and down the Center Hall, as pleasantly jittery and keyed up as she was before tennis matches on days when she *knew* she was going to play well.

The chief usher intercepted her near the Yellow Oval Room. "Mr. Fielding is on his way upstairs," he said.

"Oh. Thank you." She walked—ran—swiftly down to the East Sitting Hall, where they were going to hold the interview this time. Humphrey was asleep on the low table in front of the couch, and she lifted his front paws to dance with him for a few seconds.

"Good afternoon, Miss Powers," Preston said.

She released Humphrey, who began washing to recover his dignity. She just blushed. "Um, good afternoon."

"Good afternoon," Ms. Wright said, smiling.

They all sat down, and Meg resisted an urge to swing her feet onto the table and be cocky as hell. Jorge came in, and Meg decided to have coffee along with the others, in order to seem terribly mature. She would endeavor to be sly about the many sugars she put in.

"I'm very sorry about what happened," Ms. Wright said.

Meg nodded. "Thank you. Things are much better now."

"I'm glad to hear that." Ms. Wright uncapped her pen. "I also want to apologize about the way the interview went last time."

"I think it was my fault," Meg said. "I'm afraid I'm not very good at this."

"I'd say that you're unusually good at it." Ms. Wright scanned her notes, then looked up with a smile. "Well. I'll start you off easily. Tell me how you're feeling these days."

"Pretty good," Meg said. Then, she grinned. "Maybe even *great*."